# THE PAYBACK ASSIGNMENT

by

Austin S. Camacho

Copyright 2005 by Austin S. Camacho

All rights reserved. No part of this book shall be reproduced or transmitted in any form or by any means, electronic, mechanical, magnetic and photographic including photocopying, recording or by any information storage and retrieval system, without prior written permission of the publisher. No patent liability is assumed with respect to the use of the information contained herein. Although every precaution has been taken in the preparation of this book, the publisher and author assume no responsibility for errors or omissions. Neither is any liability assumed for damages resulting from the use of the information contained herein.

This is a work of fiction. Names, characters, places, and incidents either are the product of the author's imagination or are used fictitiously. Any resemblance to actual events or locales or persons, living or dead, is entirely coincidental.

ISBN: 0-9762181-4-3

Cover design by Kamron Robinson

Published by:

**Intrigue Publishing**

Intrigue Publishing
7707 Shadowcreek Terrace
Springfield, VA 22153 USA
Telephone: 703-455-9062

Printed in the United States of America
Published May 2005

# THE PAYBACK ASSIGNMENT

# PROLOGUE

"This hardly seems like the time or place for this conversation," Marlene Seagrave said between sips of champagne. "I'm not sure I'm ready to ruin my figure that way."

Adrian Seagrave scanned the room, his eyes sliding over the other wealthy couples.

"You may have been a beauty contest winner when I married you..."

"I think maybe that's why you married me," she said.

"...but too much good living has already loosened your figure, my dear. Before you grow too far, I want an heir."

Marlene spun off under the grand chandelier. Her shorter husband had to sprint to keep up with her. Marlene inspected the other wives as she passed through the festive crowd. She was younger than most of the women in the Canfield Casino that evening, because Mrs. Whitney generally invited old money to her Saratoga Springs soirees. But many of these more mature women looked great. They watched their diets, went to a health club, and generally took very good care of themselves. Better than Marlene had lately, she had to admit to herself. Her legs were not what they once were, back when she was Miss North Carolina, and her abdomen had swelled just a bit with what women called a pooch. Still, her complexion was as clear as ever, her natural blonde hair retained just the right amount of curl, and she knew her face was still striking.

Besides, she was still in far better shape than her husband, and weighed considerably less. She turned to review his appearance. His once-handsome face was beginning to sag under the weight of a double chin, and his hair was rapidly deserting his scalp. Of course, she knew that all of that was beside the point.

As a waiter walked by she captured another glass, exchanging it for her empty one, throwing words over her shoulder at her husband. "You want. You want! When we met it was always what I wanted. That's the man I fell in love with. Now it's always what you want."

He seized her arm at last, stopping her forward progress. Noticing the attention they had drawn, he forced a wan smile. "I think, my darling, that you've had enough champagne for one night."

"Think so?" she asked, taking a sip from her fresh glass. "Think about that one. You'd have a better chance at getting me pregnant if I was a little drunker."

"All right, I get it." Seagrave sidled up to her, his little pig eyes pressed almost closed by a bigger smile. "I'm being selfish. Is that the message? Okay, Marlene. What do you want?"

His voice, once so seductive when it got tight like this, now chilled her. This was not the way she imagined her marriage would turn out when she said those vows seven years ago. Everything came down to a negotiation with him. He assumed that her comfortable life justified the neglect. He expected her to tolerate the other women. Now he wanted an heir, a foal from his prize filly, just like the Saratoga horse owners around her. She knew that she could always leave, but the Seagrave fortune was as seductive as the power it gave him was chilling. She glanced around the room, and her eyes settled on a handsome couple holding hands beside the roulette wheel, which was only spun during fundraisers. They were so obviously in love she could spot it clear across the room.

At the woman's throat, pinned to her Halston original, was an antique diamond brooch of uncommon delicacy and beauty. Surely no woman would give up such a prize. Aside from its enormous monetary worth, it must have even greater sentimental value. It wouldn't be for sale at any price. Marlene caught her husband's eye and pointed subtly at the prize.

"I want that."

Adrian Seagrave flashed his teeth, much as a shark does when it spots its prey. "All right, my dear. As always, you will have what you want."

Even that casual promise chilled her.

# -1-

It was hot, sticky, muggy country even at night, thickly overgrown, infested with every kind of disgusting insect in creation. Bugs and birds competed to see which could create the most irritating sounds. The river they sloshed through carried the stink of sewage. Mud sucked at their boots. Leeches clung to anything that moved. A field of brilliant stars and a sliver of a moon did little to illuminate the potential animal and reptile dangers lurking in the darkness.

"You know, Mike, I've asked myself a million times," Morgan Stark whispered. "Why do we always get ourselves involved in other countries' petty political bullshit?"

"Well, because there are still times when the U.S. government just refuses to get involved," Mike answered with a grin. "Because the U.S. military can't be everywhere, fixing everything on the planet. And for the money, of course."

The men made little sound, despite the water flowing around their knees. The river they waded through was really little more than a stream in Belize. The tiny backwater nation southeast of Mexico was South America's version of a postage stamp country.

Up ahead, the point man flashed his light. It was okay to move on. The sun would rise in half an hour or so. They were right on schedule. Morgan signaled his seven followers to move out. All wore camouflage uniforms, black berets, combat boots, and a wide variety of personal weaponry.

Morgan Stark, team leader, was a couple of inches over six feet tall and a slim looking two hundred ten pounds, with heavily cabled forearms showing below rolled up sleeves. He was the only black man in this racial grab bag of professional mercenaries. However, if someone had asked his men to describe him, they would have first mentioned his long, quick fingers, the little mustache he still kept within Army regulations, or perhaps his sharp, clear, light brown eyes. In their business, you learned to judge a lot by the eyes. But in the world of professional mercenaries, color was almost an afterthought.

They moved along through the river, about two meters from shore, because it was faster and easier than travelling over land. Unfortunately, the map in Morgan's head indicated it was time to branch off into the tropical forest.

The tiny light flashed again, just as Morgan was about to crest a low hummock. This close to the target, silence was mandatory, making the light their only reasonable means of communication. That flash warned Morgan of nearby patrolling security personnel. Not that he needed such a warning.

He pressed himself up over the edge of the earthen mound, his fingers tangled in the thick undergrowth. In the near darkness, he found himself face to face with a uniformed guard. Neither Morgan nor the guard reached for a weapon. The guard's dog looked as startled as its master did. To Morgan's eyes it was more wolf than dog, huge and gray in the darkness. It was a Belgian shepherd, the type the Israelis used for border patrol. Slowly a growl began in its throat and it bared its teeth for war.

For the money, of course! Morgan repeated in his head. Those weeks ago, when he first accepted this mission, he had no doubt the money was worth it. Watching saliva drip from this beast's fangs, he was not so sure.

## -2-

A friend of a friend had made contact with Morgan, as usual. The go-between was a well-known sub-contractor named Stone. Morgan had arranged a meeting, but still he had circled the little bungalow on the outskirts of Brussels four times before going to the door. On the last and closest circle, he noticed a Renault parked across the street and three houses down. The man inside it puffed on a cigarette and read the paper as if he were merely waiting for someone. Maybe he was.

Morgan pulled a map out of his pocket, and walked to the car with a confused look on his face. In bomber jacket and aviator sunglasses, he hoped that he looked like a befuddled tourist. The driver, a small dark man with a thick Gallic nose, looked up as he approached. Morgan saw him start to reach under his seat, but he withdrew his hand as if reconsidering something.

Once beside the car, Morgan began to gesture and mutter at the map in silent mime. At first the driver stared straight ahead. When Morgan stared at him helplessly, the driver released an exaggerated sigh and rolled down his window. Morgan mumbled helplessly.

"Pardon moi, monsieur, ou est le palais? Je suis... oh hell, je ne parle pas Francais tres bien."

"My English is better," the driver said in an exasperated tone. "You are looking for the Royal Palace?"

"Not really." Morgan leaned close. "Just half wit lookouts."

His left hand shot inside the car, clamping onto the driver's throat. When both the driver's hands locked onto Morgan's arm, Morgan pulled his right hand back, then snapped it forward. The heel of his palm thumped against the driver's temple, and the man slumped over, unconscious.

Jogging across the street, Morgan leaned into the bungalow's door as he rang the bell. He waited a long ten seconds before locks began to turn inside. The door opened, and Morgan followed it in.

The parlor was empty except for four chairs around a small table. The house was cool, but it carried the musty smell of vacancy. Morgan assumed it was only used for meetings like this one. A coffeepot sat on the table, along with two cups and a creamer. Two sugar cubes and a wafer rested on the edge of each saucer. There was also a note pad at each place, with a ballpoint pen. A telephone rested on a scrambler near one end of the table. It was all very businesslike.

The man who had admitted Morgan sat at the opposite end of the table. He was a good two inches taller than Morgan but thin enough to imply frailty. A full shock of white hair made him appear older than he really was. His eyes did not quite match his hair, but Morgan had to strain to see the hint of blue there.

Morgan turned a chair so its back was to a corner. He sat with his toes braced on the floor, as if he were ready to leap at any moment. He opened his jacket and eased a hand toward his shoulder holster, all the while glaring hatred at his host.

"A problem?"

Morgan responded in a harsh baritone growl. "I told you not to post anyone, Stone. You put an armed man out front. May as well put up a sign saying there's some kind of clandestine business going on in here. I took him out before I came in. You're lucky I didn't kill him."

"Standard procedure." Stone's voice was so controlled, so bored sounding, it was almost a monotone. "I hope you didn't hurt him too badly."

"He's okay, but he'll have a hell of a headache when he wakes up. Now, why am I here?"

"Coffee?" Stone reached for the pot.

"No. You got work for me or what?"

Stone poured the thick, dark brew into his small cup as if he had nothing else to do that day. "Yes," he said, adding a sugar cube to his cup with no greater haste. "A brief job in Belize. You know the place?"

"An American ally on the Caribbean," Morgan said. "Good game preserves. Great scuba spots. Nothing going on down there right now."

"So it would appear. However, like many of the smaller countries in that hemisphere, the communist party there has not evaporated. Politically speaking, someone doesn't like the direction in which that little nation is going." Stone's voice was almost hypnotic, and Morgan made a serious effort to stay alert while listening to him.

"Uh-huh." He watched his host sip his coffee. "Someone. Your principal. Who shall remain nameless?"

"Of course, for your protection as well as his. There is a man named Carlos Abrigo. I won't bore you with the details, but he is a very influential man in the Belize national assembly, the head of their committee controlling exports. And he is leaning heavily to the left."

Morgan nodded, keeping silent for a moment. He reasoned that the mysterious customer really wanted more favorable trade arrangements or something of the sort, but what the hell. The target was a commie and that was all he needed to know. Cuba was sufficient proof that communism was not a dead philosophy, or a defeated enemy in the Western Hemisphere.

"So? You want this guy to disappear? Not my thing. I'm a soldier. Sounds like what you need's a hit man."

"What I need is a professional who can carry out a raid on a well defended compound," Stone replied, unruffled. "Abrigo lives in a rural area, some distance east of Belmopan, the capital city, in a veritable fortress of a forgotten mission. He maintains a staff that includes some thirty armed guards. They are labeled law enforcement, but are in fact military personnel."

"Politics as usual in South and Central America," Morgan said. So you want me to kill him?"

"We need his influence terminated permanently."

Morgan almost laughed at Stone's subtlety. "Fine. Sounds like a simple enough assignment. I won't know how simple until I've had a chance to do a thorough recon."

"I can provide you with maps and details of the target's defenses. You see, this assignment is time dependent. It must take place within the next thirty days. My research tells me you're the best professional available for the job. Will you take it?"

After his recent work in Sierra Leone and a messy bit of business in the Sudan, Morgan was looking for something quick and easy. This certainly looked like it. He figured he'd signal his interest by throwing out an opening price, just to start the haggling.

"I'd have to assemble a team. Equip and train them. Plan for identity concealment afterward. And of course I'd have to see the defenses before I gave you a firm estimate. But, based on what you've said, I figure I can handle what you require for a total cost of, say, two hundred fifty thousand American dollars. Plus expenses."

Stone listened impassively, then nodded and picked up the telephone. He pushed one button and waited for the speed dial to go through its motions. After a few seconds it was clear that a connection was made, but Stone didn't say hello or begin a conversation. He simply said Morgan's last name and the amount he had mentioned. He listened for a moment, his face impassive, and nodded once before resting the telephone in its cradle. Stone had an excellent poker face, and Morgan could not predict the answer.

"This amount is acceptable," Stone said, his words falling like ice crystals. "My client will supply advance intelligence and transportation to and from the site. You will of course deal only with me in this matter."

"Naturally."

Stone sipped from his cup, but kept his pale eyes on Morgan. "I will deposit one quarter of your total fee into the account you name, to cover set up and acquisition costs. The remainder will be transferred to you when the job has been completed to my principal's satisfaction. You have complete autonomy as far as training, equipping and paying your team, and for the actual planning of the event. These are the terms. Are we in business?"

Morgan suppressed a smile. "We are."

## -3-

That business had brought Morgan to this frozen moment in the Belize jungle. While he watched, a big hand reached out of the darkness behind the uniformed guard and clamped across his face. That would be Smitty, the point man. Morgan heard a thump as the guard's head arced back and his body jerked forward, as if something had hit the small of his back.

Nerveless fingers dropped the harness leash, and the huge dog leaped forward. Morgan's right hand reached to the back of his belt. When he brought it forward, it was filled with the handle of his fighting knife. He held the knife in a reverse grip, its spine pressed along his forearm.

In less than a second the dog was on him, close enough to smell its breath. The beast hung in midair, its jaws set to snap over Morgan's face. His arm swung in front of him, the edge of the blade slashing across the dog's throat. Momentum carried the beast forward, its bulk smashing into his chest. Slammed to his back, Morgan felt hot gore pumping onto him from the animal's slashed throat. Even above the natural stench of the jungle, the odor made him gag. Revolted, he thrust the body away, watching the dog's final death throes before rolling to his knees and looking over the mound again.

He saw another flash of light, then two more. All clear. Shaking off the picture of the huge dog charging him, he signaled his men to continue.

Swinging machetes, the small group of professional soldiers moved through the brush at an aggressive pace. His point man aside, Morgan led the way, feeling sweat pooling in his boots and sliding down his back beneath his belt and other carry straps. He wished he could stop someplace and wash the blood off his uniform, but he knew the mission needed to proceed as planned. As he trudged on, Crazy Mike drew up beside him, smiling despite their exertion.

"The other outer ring guards will find the bodies," Mike said.

"We're less than ten minutes from the target," Morgan replied in hushed tones. "By the time they get back to the compound they'll find us there."

"We might move a little faster if you weren't so..."

"What? Paranoid?" Morgan asked.

"Over prepared." While Mike had a machine gun slung across his back, Morgan carried a greater variety of tools. He liked to travel with everything he might need. In addition to the machete he used to carve his path through the brush, he wore a shoulder holstered pistol, a fighting knife at his back, a submachine gun at his side, a pair of boot knives, and several extra fully loaded magazines. As Mike had hinted, it all added up to a lot of extra weight.

"You know my attitude," Morgan said. "Better to be over prepared than dead."

"Yeah, well there's no sense killing yourself before..."

"Freeze!" Morgan snapped with unexpected urgency. Mike stopped in mid-swing, holding an awkward, twisted stance. Behind them, the rest of the team dropped to one knee, their rifles thrust forward.

For a full minute, no one moved while Morgan looked around in all directions. When Mike started to ask "What?" Morgan silenced him with an upraised palm. Having checked everywhere else, Morgan looked toward the damp ground. He bared his teeth and muttered "Jesus" under his breath.

"Mike. Don't panic or anything, but your left boot is pressed against a wire. It's pretty taut and I'm afraid whatever it's attached to might go off if you back off. See anything?"

"I can't even see the damned wire," Mike answered. "I don't remember any mines or snares on that map Stone gave us."

"That's because there weren't any. This is probably new since his recon. Now you just hold real still and I'll try to keep you in one piece, okay?"

## -4-

Morgan was sure he remembered every bit of intelligence Stone had given him, even though he had not had much time to study it. A month ago, he had been faced with the task of gathering a team, based on the size of Abrigo's guard force and the defensive measures he had taken.

Crazy Mike was the first man he had contacted. A big ruddy Texan with a broad, blunt nose, known for his fearless antics, Mike was a good man to have at your back. A quick phone call had brought him in. The day after his conversation with Stone, Morgan was sitting under a tall pecan tree on Mike's south Texas ranch. After so much time in the tropics, Morgan had almost forgotten how clear and blue a sky could be, and how fresh air could smell.

"After that time in Laos I didn't know if I'd ever see you again." Mike poured more Jack Daniel's into Morgan's glass as he spoke. "Which would have been too bad, because I really dug working with you. I mean, a guy needs a team leader he can trust, and you're just about the best NCO ever led me through the bush. Yeah, that was a good time, but it seems like our time's passing. Ain't done much work since then, except some demolition work in Saudi. And since I ain't up for getting married, life's pretty boring. Nobody to fight with."

"Well, you got a lot of heart, Mike, and I know you worked in Belize before. I figured you'd be just about perfect for this thing."

"And then there's this place, right?" Mike tipped his head back, draining his glass. "I mean, you'll need a training site and a staging area."

"You read my mind, pal. I could use your land and your connections. I've already called Smitty and Josh, a couple of guys I worked with in Angola, but if you know a few more fellows like you, looking for work, give them a call. I figure on an eight man team, counting me."

"I know just who to get." Mike stared off across his flat green landscape at horses standing idle in a distant corral. "So, how's the money? I mean, for gear and such?"

"According to Stone, his principal's got pretty deep pockets. He's paying expenses as I make them. So I'll be on the road for a few days, finding the right equipment. Tell the new guys they don't have to go out of pocket for anything. I'll supply a couple sets of BDU's, all the weapons and ammo, field gear, bivouac gear and so forth. And they'll each take home twenty thousand for a month's work."

Mike's jaw dropped. "Twenty grand? You kidding?"

"Nope, that's the pay. In your case, I'll toss in another ten grand for you for the use of your land for training up. Fair?"

"More than." Mike leaned back, his broad chest stretching his tee shirt to its limit. "What about recon? We got time?"

"Don't need it," Morgan said. "Apparently the client's connected too. Stone's got a description of all the security at the site, inside knowledge of the status of the unit protecting the mark, and even satellite photos of the whole layout. Believe me, this will be a piece of cake."

Morgan had spent a few hectic weeks making arrangements, and a couple more working with Stone to charter a boat. Then, only the previous day, his team had taken a choppy sea voyage down from Texas across the Gulf of Mexico. They watched the Cuban coast drift past in the distance as they sailed into the Gulf of Honduras. Despite the tricky coastline south of Belize City, he had them dropped off due east of their target. In two inflated boats called MARS craft they had paddled silently to shore.

After stowing their boats and hiding them well on shore, they hiked in, to within a couple of miles of the target, and spent the night in the jungle. They had slept in hammocks under heavy netting. Lying there, suspended over the jungle floor, it had seemed to Morgan that he had spent most of his life in hot, humid places like this. Mercenaries never got much work in the temperate zones, he reflected. They always landed in Africa, or Southeast Asia, or South America.

## -5-

In the predawn gloom, Morgan pressed two fingers against Crazy Mike's shin and found the thin wire. Sidestepping, he slid his fingers gently across the wire, moving by feel more than sight. His breathing was slow and deep as he moved, bent over almost double, gently pushing fronds and branches away with his left hand.

He found what he expected just a few feet away. Its convex face toward him, the familiar olive green device stood there on a pair of thin steel blade legs which were jammed into the ground.

"Claymore mine," he said, not daring to speak loudly enough for anyone else to hear. He had planted dozens of these things since his Vietnam days, and now he faced one. A hand detonator was strapped to a tree trunk with green duct tape, the stuff Morgan had learned to call hundred mile an hour tape in the Army. The stiff wire pressed the detonator lever in. If the wire were pulled any farther, the lever would move enough for contacts to connect, sending an electric spark down a wire to the blasting cap screwed into the top of the mine. The resulting explosion would scatter eight hundred BB sized steel pellets in his direction, turning him and Crazy Mike into bloody fragments.

Even if Mike tried to back off, the hook-shaped grommets of his speed-laced boot might pull the wire or press it enough to set the mine off. Kneeling, Morgan pulled his Gerber Multiplier survival tool from his pocket. Flipping it open, he folded the handles together, exposing the jaws of its pliers. The first inch of the jaws was sharpened to be wire cutters.

"Over prepared," he muttered to himself, kneeling. His BDU pants soaked in dampness from the ground, but he wasn't concerned with his knees being wet. He did wipe his left hand down his pants leg, rubbing it free of sweat. He took three deep breaths, holding the last, because he knew that the slightest shaking of his hand could kill them when he reached to cut the wire. Guiding on his outstretched fingers, he gently wrapped the tool's wire cutters around the thin strand. Tightly holding the wire on the side toward the mine, he slowly closed his left hand.

A quiet "snik" told him the wire was cut. After releasing his breath, he slowly released the held wire.

A moment later he was beside Mike again, whispering, "All clear."

"Thanks, man." Mike grinned in the darkness. "Saved my bacon again."

"Don't thank me. Just be ready to join me in a discussion about sloppy intel with Stone when we get back to civilization."

More cautious now, the team moved on toward their target. Five minutes before daylight, they came within sight of the mission walls. Those stout barriers were little more than solidified shadows in the crescent moon's pale glow, but Morgan could imagine their moss-covered stucco surface. With the wall in sight the group split up for each man to handle his prearranged assignment. Smitty and Josh headed for the edge of the clearing facing the front gate. They each carried a Mannlicher SSG double trigger sniper rifle. The rest of the team moved to the rear of the compound. Morgan could see only five guards on close patrol. This would be as easy as he first thought.

Back on Crazy Mike's ranch, his team had spent ten days rehearsing this assault. They had built a wall, based on the photos and information Stone provided, and practiced with full-scale mockups until each movement was a conditioned reflex. Now Morgan lifted his watchband's cover strap, counting seconds until the real show started. Three. Two. One.

"Party time," he whispered.

Around front, two rifle shots split the silence, almost as one. In the wake of those blasts, like thunder rolling across the sky, everything jumped. The two guards at the front flew against the gate. The other three perimeter guards ran around to the front. Morgan and his five men moved quickly to the rear wall of the fortress.

At its worst it was no more than seven feet high. Lee leaped up, hoisting himself to the top. Straddling the wall, he heaved his "Willie Peter," a white phosphorus grenade. It flew entirely past the main house and landed on the roof of the garrison building beyond. Then he dropped back to the ground outside the wall just before the blast.

According to NATO rules of engagement white phosphorus is used only for signaling. Their interpretation of the Geneva Convention forbids its use as an antipersonnel weapon. It does indeed explode and burn with an intense white light. It also releases enough heat to melt through the armored skin of most heavy battle tanks.

Morgan hopped up, hooking the top of the wall with his fingers, and pulled himself up until he could just see over its edge. In the distance he could see the first dim light of the new day approaching. Then the grenade went off like a miniature sun on the flat roof of the barracks. Dawn had come up in Belize with a bang.

While Morgan scrambled over the wall, Fallon was boosting Crazy Mike up to straddle it. Mike carried an M249 machine gun, the lightweight weapon that the United States Army designated as the SAW, for Squad Automatic Weapon. Mike quickly slid an ammunition box into place beneath his weapon and yanked the charging handle hard. The two hundred round belt within the box was now engaged.

Morgan dropped into the compound unopposed. Racing across the courtyard, he could picture all the action around him, just like a film running on a screen in his head. Maybe fifteen of the off duty guards would have escaped their building before the explosion. Crazy Mike would be cutting them down with the SAW by now. The other six mercs would be picking off stragglers with their AKM's. Smitty and Josh would have long since cut down the other three outside guards from the safety of their concealment. If any of the outer ring guards with the dogs came within sighting distance of the compound, the snipers would eliminate them too.

Reaching the main house, Morgan swung his submachine gun around on its sling so he could fire from the hip. A startled soldier stared out the first window Morgan came to. He cut the soldier down and shattered the window with a single three round burst. Leaping inside, he searched through the building for other occupants. His movement was fast and thorough, yet unhurried. It took him barely a minute to locate the only occupied room.

Soon he was standing in the bedroom doorway, shaking his head. Like most men of "power," Carlos Abrigo proved useless when the crunch came. He stood in the middle of the floor in a pair of silk pajamas, looking back and forth in confused horror. To one side a woman in a matching nightgown screamed louder than the gunshots outside. What an idiot, Morgan thought. Thirty guards on staff, but only one had been in the house and only six on night duty within easy reach of the house. Typical commie politico. Morgan had a hell of a lot more respect for the average guerrilla. At least he was willing to put his money where his mouth was.

Abrigo yanked out the drawer of his end table and produced a small pistol. Terror twisted his face into a horrible caricature of a man. His shaking hands waved the weapon in Morgan's direction.

Morgan carried a Jeti machine gun. This Swedish weapon, smaller than an Uzi, sends its bolt up an inclined plane when recoiling, which eliminates the familiar muzzle climb found in other submachine guns. A four shot burst from that death machine slapped Abrigo against his bedroom wall and into Belize national history. Gunned down by terrorists, as the papers would say. A thorough man, Morgan knelt, feeling for a pulse in the fallen man's neck. It was unnecessary.

Abrigo's female companion had never stopped screaming, her fists balled up in front of her chest. "Woman, shut the hell up," Morgan snapped as he strolled out.

Outside, all was quiet. He could only imagine the speed and efficiency with which his men had cut down the stragglers. The remains of the barracks crackled like a warm, cozy fireplace.

Morgan clambered over the wall and pointed to Lee, who fired three shots into the air. That signal would tell Smitty and Josh it was time to retrace their steps. By the time the Belize Army arrived and followed their trail, they would be well out to sea.

\* \* \* \* \*

"Hey, Morgan. We get twenty grand apiece, right?" Smitty asked, his dirty blond hair in his eyes again. Bright sunshine filtered through the vegetation above them dappled his face with soft shadows.

"Isn't that what I promised you? Now, what you going to do with all that money?"

"Me?" Smitty looked confused for a moment. "Well, you know my dad ain't doing so well. I figure I better help out with his mortgage. It'll sure come in handy but, damn. It seems too easy."

Morgan nodded his agreement. As leader, he would net ninety thousand dollars for one hour's dirty work this morning. Despite Stone's insistence to the contrary, this had not turned out to be a combat mission after all. In truth, it had turned out to be an execution, pure and simple. As if executions were ever pure, or simple. The slaughter of Abrigo's poorly trained protective force had been almost incidental. Perhaps the client had wanted to send some message to Abrigo's backers, but an assassin could have handled this business much more cleanly. All things considered, he preferred combat and would never even consider a mission profile like this one again. On this assignment they had been over-manned and over-gunned. And they would certainly be overpaid.

At that moment the team broke the jungle line and stood within sight of the coastline. Morgan's aching eyes welcomed the sight of the cool blue expanse of ocean and the large yacht that had delivered them to these strange shores. She stood at anchor, no more than a quarter of a mile out. Without being told, Lee fired the three-shot signal that signified the mission's success. The blast echoed through the jungle, but at that point, seconds away from leaving, Morgan figured a little noise could not make any difference. Besides, once a job was done he figured it was time to relax. His arms were feeling leaden and his steps shortened.

"You look kind of washed out, Morgan," Mike said. "I don't know what happened in that house, but you look like it wore you out."

"Well, it wasn't the combat I was expecting," Morgan said. "And the truth is, I never get tired until it's all over. Guess it just hit me. Not that it matters. All that's left is for us to paddle our inflatables out to our patiently waiting transportation." What he really needed, he thought was a cup of hot, fresh brewed coffee. He was dirty and exhausted. A real bed, a hot meal and that coffee would square him away.

But, as he approached the landing boats, his head suddenly snapped up. He was getting that old familiar feeling. That funny tingle at the nape of his neck. That jangling of nerves that told him something was wrong, that he was in deadly danger. He never questioned where it came from or why it came, but he knew it had saved his life more times than he could count, most recently that morning in front of the tripwire. But, where was the danger? Neither the local army nor the police could have found them so quickly. Was some jungle beast stalking them? Could a survivor from Abrigo's compound have followed them? He was staring around for some clue when Smitty shouted.

"For Christ's sake, Morgan, look." All eyes turned seaward. The boat they had returned to looked smaller than it had before. A barely visible wake showed behind her, and she was turned at a slightly different angle to the shore.

"Son of a bitch," Morgan snarled. "She's heading out to sea without us." As he said it, he cursed himself for not demanding full payment in advance. Now his unknown customer could figure to have his dirty work done for a quarter of the agreed price. No wonder he had agreed to such a high fee. Where had Morgan read it? If something looked too good to be true, it probably was.

"Well, what now?" Josh asked. Seven pairs of eyes turned to rest on Morgan Stark.

"Sorry guys. I guess I screwed us all."

"Hey, not your fault," Crazy Mike said with a grin. "Stone's been around this business a long time. We've all worked for him before. You can't figure a guy with his experience and reputation to pull something like this."

"Well, it's done," Morgan sighed. "We're dozens of miles from anywhere good. I give the federales about twenty minutes to get here. Like amateurs we left a trail behind us a blind man could follow, and those signal shots will pinpoint us for sure. I think maybe we better split up."

"Mexico's only about a hundred fifty miles away, but they're on pretty good terms with Belize, so they'll be bottling up the border pretty fast," Lee said.

"Panama's good," Fallon said. "We can get lost there easy and get in and out easy. Of course, it's a bit of a hike from here."

"Okay," Morgan said. "Here's the best way to play it. We'll make two teams. Four go south, four go north. Anybody who makes it out can find me in the usual way. I'll make your money good. Okay?"

"In that case, I'm going with you," Mike said. "If you get caught, nobody gets paid."

Everybody chuckled, and they began the process of choosing teams. Despite the tension inherent in a mission gone wrong, Morgan knew that their professionalism would keep them in a positive frame of mine. As long as leadership is confident, the men are confident, he thought.

Then Morgan's head whipped around, his eyes riveted on the jungle they had just left. His men's laughter and light hearted banter trailed off, replaced by the grinding screech of an ill-tuned transmission.

## -6-

"Scatter!" It was all Morgan had time to say before the fireworks started. His senses registered chaos all around him as he scrambled for cover. Gunfire came from everywhere. Four of his men fell in as many seconds. Dirt and foliage was scattered through the air.

Five jeeps stood at the tree line, and Morgan figured more must be hidden beyond it. His jaw dropped open when he saw Crazy Mike standing straight up at the edge of the shore, returning fire with his M249. The lead vehicle crumpled as 7.62 mm NATO rounds chewed it up at the rate of six hundred rounds per minute. Knowing that some of those rounds would find the gas can in the back, Morgan clenched his eyes shut just before the jeep exploded into shrapnel. The piercing blast tortured Morgan's ears, and a thick black cloud burst skyward.

Mike's courageous cover fire, and the explosion it caused, gave the remaining men a chance. Morgan saw at least two of his teammates make it back into the forest, unseen by their attackers. Over his shoulder he saw Mike grinning like a child on a roller coaster, before a hail of bullets knocked him back onto the shore. He could not think of that now. There would be plenty of time for mourning the dead later. Now he had to move if he was to avoid joining them. And he had to be fast, but quiet. He circled wide, creeping through the woods like one of its native animals. Tall grasses and ferns slapped at his face as he crawled through the underbrush. He continued to move in a shallow arc until he got behind the convoy. Crouching in the undergrowth, he saw there were seven jeeps, each with a four-man crew. All of the soldiers were armed with automatic weapons, a random mix of M-16s, AK-47s and older rifles. Old Abrigo must have been far more important to someone than Morgan had guessed.

The jeep train stood just in front of a slight rise. Morgan moved slowly, silently toward it. By the time he reached the dense underbrush of that rise, the nature of the fighting had changed. What had been a blazing firefight just moments before had degraded into a running guerrilla battle. Now he heard only an occasional shot.

He imagined his men, those who survived, were long gone, faded into the bush, on their way to another country. These under-trained Belizean soldiers were probably just taking sound shots at shadows, or, with any luck, each other. This was the time to make his move, during the confusion. He had made one decision. He did not intend to walk out.

After scanning the options he selected an isolated jeep. Half of its crew was out chasing "terrorists" in the woods. The driver sat in the jeep, smoking a cigarette. His partner leaned against a tree some ten feet away, cradling an old M14 rifle in his arms. He stared dreamily in the direction of the last few shots.

Morgan's chances would not get any better. Moving with agonizing slowness, he crept toward the standing soldier. He traveled with the stealth and patience the United States Army taught him years ago when he was an underage tunnel rat for MACVSOG, the so called Studies and Observations Group of the Military Assistance Command in Vietnam. They trained him well, but he perfected his skills after the war, during years of experience in every kind of dangerous environment on earth.

He breathed silently through his mouth, ignoring the insect bites, the stench of rotting vegetation on the forest floor, the sweat stinging his eyes. Using light and shadow perfectly, he was practically invisible in the noonday gloom of the triple tiered jungle. He stopped barely seven feet from his intended victim. His hand slowly slid down his right leg. From his boot he drew a blackened double-edged throwing knife. With his other hand, he smoothly slid his machete out of its belt sheath.

The young soldier with the rifle was apparently day dreaming, probably about some young lady back in town. Morgan imagined him inventing his story of this day's adventure. How many terrorists could he say he killed? Twelve? Fifteen maybe?

Of course, Morgan could only guess at the soldier's thoughts as he stared off into the woods. Whatever occupied his mind, he did not notice the tall, grim black man rising to his full height behind him. Morgan's left arm drew back and arced down sharply, burying the twenty-four inch tempered steel machete blade between the man's neck and left shoulder, not quite deep enough to touch his heart, but certainly deep enough to do the job. Almost in the same motion, Morgan's right arm blurred. The driver was still fumbling with his rifle's safety switch when the blackened throwing blade buried itself hilt-deep in his throat. His eyes were wide with shock, blood still spurting from the wound when Morgan kicked him out of the seat and fired up the jeep's engine.

With grinding gears and a certain amount of swearing, he managed to get the clumsy vehicle turned around on the narrow trail and headed out in a burst of loose dirt and dead leaves. Five or six soldiers waited up ahead, startled by his sudden appearance. Morgan hardly considered them an obstacle. Driving with his left hand, he unlimbered his Jeti and cleared the road with one quick burst. Driving between the scattering soldiers, he yanked the wheel, dragging the jeep around a sharp curve. But what was that in the road up ahead? Some sort of obstacle. A body?

"Oh, God," Morgan murmured. It was Smitty, lying face up, his dirty blonde hair still in his eyes. Those eyes stared skyward in death now, a rifle still clenched in his right fist.

Everyone who could have seen which way Morgan had gone was dead. Still, stopping now would mean an increased risk of detection, even pursuit and capture. Turning around would be suicide. Besides, the trail was too narrow to even swerve without ramming his bumper into a tree. He really had no choice.

Gritting his teeth, he down shifted and gunned the engine. His stomach clenched as he bumped over Smitty's body, the sound of cracking ribs reaching his ears. He feared he would be sick. He squeezed his eyes tight for a moment, swallowing hard.

When he looked up, he spotted a lone rifleman on the edge of the dirt road, maybe sixty meters ahead. The soldier was taking slow, careful aim at the target rolling toward him. Morgan pointed the Jeti, squeezed its trigger and heard the hollow sound of an empty magazine.

"Damn!" Dropping the submachine gun on the seat next to him, Morgan yanked his Browning Hi-power from its shoulder holster. One bullet smacked the jeep's hood, just before Morgan fired. The rifleman's head exploded under his helmet. Morgan pressed the accelerator to the floor, passing the rifleman's body before his helmet hit the ground. Morgan glanced briefly at the corpse as he passed. It was a little more personal when you hand loaded your own ammunition.

He kept the jeep rolling unerringly north, a talent having nothing to do with his training, but rather a gift he had possessed since birth. He had an unnatural, uncanny sense of direction and distance. Someone had once told him he was psychic or something, but he couldn't care less what others called it. All he knew was, he had a grid map in his mind on which he could see himself moving. And he never needed a compass, because he could literally feel magnetic north. For him, getting lost was a complete impossibility.

So he would drive to Mexico. From there he would go on to the United States. He would track down Stone, and through him, his mysterious boss. Someone was going to pay and pay big for cheating him, for stranding him, for getting his men killed. Someone was going to pay, and soon.

## -7-

Jonathan Stahl saw himself as just another wealthy man in a crowd of wealthy men. The Acapulco beach on which he stood was cluttered with the rich and a few of the famous. All of these men had leased absurdly expensive vacation villas not far away. And they all had boring wives who insisted on spending the evening at the party on this particular beach. After all, they had to show off their expensive gowns, and shoes and jewelry. He had to admit some surprise that the party crowd had chosen the Hotel Plaza Suites for their Acapulco gathering. But then, their piece of the beach was as lovely as any other under the spectacular field of stars that was spread like diamonds on black velvet above them.

Stahl considered it a tragic waste to be listening to the surf gently tapping the sand while wearing a tuxedo. It helped that the hostesses had greeted them with traditional flower leis. And the chefs were doing marvelous things with prawns, kabobs and more exotic fare on charcoal grills, spreading mouth-watering aromas across the beach. The breathtaking displays set up by hotel staff and swaying coconut palm leaves combined to create a spectacular setting that put him in a serious party mood.

When a woman eyed him, it made him feel as if maybe he wasn't just one more man on the beach. Looking around, he thought he was perhaps a shade thinner, a bit taller than some of the others, and the gray starting to show at his temples could be seen as distinguished.

For whatever reason, the beauty standing at one of the portable bars was looking him over. What distinguished him from his peers in her eyes? He really did not know or care. All that really mattered right then was that Victoria was off making one of her interminable visits to the ladies' room. That meant that he could return the beauty's stare and maybe even risk a smile. Could she possibly be there alone?

This girl apparently took his smile as an invitation. When she stepped away from the bar Stahl's breath caught in his throat. She was stately, perhaps five feet nine or ten inches, and quite svelte in an emerald gown clinging tenaciously to her hips. She wore no watch, no jewelry of any kind except for one finely cut emerald on her left hand. He knew it was a cliche, but the only phrase he could think of to describe her skin was peaches and cream. Not just her face, but her shoulders and the satin globes bursting from her bodice as well. Her gown was simple, sleeveless and low cut, with a slit up the left side exposing long, well-muscled legs as she walked toward him. Her hair was that deep fiery red that can only be natural, and it hung to the small of her slender back. Her nose was proud, her cheekbones high, her lips wide and challenging.

Every element of the picture was a point of beauty. Despite all this, her most striking feature was certainly her eyes. Slanted almost like a cat's, they matched the color of her gown and glinted with life.

"Hello," she said, stopping just out of reach. Her voice was summer honey with the slightest hint of Irish brogue. "They call me Felicity. And you are...?"

"Stahl. John Stahl." Although flustered, he recovered quickly. "I'm glad to know you, my dear. I must say you're the first new face I've seen in this crowd in quite a while." He left the obvious question unvoiced.

"Oh, I'm recently widowed," Felicity said, sipping from a highball glass. "My husband was, well, he was a bit older than I. He was well prepared for the worst. He took care of me. So now I'm looking for a way to get rid of some of this money. When I heard about this beach party, it sounded like a good place to start doing that. And I thought I might find some other things I've been missing."

Felicity had stepped closer. While she spoke she ran her free hand down Stahl's side in a manner that he found quite disconcerting. His voice failed for an instant. Another, shriller voice chimed in from behind him.

"You won't find them here, missy," Mrs. Stahl snapped. She was a smart looking blonde, although a bit shorter and somewhat older than Felicity. She wore bright red lipstick and nail polish. Her evening gown was basic black. At her throat sat a brooch holding a brilliant diamond, surrounded by pearls, in a marbled green malachite setting.

"You should be less suspicious, madam," Felicity responded coolly. "And you should show more appreciation for what you do get from your husband. That single bauble you're wearing is probably worth something in six figures. A man deserves a little more respect from a woman at those prices."

\* \* \* \* \*

After her one stinging remark, Felicity O'Brian turned and walked off across the sand. The outburst had caught the attention of others nearby who were busy looking embarrassed when she passed them. Behind her, Felicity could hear heated words passing between the Stahls as she left. That was good. They would probably argue for an hour. Then they would join the rest of the party when it moved to the rocky lookout at La Quebrada to watch the courageous native divers fly into the air and down into the waves. They would not be headed for home anytime soon.

Felicity went into the hotel, found the ladies' lounge and walked to the farthest stall. After locking the door she perched carefully on the edge of the seat, not wanting to risk getting her gown wet. She drew an odd looking metal device from her purse. It resembled a tiny waffle iron, with a pattern inside that looked much like a key blank when she opened it. Next she removed a key from a key ring and placed it on top of the blank. She had taken the key ring from John Stahl's pocket quite easily, without his noticing. In her opinion, a man of Stahl's financial standing shouldn't even carry a front door key.

She partially closed the double handled tool she held and turned the tiny screws on one side. The screws moved the cutting blades inside. When they were in place, pressed against the edges of Stahl's key, she used both hands to squeeze the handles together. After a few seconds of pressure she heard a subtle pop, and tiny bits of metal clattered to the floor. When she opened the odd device, a smile lit her face. Beneath the key she had placed inside lay an exact duplicate. She took a deep breath and let it out slowly. Well, that was it. The preparations were over. The job was on.

She replaced the original key on its ring. On her way out of the hotel, she dropped the "borrowed" key ring in front of the men's room door. She was confident that someone would pick it up before long and hand it in to the hotel management. Some ambitious employee, anxious for a fat tip would announce his find and search until he returned the keys to Stahl. He would probably tell them he did not remember dropping his keys, but since he had them back he would think no more about it.

Felicity enjoyed the ocean breeze and the electric scent of the Pacific until the valet brought her car around. She slid down behind the wheel of her jet-black 300 ZX turbo and smoothly moved out onto the wide avenue. Her compact disc player filled the vehicle with a Bach violin concerto as the air conditioner quietly fought against the night's humidity. Some of the newer cars had much better environmental controls, but she had bonded with this one the day she bought it. She liked the feel of the car, the throaty roar of its engine. Some cars are helpful tools. This one was a friend.

Traffic was heavy for ten p.m. She competed for road space mostly with aging Volkswagen Beetles, little Fiats, tiny Renaults, and a variety of other small, older cars whose drivers made liberal use of their horns. Like most of the city's major streets, this one had a wide median strip, adorned with tall sculptures. She was looking for a particular monument, which was her landmark.

She drove slowly because there was a statue or something at almost every intersection, all quite similar to a foreigner like herself, similar enough to be annoying. Some were historic figures, but most were modeled after members of an ancient pantheon of gods, part human, part bird or snake. Finally she spotted it. It was some sort of unpronounceable Mexican god, but the body parts matched her memory of the one she was looking for. She cornered sharply, down-shifting and rocketing down the narrow lane, pushing her sleek sports car over ninety miles per hour.

She knew exactly where she was going. She had done her research well, including a lot of surveillance during the last thirty days. The contractor who contacted her more than a month ago was impatient. He had an anxious client who wanted a particular antique jeweled brooch. Apparently the client had tried to purchase this piece through an agent, but to his surprise the present owner refused to sell. So he decided to hire a professional to retrieve it.

While one part of Felicity's mind focused on driving, another considered the unusually fine and exceedingly rare item she had been asked to acquire. The only reference she had found to it listed its value at eighty thousand dollars. To put that in perspective, she reflected on an antique diamond bangle bracelet from St. Petersburg she had acquired the previous year. It bore the fine workmanship she expected from Tsarist Russia's imperial capital, its top prong-set with five large diamonds, each enclosed within oval frames channel-set with rose diamonds in a figure eight design. It barely brought four thousand at auction. The finest brooch she could recall, an art deco Belgian piece, platinum and white gold set with twelve carats worth of perfect diamonds, had fetched thirty-two thousand.

It seemed clear that tonight's target meant more than money to the client. Felicity would receive half of its current market value on delivery, a quick forty thousand dollars. Even with her lifestyle, she could relax for a couple of months after this one. The contractor had given her the present owner's name and offered her other assistance, but she had declined. Felicity was both a technician and an artist, the best at what she did, and she preferred to work alone. That way, she stayed in complete control.

With a slight squeal of tires, Felicity turned left down a still narrower road. She had now left streetlights behind, and was only a couple of miles away from her diamond treasure. She had already come to think of it as hers, even though she had only seen its image and the replica attached to Mrs. Stahl's gown. One good look had told her Mrs. Stahl was not wearing the real thing, although Felicity had to admit that she was adorned with a magnificent copy. Felicity was confident of two things. One, that the real brooch spent its life at home in a safe. And two, that she was the only person at the beach party that night who could have guessed that they weren't looking at the real thing.

With only moonlight to guide her, she pulled her car off to the side of the narrow road a couple of hundred feet from Stahl's front gate. A seven-foot wall surrounded the villa. A row of dahlia bushes, probably imported from the mountains, stood at its base. Their round, red, flowers bowed their heads, lending their almost imperceptible scent to the air. Because she didn't want to crush them, the bushes would present more of a challenge than the barbed wire topping the wall. What lay beyond the wall, well that was another story.

It was still quite warm outside when she stood next to her car and stripped. With cool efficiency she squirmed into her working clothes: a pair of black tights, a black stretch turtleneck pullover, and black suede boots. She strapped her hair back with a wide, black elastic band. A slim black shoulder bag from the car's back seat completed her outfit. She had pre-packed it with everything she would need for this job. She paused for just a moment to stare up at the densely packed stars above her, filled her lungs with the sweetly scented air, and headed for work.

The humidity was oppressive. Her skin was already damp and sticky after the brief jog to the wall, and she was feeling the weight of her long, thick hair. Someday she would overcome her vanity and cut it to a more convenient length. For now, she crouched beside the stuccoed stone wall and went over Stahl's security system in her mind one last time.

Two fierce Doberman pinschers roamed on the other side of the wall. Beyond them, the house itself was wired with a variety of alarms. Touch a window or wall and the police immediately got a ring. The alarm on the safe was wired separately. Dogs roaming freely meant that Stahl had decided against motion sensors or electric eyes outside the house. However he had installed an independent electric eye to stand guard in front of the safe. That information had been expensive, and she never did manage to find whoever installed the safe so its exact location remained a mystery. Oh well, she did not want it to be too easy.

Felicity drew two large, raw, boneless steaks from her utility bag and flipped them over the wall. As they thumped to the ground, she could hear the pair of canines running. Seconds later she heard the dogs snarling. That menacing noise was quickly replaced by the slavering sounds of an animal feast. In her head she began ticking off seconds, something she did with unusual accuracy. According to her supplier the drug in the meat would take effect within two minutes. She could count the time off with accuracy to rival any stopwatch.

Two minutes later, she hopped over the bushes to grip the top of the wall under the barbed wire. When she hoisted herself to the top of the wall and looked down she saw one dog sleeping on his side. The other one slumped over as she watched. One obstacle down, she thought.

She dropped to her feet again outside the wall. From her shoulder bag she pulled a simple leather square, about two feet long on a side, and tossed it over the wire. Hopping to grip this, she flipped herself over the wall. Her landing was steady, on all fours. She sprinted the fifty yards to the door.

All the outside pressure alarms were wired through, and controlled by the front door lock. It was an expensive option, and more complex than it needed to be. It's primary advantage was that it prevented Stahl from having to memorize a deactivation code. She would have designed things differently, but she was glad this was the system she had to face. She simply pulled out the key she had made and slid it smoothly into the lock. As she turned the key, the deadbolt slid back and all of the alarms except for those on the safe were turned off. Smiling, she opened the door and walked in as if she belonged there.

The villa was a scaled down mansion, but she did not need a light to find her way around. The floor plan was locked within her photographic memory, and she could call it up like a diagram displayed on a screen. The living room, with its semi-circular sofa, was adjacent to the dining room and overlooked the patio. That gave the ground floor an opening for fresh air to flow through. That sliding glass entrance overlooked the swimming pool and even at night offered a magnificent view.

Knowing that the staff left at night, Felicity headed straight up the long staircase. The Stahls' love of entertaining showed in their choice of a villa with five bedrooms, each with its own full bathroom. Thanks to proper research Felicity was able to continue down the short hall into the room the Stahl's had chosen. It was the vast space that she expected, overly decorated with vanity table, love seat and plasma television, but tasteful despite all that. Plus it simultaneously looked out over the Acapulco Bay, the city and the mountains. But now that she was there, she didn't have time to admire the view.

Again she reached into her bag. This time, she produced a palm-sized disc with an earphone attachment. Fitting the earpiece into her left ear, she began probing the walls, staying between three and four inches away from the tasteful blue flowered wallpaper. She worked around furniture, paying special attention near light switches and electrical sockets. It was slow, tedious work. The tension in her neck grew as the minutes crawled by.

She was beside the king-size bed when the quiet beeping began. Pressing her hand unit to the headboard caused the volume to rise to maximum. With a smile she returned the tiny metal detector to its home inside her bag and began probing the wood with long delicate fingers for a trip lever. She knew she was close.

The button turned out to be under the solid oak headboard's top shelf. She had to press it in and push it to one side. As she did this, the entire headboard slid smoothly to the right, revealing a built-in safe, set flush with the wall.

Staring at the recessed steel door, Felicity heaved a sigh of relief. Until this minute, she faced the possibility that she might be unfamiliar with the safe's protective system. Luckily for her it was a common Model Number 14 Fort Knox inset wall safe, at least three years old. She knew exactly what type of integral alarm would be used. She stepped into the hallway, moving to the nearest linen closet. Behind a stack of satin sheets she found a control panel on the wall. It required only two quick adjustments with a cross-tipped screwdriver to deactivate the alarm. Certainly a switch in the bedroom somewhere did the same thing, but there was no reason to waste more time searching for it. Now that all alarms were off, it was time to return to the safe and get busy.

Felicity's profession required her to be very knowledgeable about safes and security systems. She had studied these devices for several years, researching like a candidate for a rather specific Masters degree program. This particular safe was a fairly old, basic tumbler type design. Stahl had been penny wise and pound foolish not to install a more up-to-date electronic type. She knew how to deal with the latest mechanisms too, but this one called for some of her old school skills.

She had to kneel on oversized pillows at the head of the bed to reach the safe door. She stuck a magnetized amplifier to it. A short wire led from the amplifier to an earplug. Once she had that in place in her left ear she began turning the dial slowly, picturing the disc shaped tumblers behind it. Listening for the clicking noise as each tumbler aligned with the bolt release mechanism, she soon deciphered the combination. When the last number fell into place, she turned the lever and pulled open the square steel door.

When she looked inside, her breath caught in her throat. God, it was a beautiful piece of work, she thought. It seemed quite at home surrounded by a stack of currency and a pair of pearl necklaces. She had a special weakness for Russian malachite, the green marbled semiprecious stone which, in this case, served as a setting for one of the most perfect teardrop diamonds Felicity had ever seen. Finding this kind of clarity in a three and a half carat diamond would be a thrill, even if it weren't mounted in her favorite stone.

During her research, she had learned how this pendant had passed through several generations of Russian royalty. It was created originally for Sophia, wife of Ivan III, late in the fourteen hundreds. It was Ivan the Terrible who added the halo of perfectly matched pearls, and the smaller but equally exquisite square cut rose diamonds at the four compass points, just inside the pearl circle. After that, it passed in and out of royal houses as a gift, and sometimes as a bribe. Women had lied and laid for it. Czars had bled on it. It had been shown off with Faberge eggs and worn with priceless furs. And now it had fallen into the hands of a pretty young Irish thief.

She briefly wished she had spotted this luscious treat for herself, but reminded herself that forty thousand dollars would allow her to be lazy and pick her shots for a while.

Respectfully, almost lovingly, she lifted the glittering prize from its resting place, replacing it with a flawless copy from her bag. This imitation was even better than the one Mrs. Stahl was wearing that evening. If, as Felicity expected, the brooch was seldom pulled out and inspected closely, weeks could pass before anyone discovered the theft. The incident at the beach party would be long forgotten by then.

All that remained for Felicity was the simple task of covering her tracks. She locked the safe. She closed the headboard. She neatly remade the Stahls' bed. She turned the alarms back on, leaving as she had entered, locking the door behind herself and dropping the key casually into her bag. Just being outdoors made her less tense. Once out of the house, the job was almost over. Relief flowed down her body, relaxing muscles and senses.

But an unexpected sound snapped her head around.

It was a low, rumbling growl.

## -8-

One of the dogs was up. Her heart tripled its pace as she realized the drug did not last as long as her supplier said it would.

"Nice doggy," she said, with a waver in her voice. Hesitantly, she stepped away from the door. After all, there was no going back. All exterior alarms were now activated again and she had no time to fish around in her bag for the key.

Felicity met the dog's eyes as she began her slow movement toward the wall. The beast bared its teeth, starting forward on unsteady legs. It still looked groggy, and seemed to be having a hard time keeping its balance. She backed slowly away from the house, one hand extended. If the dog was sleepy enough, she might still escape this situation with her skin.

Even as she thought that, the second dog raised his head and the first one began trotting toward her. Forcing her constricted chest to expand, sucking in a great gulp of air, she turned and leaned into the fifty-yard sprint to the wall. She heard the padded feet, so fast, behind her. Teeth gnashed, and she imagined the jaws open behind her, reaching for her legs.

A dozen feet from the wall she began her dive. She heard slavering jaws snap shut inches from her legs as she grabbed her leather pad and vaulted over the wire. Behind her, the dogs hit the wall, barking and clawing as if they could climb after her. On unsteady legs, Felicity paused for four or five deep inhalations to regain her breath. Then, mindful of the noise, she snatched her leather pad, stuffed it into her utility bag, and ran for her car. Bouncing into the driver's seat, she jammed the sleek, black craft into gear and sped off down the dark lane.

Felicity evaluated her performance while she drove. She completed the entire operation in just under twenty-two minutes. Right on schedule. But those dogs should have slept for another fifteen or so. She had risked capture a thousand times over the years, but had never purposely risked her life. Now here was more evidence why it was unwise to trust anyone else when she was on a caper.

Two miles but less than two minutes later, the 300 ZX pulled to the side of the road again. Now she took a deep breath and released it in a long sigh of relief. She loved the tension and excitement during a caper, even when things got a little more exciting than planned. But afterwards, as her adrenaline level began to drop, she all but collapsed. Only now did she feel the perspiration. She became aware of the clothes clinging to her body, the sore muscles from the climbing and jumping and...damn! A broken nail on her left hand.

After the initial reaction, a slow, contented smile spread over her face. Lethargically, she got out of the car into the waist high grass. Staring at the skyful of stars above, she leisurely stripped, freed her hair, and toweled herself briskly. Just for a moment, she let the fresh air cool her naked form. Her skin now aglow, she donned her evening wear once again. Bending over, she brushed her hair out thoroughly before returning to the car.

In her vanity mirror she meticulously removed and reapplied her makeup. Once satisfied with her appearance she flipped on the air conditioner and drove back toward the city. Driving with her left hand, she fished around in her bag with her right until she found the key to Stahl's leased Acapulco villa. At the first major intersection she powered down her passenger side window and tossed out the key to Stahl's villa. Now the caper was really over.

She drove back to her hotel at an even speed through the poorly lighted streets, feeling the Nissan's power surrounding her. This woman was a true loner. Had been since she saw her parents blown to bits in her native Belfast suburb. Sex she could pick up whenever she felt the need, and always on her own terms. She considered that one of the privileges that beauty granted a woman in this world. As for companionship, she never felt the need for it.

Never, except in rare moments. Only at times like this, the mellow times, did she crave...something. But what? What was missing? Perhaps someone who would understand. No, not just that. She wanted contact with someone else who was good enough to appreciate her expertise. After all, she could not go boasting about the kind of skills she had to just anybody.

The restlessness was setting in as she pulled into her parking space. She considered a quick swim, but decided it would not help. The Hyatt Regency Acapulco was quite comfortable, even luxurious, but that wasn't what she needed now. She needed to move. She needed home. Plans formed in her mind as she stepped down the hall to the elevator. She saw no sense in putting it off. She would get to her room and make a reservation on the first plane out to her Los Angeles place. She would have the car shipped. That would take days, but she had the new Mercedes CLK Cabriolet convertible waiting in the garage at her California apartment building. She could drive it until her beloved Nissan arrived.

But, as she approached her room door, Felicity's head snapped up. She was getting that old familiar feeling. That funny tingle at the nape of her neck. That jangling of nerves that told her something was wrong, that she was in danger. She never questioned where it came from or why, but she knew it had helped her avoid capture on any number of occasions.

Slowly she backed away from the door, her mind spinning. Was there a burglar in her room? Not likely, but who else? Why would anyone be after her? She returned to the elevator and pushed the button, already mapping out alternative travel arrangements. By the time the doors slid apart, she had her next move planned.

"Why, Miss O'Brian, don't you like the room?" The tall thin man in the elevator was neatly dressed in a blue cotton suit and held a small automatic pistol aimed at her navel. A shorter man stood beside him, with darker skin and straight black hair. She froze, feeling bad news approaching. The tall man pointed, and his partner took off toward her room. They must have a friend staked out in there, she reasoned. It was a very simple, very professional trap.

"Please join me in the elevator," the tall man said in a smooth, accentless voice. "I'll give you the layout before the two apes return. My name is Paul. I was sent to retrieve something which you recently acquired at the request of my employer."

"Fine, fine, only, why the gun? Just come back tomorrow after I've had some sleep and a shower. We'll verify the funds deposited in my account and I'll give you the package."

"I'm sorry," Paul said, "but there's been a change of plan. You will give me the antique brooch now. There will in fact be no exchange of funds. You will not interfere with my departure. My orders are rather liberal beyond that. I'd rather not kill you, but if I must..." Leaving that threat hanging in the air, he stretched out his left hand, palm up.

Felicity stared into his ice blue eyes. They were the eyes of a professional, a man who could kill without remorse. For neatness' sake perhaps, he would avoid killing if that course proved convenient.

People who have never been there often wonder if they would hesitate at a time like this. However, when one looks death in the face, one's values become very clear. Her face formed a tired smile and she shrugged her shoulders.

"What the hell," she said. "I can always steal another priceless antique brooch." Slowly she reached into her bag and produced her glittering prize. She tipped her hand and watched the brooch slide off her palm and land in Paul's. "By the way," she said, "What in the world led you to me here? I don't announce my travel plans and I don't use my real name. Besides, there must be hundreds of hotels in Acapulco."

"Over two hundred and fifty, actually," Paul said.

"So how'd you find me?" she asked.

"I'm thorough."

When the other two men returned, Paul turned off the emergency button allowing the car to descend. Then he passed the brooch to one of his partners, a pudgy man in a crumpled plaid suit. He examined the brooch with a jeweler's glass, and verified the object's authenticity with a nod of his head. The third man, evidently a native, stared at her with undisguised lust.

Paul maintained the perfect distance from her, out of reach yet in complete control. Leaving the hotel by a side door, the small group entered a black Cadillac limousine. Pudgy drove, Paul shared the front seat and Felicity sat in the back with number three. Paul's automatic stayed on her the entire time.

"We have a long drive ahead of us," Paul said. "We must meet a large yacht on the East Coast, somewhat south of Mexico. If you cooperate we shall leave you alive in a, er, rural area somewhere along the way."

At the edge of the city, the limousine pulled up behind a large four by four type vehicle. Felicity found these vehicles, so popular in America, to be foolish conceits. They were expensive toys, she thought, for people who thought they wanted an army jeep, but with the luxury of a high cost sedan. This one was an Isuzu Trooper, brown with tan trim, with windows and a roof and carpet just like a real car. Unlike most such vehicles she had seen in the States, this one appeared to actually be meant for off road use, with extra large tires with huge, deep treads. That made her wonder just where they were going.

Paul guided her to the new vehicle with his gun. Her three captors assumed their prior seating arrangement and they drove away, apparently abandoning the Cadillac. Before long, they were cruising smoothly down the asphalt road. The tires whined on the highway but it did not last long. Soon the asphalt faded to gravel, then into dirt.

"I take it there's no decent road leading to wherever it is we're going, eh?" Felicity asked. Her seatmate grinned, and Paul pretended to not have heard her implied question. That made her doubly nervous.

The air was close in the Isuzu, and conversation was minimal. Without the radio playing, road noise and wind shear were the soundtrack of their journey. The tropical scenery was pleasant, filled with trees and flowers whose names she had never bothered to learn, but it didn't take long for the monotony to wear her down.

Her traveling companions didn't seem at all affected by this annoying form of sensory deprivation. They continued rolling, on into the night. In the darkness she knew there was very little chance she could remember the route. With few useful alternatives available, no information on which to build a plan and apparently no immediate danger, she did the only thing that seemed useful and reasonable. She closed her eyes, settled her breathing and went to sleep.

She awoke when the Trooper pulled to a stop. She knew instinctively that four hours had passed. Pudgy and the Mexican each took a rest stop behind a tree. Pudgy returned to the car, but his partner stood beside the vehicle when he returned.

"Would you like to go into the woods to relieve yourself?" Paul asked her.

"I'd go just for a moment of privacy, I would."

"Sorry," Paul said. "I will have to watch you, of course."

"In that case, never mind."

Four hours later, soon after daybreak, they stopped again. The Mexican took down one of the three ten-gallon gasoline cans on the rear of the Trooper and emptied it into the gas tank. Paul repeated his offer to her and this time, she grudgingly accepted. She took fifteen long paces away from the narrow lane and found a spot between two healthy trees. Flashing defiance, she stared into Paul's eyes while she hiked up her dress, slid off her panties and lowered herself. It was not the first time Felicity ever squatted in tall grass, but she viewed Paul's presence as an invasion. He kept the gun trained on her, but handed her a roll of paper when she was in position. And when he heard the sound watering the ground he turned his eyes away. It was a small gesture but somehow it had value to her.

When they returned to the vehicle, Pudgy stood at the back opening a cooler on the tailgate. He distributed breakfast sandwiches and bottles of water. Back in the SUV, the kidnappers returned to their original seating plan.

This routine continued throughout the day and into the next evening with little to occupy Felicity's mind except to count the minutes and try to guess where they were going. She slept a lot, but her body would only accept so much of that. So she sat, twenty-five hours and forty minutes after her abduction by Felicity's flawless reckoning, trying to catch a glimpse of the world outside the vehicle. It was deep in the night again, a dense field of stars and a sliver of a moon lighting the sky. It was the Mexican's turn to share the back seat with her. When she noticed him staring at her she turned to face forward and concentrated on the road, such as it was. Felicity's captors had spoken very little during the trip. Felicity had been similarly quiet, primarily because she had nothing to say to any of them. Her seatmate must have taken her silence for fear, or uncaring. Leering, he reached out to stroke her arm with a sweaty hand.

"We could have some fun with this one," he said, grinning through crooked yellow teeth. His accent was a chilling cartoon caricature.

"You wouldn't enjoy it," she said evenly, continuing to stare straight ahead. "I'd just lay there still. Be like having a dead body, it would. And just before you finished, I'd reach underneath, sink my nails in deep and rip your balls out." She smiled pleasantly, as if she were having a very pleasant dream.

"Bitch!" His sweaty palm arced over, slapping hard across her face. Paul signaled with his gun for the Mexican to back off. She turned back toward him in slow motion, looking up from beneath a rumpled mass of red hair. Her emerald eyes glowed out from the shadows. Her voice was polar ice.

"What's your name?"

"Paco," the Mexican said, grinning. Then he saw her frozen smile.

"Paco," she cooed, "You're a dead man."

At that point Paul signaled to the pudgy driver. The four by four vehicle pulled over into the trees. Vegetation blocked the left side door, next to Paco. Felicity's only looked that way because the tropical grass grew so high.

"I believe this is your stop, Miss O'Brian," Paul said, pointing for emphasis with his gun. "Take some advice. If you're smart, you'll accept this loss maturely and move on to other projects."

She stepped out of the vehicle with her head high, her jaw jutting forward. "Tell your employer that he hasn't heard the last of me. We'll be meeting up face to face before too long."

She slammed the door hard, and the sound echoed through the emptiness. As the Isuzu pulled away, the night noises closed in on her. Darkness held no terror for her, and she recognized the sounds of crickets and frogs from her youth. But without knowing what other wildlife might be around, traveling at night would be stupid. Knowing only a couple of hours separated her from daylight, she found a thick, squat tree and climbed into its branches. There she curled up as best she could to wait for dawn.

"We will meet, mister mystery man," she muttered to herself, "And you're going to regret double-crossing this girl."

## -9-

The baked sand of the narrow road burned into the soles of Felicity's feet. It was a pain she accepted. She could not have walked another step in those damned high heels.

She had shivered through the night but fear had kept her awake. When dawn finally came she had started walking. Within an hour she was barefoot. That was no big deal. She spent most of her youth that way anyway. An hour or so later she discarded her hosiery. Soon after she tore off her gown to just above her knees. Thai silk gowns, she soon discovered, do not rip easily. Just getting a hole started cost her another fingernail. It hurt, but the gown was too restrictive for walking. She needed the mobility.

She ached everywhere. Hunger gnawed at her belly. Not the first time in her life for that, either. She was very thirsty too, but she ignored it. Hatred, gleaming in her eyes, was all that sustained her.

Her beautiful hair had become a matted, tangled heap. Her body was bathed in sweat. Her eyes ached from facing the blazing sun. She walked on the road, out of the shade, only because the cloud of insects was thinner there. Still, bites covered her sunburned arms and legs. For the first time she cursed her heredity, source of the fair skin that had always been a point of pride for her.

Funny, she thought, what you don't know about jungles if you've never spent time in one. Even after watching so many old

Tarzan movies, she never realized the jungle was so noisy. Most of what she heard sounded like the racket birds might make but, Jesus, they were loud. And then there was the smell. The air seemed thick with an odor halfway between sewage and death. Plus, the humidity was unbelievable. Not only did this make breathing difficult, but it caused the stench in the air to cling to her burning, itching flesh.

Worst of all, she had no idea if she was even pushing on in the right direction. She saw no landmarks, and the scenery was totally monotonous. She felt as if she was walking on a monstrous treadmill, a lone, lost hamster spinning her wheel, expecting somehow to make progress. Yet she continued.

She made it ten twenty-six a.m. when she first heard the new sound. An engine, she thought, and it seemed to be getting louder. A vehicle, heading her way! For a brief moment, she reflexively tried to straighten her dress and touch up her hair, before realizing what a hopeless effort that would be. She was just a ragamuffin on the roadside. Besides, being realistic, she figured that her chance for rescue would most likely turn out to be a simple local farm boy approaching in an old pickup truck. He would probably beat her, rape her, and dump her in the next jungle.

Then again, maybe that was not the worst possibility. As the vehicle approached she identified it as an aging, green army jeep. A big black man in camouflage fatigues was driving. He stared stonily ahead, keeping the vehicle centered on the bumpy road. That rattling tin heap must have been travelling at a good seventy miles per hour on the narrow dirt track. Would he roll right over her?

At the last possible instant, she nimbly leaped to the side. The silent driver locked up the brakes. The jeep ground to a halt directly in front of the girl. The driver's head never turned.

"Get in," he growled in a hoarse voice. It took Felicity only a second to weigh her options and decide that any company was better than being alone in the jungle. With a shrug she put one hand on the dashboard and the other on the back of the seat to lift herself up. But with one foot in the jeep, she froze. Her eyes were riveted on the small submachine gun lying on the passenger seat.

That sight prompted her to look up and reevaluate the driver. He carried the foul stench of river water and was covered with a talc-like layer of road dust. He seemed to her to be armed like Mad Max in those old movies, fairly bristling with knives and guns.

Maybe, she thought, she would just catch the next ride.

"Well, you're no prize either," the driver snapped, seeming to read her mind. "Come on! It's either me or the coral snakes and rattlers."

Her eyes bulged. Snakes? She had not thought about snakes. She was probably surrounded by every type of reptile on earth since she stepped out of the Trooper, without seeing one of them, slithering there in the underbrush. Gingerly she picked up the gun, which turned out to be heavier than she expected it to be. She placed it on the jeep's back seat with both hands, then climbed into the passenger seat. Her behind had barely touched the seat when the driver slammed the gas pedal to the floor. The jeep bolted forward like a spurred stallion, slamming Felicity back into the hard seat.

With a hot wind whipping her hair around like a racing pennant, Felicity stared at her stone-like chauffeur. Upon closer inspection he was striking, his face not really handsome but somehow arresting, despite his need for a shower and a shave. His skin was the color of polished oak, his crinkly hair cut short. He displayed the broad shoulders of a champion swimmer, but he had a weight lifter's chest. His brown eyes were sharp, clear, and alert. While she examined him, she searched for the right way to say thank you. Before she could speak, he tossed a question into the silence.

"Name?"

"Felicity," she responded, starting to blush a bit. "Felicity O'Brian. Listen, glory, I wanted to thank you, and I didn't even think to ask your name."

"Morgan Stark," he said, smiling slightly. "And you certainly can thank me. I drove a few miles out of my way to pick you up."

Felicity wasn't sure how that could be, but she decided to let his remark lie. The silence lasted for a good two minutes. This Stark fellow was obviously not a man who was troubled by long silences. While they bumped down the narrow path between tropical trees she thought about his last comment, eliminating all of the obvious answers. Finally she had to ask.

"Okay. I give up. How could you know I was out there?" She found herself smiling broadly when he finally turned to look at her.

"I don't know, lady. Really. I just felt this pull, you know? Somebody over this way, in trouble. Alone. Maybe lost. But not scared."

"I see." She was about to elaborate when a sharp curve almost threw her out of the jeep. "Are you in a particular hurry, Mister Stark?"

"Well, actually, there is a small chance that most of the local army is on my trail. I think I lost them, but I don't like to push my luck."

"The army?" She was grinning uncontrollably now. "I seem to have hooked up with quite a character. Just exactly what did you do?"

"Well, let's just say I got caught on the wrong side of a little local political conflict."

"Oh." What did that mean? This guy was obviously no South American soldier. She saw no United States insignia on his uniform, or any other kind for that matter. Could he be one of those soldiers of fortune she had heard about? A mercenary? He must be, she decided. Felicity's mind was alight with a dozen romantic notions concerning "mercs." Was he a hardened killer? A professional soldier? A bored adventurer? Perhaps all of these. In any case, she was instantly fascinated.

"What about yourself?" Morgan asked. "How did you come to be alone, in the jungles of Belize, miles from civilization, and so, well, inappropriately dressed?" This guy sounded mighty literate for a grunt type field soldier to her. She figured she had best tread lightly.

"Well, the truth is, a business associate of mine decided to play a little trick on me."

"A double-cross, eh?" Morgan asked. "Well, whatever 'business' you're in, I'd say you ought to be speaking to your 'associate' again soon, with a brick."

The two travelers glanced at each other. She decided she liked his smile and got the impression he liked hers. After the brief nonverbal exchange he turned his attention back to driving. She stared ahead too, down what looked to her like an endless dirt track. Expecting a long ride, she settled in and got as comfortable as possible on the stiff green seat.

"How long you been out here?" Morgan asked.

Felicity looked down, shaking her head in self-mockery. "Gawd, I spent the night in a tree."

Nodding, Morgan reached up under his seat and presented her with a green plastic canteen.

"You dear, sweet man is that water?" A shake told her that the canteen was about two thirds full. She gratefully accepted it, starting to guzzle greedily. The water was warm, but it was wet and clean, and she hadn't known how thirsty she was until she tasted the first precious drop.

"Slowly," Morgan said. "If you drink too fast, you'll give yourself cramps. How long since you've had any water?"

"I don't know," Felicity said between swallows. "Late yesterday afternoon I guess. Is this all we got?"

"Afraid so," Morgan said. "And we won't have any more for a while. The next safe town is about thirty-five clicks away. I kind of need to stick to small towns until we hit Mexico. We can get something to eat and drink in the next town, though, okay?"

Felicity nodded. "Hey, can I ask you a question?" When Morgan shrugged, she continued. "You sure seem to know this area awfully well. How is it you know which way to go?"

"Got a map," Morgan said. "The next town is almost due north."

"Oh. You've got a compass too, then."

"Nope. Don't need one. Always know where north is. Now, any more questions?" His face flashed defiance, as if he expected an argument.

"Well, yes. What's a click?"

"A kilometer," Morgan said, flashing a sarcastic smile. "Thirty-five clicks is about..."

"I know what a kilometer is. Thirty-five kilometers is a little over twenty miles, I'd guess. Not far, really."

However, fifteen minutes later, their transportation almost vetoed their plan. The jeep slipped completely out of gear. Morgan almost growled, but despite his playing the pedals furiously, it happened again. Noxious fumes belched out of the undercarriage. Morgan's right arm knotted as he yanked and shoved the gearshift lever. It made Felicity think of a cowboy pulling on the reins, trying to force a bucking bronco to stay in a lane. Alternately cursing and pleading, Morgan managed to cajole the vehicle to the edge of a dirt street village in first gear.

"Any idea what's wrong?" Felicity asked. Morgan looked at her as if she just asked him what the steering wheel was.

"Oh, nothing except a burned out transmission. Probably just hasn't been serviced right. No big surprise."

"Well, how far are we from any place worth being?" she asked as they descended from the jeep.

"About five clicks from the border."

"Three miles," Felicity said. "Not that bad. How about to a real city?"

"Two hundred and seventy miles from Merida. Long walk," he said. "Especially with..." his voice trailed off.

"With what?" she asked. "Excess baggage?"

"You said it, I didn't."

"I'll try to keep up," she said. "Now, do you suppose we can get something to eat in this place?"

A sharp look told her she might be pushing too hard. Grabbing up the canteen and shoving his submachine gun into a sack from the back seat, Morgan headed toward town. The track they were on slowly swelled to almost twice its width. It appeared to be the village's main street. In fact, Felicity began to suspect it was the only street. Despite his long, powerful stride, she followed close behind her rescuer. His grim visage would intimidate anyone they encountered, including her. She simply could not understand why some people can't try to make the best of a bad situation.

As they passed a couple of small shacks Felicity got the feeling she had seen this very village in an old spaghetti western. Unwashed children played in the unpaved street, which was lined with wooden buildings. The few vehicles she saw parked haphazardly between or behind buildings all appeared to be 1960s vintage.

They walked into a small cafe, which also looked like something out of the Old West. A bar counter spanned one wall, in front of shelves crowded with unrecognizable bottles and obscure equipment that might be involved in the process of making coffee. The rest of the space was cluttered with round wooden tables. Only two of the tables were occupied, in both cases by older couples. The looked fairly clean, despite the fact that it smelled of hot oil and perspiration.

Morgan moved toward a table in the corner, reaching for the chair with the best view of the door. Felicity liked sitting with her back to the corner as well, but settled for the side with her back to the wall. From habit, she stood next to her seat, waiting. Morgan sat down, evidently oblivious to her. With a sigh, she seated herself. She had a good view of both the door, and his face.

Surely they made an unusual sight in this rural locale, or in fact anywhere, but the aging proprietor hastened over to them. He seemed to make a point of not noticing anything odd about them, as if he dealt with armed black soldiers and ragged barefoot white women all the time.

"Buenos dias," he said pleasantly.

"English?" Morgan asked, not looking up.

The tavern owner nodded and his smile never changed. "Good morning. We do not serve travelers often, and you two appear to have come a long way. Our menu is small, but I can offer you fresh lemonade on this hot day."

"We'll take a pitcher," Morgan said. "Strong and sweet. And a fat beef enchilada. Re-fried beans. Small bowl of chili. Twice."

The old man nodded more deeply and moved away. When he was gone, Felicity leaned toward Morgan and said in conspiratorial tones, "He speaks English!"

"Of course he does," Morgan said. "Belize is not Mexico, you know. You'll hear a lot of Spanish here, and a kind of Cajun dialect, but English is the official language. This little country was a British Crown Colony for a hundred years. Only got its independence in '81."

"Oh." Felicity fell silent. She was sure she must look like a total idiot to him, and did not want to give him any further evidence. His mind seemed light years away anyway, which suited her just fine. It gave her time to think. As always, she had a plan. It percolated in her mind while she excused herself to visit the ladies room. It too proved clean, although she didn't enjoy washing her face and hands in cold water.

When she returned to the table, she saw that Morgan had also washed while she was gone. She found him easier to look at with clean hands and face but she wished he would smile more. Soon after she sat down their food came, on chipped china plates. Morgan fell on his hungrily. Felicity poured and emptied two glasses of lemonade before she even approached the food. She finally lifted a fork full of the beans as if judging their weight, and dropped them back onto her plate.

"How can you eat this disgusting, overly spiced slop?" she whispered.

"Hey, when you're hungry, food is food," Morgan said between mouthfuls. He continued in an imitation Massachusetts accent that surprised her. "I suppose you've got the cultivated palate of a gourmet. Too bad. I've eaten too much mess hall food, in the U.S. and a few other armies. My taste buds retired long ago."

Despite her reservations, only seconds passed before the necessity of hunger drove Felicity to taste parts of her meal. Two minutes later she was eating steadily, and soon was devouring her food greedily. She had nearly finished her greasy meal when she suddenly looked up.

"Do you have any money?"

"About twenty dollars American," Morgan said. "More than enough for the meal."

"Wait a minute. You travel in a foreign country with just twenty dollars in your pocket?"

Morgan's face hardened again. "I didn't expect to be here for any length of time, and I didn't get paid for my last job."

"Hm. You know, the men who stranded me also stole something from me," Felicity said between bites of enchilada. "I'd be willing to pay you a fair amount if you'd help me get it back."

"What's your idea of fair? I'm pretty expensive help. Besides, right now I don't even know when we'll get to civilization. Hell, I don't even know where I'm going next."

"Look, I've got plenty of money, if that's what you're worried about," Felicity said, pushing the last of her rice onto her fork. "I just don't have any with me. I lost my purse in the jungle in the dark. As for how we'll get to civilization, don't be worrying your little head about it. I spotted an old pickup truck down the road. Nobody will miss it. You said Merida was less than three hundred miles away, right? We can be there tonight. I can wire for cash from there and we can fly to my Los Angeles home."

"Hold on!" Morgan said. "You're moving a little fast here."

"I thought you were an adventurer. Besides, do you have anywhere else to go?"

"Well, I guess not," Morgan said after a few seconds.

"Well then, I say let's be off."

\* \* \* \* \*

They were approaching the end of the road when Morgan finally accepted that this woman was serious. They stopped next to an ancient blue Chevy pickup truck. Dust covered, with just passable tires, it stood like a lonely swayback mare awaiting its rider.

"You intend to buy this old hulk somehow?" Morgan asked, grinning. "Or maybe talk the owner out of it?"

"Don't be silly. We'll just take it."

"Real nice," Morgan said, trying the door. "Just like that. It's locked, you know."

Felicity shrugged. "So?"

Morgan had decided his new companion wasn't very bright, but at that second the scatterbrained expression dropped from Felicity's face like a mask, replaced by a surprising focus and concentration. From her matted hair she drew a small sliver of spring steel, almost like a shiny bobby pin. She slid this into the driver's side door lock in businesslike manner and opened it. Under the dash, she pulled wires and twisted them carefully. The starter reluctantly turned and the engine leaped to life. Just under seven seconds passed between her sprightly "So?" and her terse "Get in!" Morgan barely got onto the running board before Felicity, with some grinding of the gears, sent the old pickup lurching forward. By the time he was inside and got his door closed, they were moving quickly enough to raise a dust cloud behind them.

They heard loud voices behind them, shouting in Creole and English, but Morgan figured that by the time the locals got another vehicle on their trail, that trail would be cold. The local police force was probably pretty disorganized, so getting into Mexico with this rust machine should prove no problem. All in all, he was impressed. She took action without a second's hesitation. He liked that. It was a pretty ballsy move for a broad.

"You know, Red, you're all right," he said, shaking her head by a handful of hair.

"Thanks," Felicity said, "but don't call me Red, okay? Nobody calls me Red. Hey, this thing's got a tough clutch. You want to drive?"

"Sure thing, Red," he said with a deep laugh. "Pull her over."

"No need. Don't want to give anybody a chance to catch us." Felicity gripped the wheel tightly and raised herself from the seat. After a couple of seconds she said, "Well, come on. Step on the gas and slide on over here." Shaking his head, Morgan pushed her foot off the accelerator with his own and pulled himself under her body, so that she was steering from his lap. Once he was in place she nimbly hopped off him to land on the seat to his right. She was giggling a bit, as if they had just performed some schoolyard prank, and Morgan had to admit her relaxed smile was infectious.

As the truck, bucking like a rodeo bronco, rolled over the endless treadmill of a road, he thought it was a good chance to take some time to think.

After a couple of minutes passed, Morgan asked, "Are you sure this 'business acquaintance' of yours stole something from you? Not that it matters, but it occurs to me that maybe you stole something from him."

"Not from him," Felicity answered. "For him." After a much longer hesitation she added, "It was a contract job. I've a feeling you know about such things. Only, like yourself, I didn't get paid."

"Oh, so you're for hire, eh?" he asked, grinning.

"Not usually. I'm self-employed, normally. But this deal looked so good..."

Felicity stopped as Morgan pulled the pickup around a curve in the narrow dirt road, and then pulled them over to the side. Her raised eyebrows silently asked why they were stopping.

"We're approaching the border," he said. "I got no problems in Mexico, but the Belize boys might be watching. This is a pretty obscure crossing point, but I want to go up and take a look before we drive on up there."

\* \* \* \* \*

As Felicity watched from the truck, Morgan walked down the road ahead. He looked like a huge man when she was standing beside him, but now he was dwarfed by the tall jungle trees lining the road. The foliage presented a solid wall of green, because tree bark was obscured by vines and moss. The tall, massive trees appeared to be woven together, as if some giant seamstress had pulled her needle in and out between them, a needle threaded with thick, leafy vines.

Morgan's uniform matched the jungle perfectly, but she followed his movement at the edge of the road. About twenty meters ahead, he suddenly stepped to the side and vanished into the brush.

"What a thief this man would make," she said aloud.

Felicity stared out the open truck window, waiting for something to come out of the jungle and bite her head off. She felt very alone, which was a feeling that had never bothered her much before. Of course, this was not her natural environment. Even the woods of her homeland didn't cause her this kind of unease. The birds there sung a different song.

She sat alone for what felt like an hour, although she knew it was barely ten minutes. As time passed, weariness overwhelmed tension and she began to relax. Just as her eyes were about to slide closed, Morgan silently stepped through the green barrier onto the road. He didn't look happy, but he wore an expression more of annoyance than actual concern. He didn't speak until he was right beside the truck again.

"These bozos have got a pair of kids in uniform up there watching the border."

"Okay," she said. "So can't you go up there and bop them on the head or something? I don't feel like driving along the border all day looking for a clear spot."

"Sure, Red. You just tell them to put those little rifles down and I'll do that."

"Don't want to shoot them, huh?" She hoped not.

"Shoot them?" Morgan said. "Look, I'm a fighter, but I fight soldiers. These are just kids."

Felicity smiled and blew a stray stand of hair out of her face. "Well then, I guess I'll just have to get them to put their guns down."

## -10-

The young Belizian border guard turned over his hidden king, raked in a handful of his partner's coins and inhaled deeply on his cigarette. Victor pushed his cap back on his head, too weary to even be angry about losing. Guarding a border crossing no one knew about was the worst duty possible. He knew they were being punished for being young. How could he prove he was a real warrior? No enemy would attack them there, except boredom. He would welcome a farmer bringing a truck full of fruit, just to have someone to harass.

Their little shack stood to the side of a road not quite wide enough to allow two vehicles to cross. Not that it mattered, Victor thought. Most of the people they had seen in the last week were riding behind animals, not engines.

His thoughts were suddenly shattered by a piercing scream. The two guards leaped to their feet, yanking the charging handles of their AKM's. They looked at each other, their hearts pounding. Victor, the younger man, jerked his head toward the dirt trail that led up to their post next to the border. His nineteen-year-old partner slowly stepped down the path, a little way into Belize. Twenty meters away he turned to face the border, smiling, and waved his partner ahead.

What they saw was the universal stuff of teenage dreams. A tall, fair-skinned woman lay sprawled in the road face down, just around the first narrow bend. One leg was curled up, her ragged gown almost, but not quite, revealing the tender flesh of her perfectly rounded buttocks.

The border guards circled their discovery cautiously. The red-haired woman lifted her head, licked her dry lips, and raised one hand in a silent request for help. The two young men broke into broad smiles, but took no action.

"They, they left me here, all alone," she said, exhaustion showing on her face. "Please, would you help me up?"

"Oh, we'll be glad to help you," the older guard said, setting his rifle aside. "Keep her covered," he told his partner. Barely able to keep a straight face, Victor pointed his shaking rifle at her bosom. The other took her arm, drawing her to him. Artlessly, he pressed his mouth to hers. Clearly sensing no resistance, he started trailing sloppy kisses down her throat, headed for her breasts.

\* \* \* \* \*

Felicity tolerated the drool on her flesh, keeping her eyes on the other border guard. The little twerp was watching the show with obvious pleasure, until a black man wearing camouflage fatigues took one long step out of the jungle and landed a solid left cross on his jaw. The other guard turned just in time to see his partner collapse like an empty uniform into the sand. Morgan grabbed the second guard's shoulder, continuing his spin into the stiffened fingers of Morgan's right hand.

It looked to Felicity as if Morgan's hand sank to the wrist in the youth's soft belly. A blast of air rushed past the guard's lips. He dropped, first to his knees, then to his face in the dirt. Morgan was shaking his head.

"And you didn't think it would work." She began brushing herself off.

"I didn't think anybody could be that dumb."

Morgan dragged the unconscious guards into the brush off the side of the road while Felicity brought the truck forward. Morgan got back behind the steering wheel and they continued north.

Felicity couldn't say that Mexico looked different from Belize, but she was somehow more comfortable after they crossed the border. Barely out of sight of the little guard shack, Morgan pulled onto a two-lane blacktop. A few minutes later they were on an actual highway. The old truck had more power than she expected, and Morgan kept it moving over sixty miles per hour. The familiar whine of the tires on a real road made her situation seem less foreign. Felicity leaned away from the breeze coming in her open window and her head settled onto Morgan's shoulder. She was surprised at how natural it seemed. He was whistling a tune she wasn't sure she recognized.

\* \* \* \* \*

"Hey Red, check this out."

Felicity's eyes snapped open and she jerked upright.

"Where are we?" she asked.

"We're tooling through the Yucatan, headed north on Route 261," Morgan said. "Now look out my window quick, or you'll miss it."

Felicity stared past Morgan, but saw only the jungle she had been looking at all day. Then her eyes wandered to the top of the tree line, and she saw what at first looked like a gold tower thrusting up into the clear azure blue of the sky. It was, on closer inspection, a chunky stone structure almost twice as tall as the trees. It resembled a giant layer cake, but with dozens of layers, each one smaller than the one beneath it.

"Oh, my. What are those? Pyramids?"

"Very good," Morgan said. "Those are the ruins of Uxmal, one of the best known Mayan cities. It's quite the tourist attraction and one good reason to visit the Yucatan. That big one is called the Pyramid of the Magician. If you dig that kind of thing, there's a hotel right up here on the right."

Felicity dragged her fingers through her snarled hair. "I appreciate the offer, but I think I'll put off sightseeing until we get someplace where I can get some cash in my hand, and after I've had a chance to settled into a long, hot bath, okay?"

Morgan shrugged. "Sure, kid. We're still a good fifty miles south of Merida. But you're missing some cool columns, temples, and an ancient cemetery, not to mention the good old temple of the phallus."

"You're making it up, now," she said, giggling as she craned her neck to watch the ruins pass out the back window.

"Who'd make up a thing like that?"

Felicity sat back in her corner of the truck's dusty cab and pulled her left foot up onto the seat so she could watch Morgan more closely. "So, you fancy yourself a tour guide as well. Well, since you'd never make anything up to fool a poor girl like myself, why don't you tell me a bit more about this job you were on."

"Tell you what," Morgan said. "I'll tell you how I ended up in Belize if you'll tell me a bit more about how you did."

"You'll show me yours if I'll show you mine, eh? Well, fair's fair."

For the next few minutes they exchanged personal stories, but their conversation did not stray beyond the events that directly led up to their meeting in the jungle. Felicity made a point of not asking anything about Morgan's past beyond that, and was grateful that Morgan showed no curiosity about hers outside of her present circumstances. Morgan did ask one or two questions about Felicity's life as a thief, but his questions were mostly about technical things. He was interested in her equipment and techniques. He really seemed to admire her systematic approach to the Stahl job. For her part, Felicity was interested in the different weapons and tools of his trade. Her interest was entirely professional. It seemed too soon to her for personal information. She may have owed him her life, but they had just met, after all.

About a half-hour after passing Uxmal they came within sight of the Hacienda Yaxcopoil, which Morgan explained was a seventeenth century estate and another popular tourist stop. Not long after that they rolled into recognizable suburbs and appeared to have left the third world far behind. Felicity made it one-forty p.m. when they motored into Merida, the major city in the southeast corner of Mexico complete with wide, clean streets and snarled urban traffic.

"You know, I love Acapulco," Felicity said. "People call it the Riviera of Mexico, but there isn't much there beyond perfect beaches. This place is much bigger and a lot more urban."

"Yeah and noisy as hell," Morgan said. "Now you want to find a hotel?"

"What I really want is that haven for lost Yank travelers, the American Express office."

They had entered the city on a main street and soon spotted an information booth. Felicity jumped out of the truck and in the time it took Morgan to sit through a single streetlight change she was back with good news.

"The American Express office is dead ahead on Calle 60," she said as Morgan pulled through the intersection. "It's at the north end of the city. Let's get going."

But after a morning at highway speeds they seemed to be crawling now, through a city as congested as Paris or London. Most of the cars there were older, but drivers leaned on their horns as much as anyplace she had been. On the way they passed some lovely parks and one impressive church, but Felicity was focused on their objective. She bounced impatiently in her seat and, when traffic stopped them half a block away from the American Express sign, frustration overwhelmed her. Morgan's jaw dropped when she popped her door open.

"I'm going on ahead," Felicity said. "By the time you find a place to park I'll likely be back."

Felicity again left the truck, waved back at Morgan and jogged through the lanes of traffic to the office where she rushed inside to tell her story.

The statuesque redhead drew all eyes when she walked across the lobby. She was relieved to see only a handful of people inside. Their conversations hushed as all turned to stare at her. Despite her discomfort, she maintained her erect carriage and commanding manner. Her practiced eye led her to the manager without her having to ask anyone. She walked up to the slightly built man's desk and lowered herself into the chair beside it.

"How can I help you?" he asked hesitantly, pushing his glasses up his nose.

"My name is Felicity O'Brian and I'm in a bit of a spot Mr…" she looked at the name plate on his desk, "Mr. Marshall. I need some traveler's checks and probably some cash for local purchases. For that, I'll need to have some money wired in from L.A."

"You are an American?" the manager asked, skepticism fighting with annoyance for display space on his face.

"U.S. resident, yes," she answered patiently. She crossed her long, bare legs to make sure she could maintain the man's attention. "I was robbed, and kidnapped by three men. They took my purse and ditched me in some jungle south of here. Look, I'm registered at the Hyatt Regency Acapulco hotel and my car's there. That should be easy enough to verify. I just need some funds for traveling."

The manager stared at her thighs, and ran a hand up through his short, sandy hair. "Have you a passport?"

"In my purse of course," Felicity said.

"I'm very sorry," Marshall said, his voice dripping with mock sincerity. "I'd like to help you, really I would but, without positive identification, I'm afraid I'm helpless."

"Is that the only problem?" To the manager's embarrassment, Felicity slid her fingers inside the top of her left brassiere cup and pulled it forward. From a pocket inside she pulled a titanium American Express card. Her right cup yielded a California driver's license. In one motion she laid them on his desk and pulled a small note pad toward herself. She wrote a name and telephone number on it and pushed it back toward him. She offered him a demure expression, actually batting her big green eyes for effect.

"Now call my banker in Los Angeles and get me some money."

While she watched, he picked up the telephone and pushed the buttons to call the number in Los Angeles. He glanced at Felicity in surprise when he heard the reaction he got from a mention of her name. When he reached the right person, he handed the telephone to her. She spoke to her American banker in a friendly but businesslike manner, and handed the receiver back to the American Express bank officer when she was finished.

"Now if you'll point me to your ladies' room, I'll let you work out the details of the transfer with him."

After using the facilities and splashing some water on her face and neck, she returned to sit calmly in front of the manager's desk. She relaxed, determined to show patience with the process while Marshall's eyes flitted around the room. His nervousness seemed to match her patience.

Neither Marshall's nerves nor Felicity's patience was tested for long. Within fifteen minutes, her bank had telexed expense money to her. The baffled manager went to a cage himself and counted out four thousand American dollars in traveler's checks and another thousand dollars worth of pesos to a dirty, barefoot girl in half a dress.

"With your card, there's really no reason for a lot of cash," the manager said. "Why carry so much?" the manager asked.

"Security," she replied. "I just feel better with the cash in my fist." She closed her hand around her money and practically skipped back to her stolen vehicle. Morgan had found a space across the street within sight of the door. She raced through the sluggish traffic, bounced into the truck and slammed the door.

"Well, shall we go get us some decent clothes?" Felicity asked. Her smile stretched wide enough to almost hurt her face. She had money again and to her, money was power.

"No. First we need to find us a hotel room."

"I beg your pardon?" Felicity glared at him. Had he told her no?

"You need a bath before you do anything else," Morgan said. "I spotted a Hyatt while I was circling for a parking space. Should suit a civilized gal like you. And you better give me that wad of money."

"Excuse me?" she responded icily through clenched teeth, her usually soft brogue coming out. "You'll not be telling me what to do. You're not in charge here. Why on earth should I be handing my bankroll over to you, a total stranger, when I'm a billion miles from anywhere?"

"Because I have pockets! If you stuff that wad in your bra you'll look like Dolly Parton."

Nonetheless, when the gas-belching, backfiring pickup pulled to a stop in the hotel parking lot, she still clutched her money in her sweaty little palm. The seventeen-story Hyatt Regency Merida was not hard to spot in Merida's skyline. The building was in no way Mexican or even Latin. In fact, the glass and silver structure was totally devoid of any local imprint. It could have been a Hyatt Regency anyplace on the planet, which gave Felicity some comfort. It would represent a total return to civilization. There was even a shopping mall across the street. As soon as Morgan parked and shut the engine off, Felicity stepped down to the ground. She had taken three steps before she realized that he hadn't moved.

"Are you coming? If I need to bathe so badly, you need to register us in a room."

Morgan slowly stood up and out of the jeep. "Not me. I'm broke. You don't trust me with your money, so I guess you'll have to do it."

Felicity's lips clenched together, but instead of an explosion of words she gave him only a fierce stare before turning and entering the lobby.

Stepping into a wall of cool air reminded her that her body was soaked with perspiration. Padding across the neutral colored carpet made her aware that she was barefoot. She glanced over her shoulder at Morgan and saw only a dangerous looking mercenary. Their appearance and lack of luggage nearly made her balk, but her arrogance overcame her pride and she walked up to the desk like a princess.

"We need two rooms for tonight," she told the desk clerk. He was dark for a Mexican, with long hair plastered down onto his head with too much pomade. His eyes moved from her gnarled hair down her tattered gown as far as he could see and slowly drifted back up to her eyes. His face said she was an undesirable guest.

"I'm sorry, but I'm afraid we have no vacancies today," he said slowly, the way he might speak to a person who was a little slow, or potentially dangerous.

"That can't be," she said. "This isn't even the high season. And I need a room now." To make her point more persuasive, she pulled her American Express card from her bra and slapped it onto the counter. The clerk stared down at it skeptically.

"Where did you get that?" he said in clear English. His eyes flashed to the bundle of cash in her hand. Did he think she had stolen the money, and the card? "As I said, I'm afraid we are fully occupied."

Felicity glanced around the room in frustration. To her right, three men sat around a table playing dominoes. They were unshaven and wore work clothes. That marked them clearly, not as guests or tourists, but local men enjoying the air conditioning. They watched her with undisguised lust, but she wondered if they were leering at her body or the money in her hand. She faced the clerk again, offering a tentative smile.

"Look, you can't turn me away," she said in softer tones.

He shrugged. "What can I do?" Then his expression shifted, from arrogant superiority to something like tentative fear. Morgan's elbows had settled gently onto the counter beside her, his arms crossed loosely. She hadn't noticed that his pistol was no longer in its holster. Probably in the sack he had placed on the floor beside his foot, but the empty holster probably still made a statement.

"I think you're confused," Morgan said, in a soft yet still menacing voice. "I'm confident that if you look again you'll find vacancies you overlooked before." Locking eyes with the clerk, Morgan showed his teeth, but it wasn't a smile. "You don't want to disappoint this lady."

Felicity could feel whatever Morgan was projecting that made the clerk's demeanor change from cool to flustered. He punched buttons on a computer console while he licked his dry lips.

"Why, you're absolutely right, sir," the clerk said. "Look at that. Two rooms you said?"

Felicity looked again at the three men in the lobby, who still looked at her the way she imagined sharks looked at smaller fish.

"One room," she said. "One room will do."

\* \* \* \* \*

Their room looked like any standard hotel room in America. Felicity entered first, noting how comfortable the two full size beds looked. A table stood by the window, under the predictable hanging lamp. Green pattern wallpaper, matching carpet and a couple of still life paintings completed the decor. Felicity headed for the easy chair beside the table. When Morgan closed the door behind them she smiled at how well the room shut out the noisy city.

The air-conditioned atmosphere had shocked her system and exhaustion hit her like a heavy fist. As she settled into the chair's deep cushions, Felicity realized that Morgan was right about one thing. A hot tub to soak in would be just the thing.

"Let me in the bathroom first," Morgan said, stripping off his shirt. "I'll only be a minute." He then peeled off his tee shirt, and Felicity was struck by the powerful muscles, trapezius she thought they were called, running down from his neck into bulging shoulders. Yes, she decided, a weight lifter for sure. He strode into the bathroom and turned on the tap in the sink. He was already washing his face, hair and neck with the tiny complimentary bar of soap when he pushed the door closed with his foot.

While Morgan cleaned up, Felicity opened the closet, surprised to find no safe on the floor. The hotel must have kept a safe downstairs behind the front desk. She never even considered leaving the room to hand her money and credit cards to the presumptuous desk clerk. Instead, she cast a furtive glance about for a safe place to stash her money. Behind a drawer? No, too obvious. Inside a lampshade? No. It was the first place she would look if circumstances were reversed. Why wasn't she bright enough downstairs to ask for two rooms? No, that was no mistake. With this much money in a strange town, she wanted a man nearby. She might not know him well enough to trust him with her meager funds, but she felt she could count on Morgan to protect her.

Finally she decided to move the nearest bed forward a few inches and claw up the carpet just enough to spread the bills out beneath it. When her money was well hidden she moved the bed back to its exact original position. No telltale lump showed on the floor, no hint of a disturbance. The sound of the toilet flushing spurred her to move away from her hidden treasure. She was standing at the bathroom door when Morgan came out.

"You look like an abandoned orphan, Red," Morgan said as she brushed past him, "but you're damned sexy for all that."

When she first entered the bathroom, she thought Morgan must have left the water running accidentally. Then she looked over and realized the sound was not coming from the sink, but the bathtub, which was almost full. Reaching in, she found it just a bit too hot. She turned off the "H" tap and waited a moment before turning off the "C". She shed her rags and kicked them into a corner, but decided to check herself over before getting into the water.

From long habit she went over her muscle tone from her neck clear to her toes. Her feet were sore but healthy. She bruised easily, and had picked up a couple of visible welts on her upper arms and legs from walking into branches. Her back, arms and legs all stung from a nasty sunburn, and tiny bumps from insect bites covered her limbs. All in all, she hurt but was not really injured. She credited her gymnastics classes with the resilience and toughness she needed in her work, and even in extreme circumstances like the last two days.

Satisfied with her condition, she stepped into the tub and lowered herself gingerly into the hot water, feeling her pulse increase. After a couple of deep breaths she lathered her body as briskly as she could stand, and washed her hair three times, emptying the bottle of overly scented shampoo the hotel supplied. Once she felt clean she leaned back, sinking chin-deep into the water. She felt weightless, with a million tiny pinpricks on her body, and her skin burned everywhere from insect bites and sunburn. Even after the rapid-fire events of the past seventy-two hours, all she needed to put her right was the total relaxation only a tubful of heat could bring.

\* \* \* \* \*

With a start she snapped awake. The water surrounding her felt cooler and was covered by an unpleasant soap film. She sprang to her feet, feeling her hair drain water down her spine. Forty-two minutes had passed since she slid into a tub of hot water. She spent that time in a deep sleep, leaving her feeling completely refreshed. A nice feeling, but it had not been her plan. In fact, she realized with mounting anger that, in her weariness, she had not really planned at all. Here she was, standing in a draining bathtub, without a stitch of clothing to put on. She remembered that the hotel supplied terrycloth robes, but they were hanging in the closet.

Surely Mister Stark was thinking of this when he maneuvered her into this damned hotel room. Well, she had plenty to tell him. But she certainly could not put her shredded dress or those nasty underclothes back on after two days in the fetid jungle. Looking around the room for cover, she settled on two large bath towels. First, she dried her body thoroughly. By carefully wrapping the towels around herself, she managed to make herself reasonably modest. Without a brush her thick hair would be impossible but she would cope with that later. She shoved the door wide open, prepared for war.

The scene that greeted her stunned her into silence. It was as peaceful as dawn over the Wicklow Mountains back home. Morgan lay face up on the far bed, barefoot and topless, with his left arm thrown over his eyes. His chest rose and fell in the slow, steady cadence that indicates a deep, sound sleep. His mouth sagged open slightly and he gave off a sound just short of a snore.

On the other bed, clothes were laid out the way a mother does for her young children, in the shape of a body. Just under the pillows there was a tie-dyed tee shirt with a bra on top of it in the appropriate place. A pair of blue jeans lay just below the shirt, topped by a pair of cotton panties. At the foot of the bed she found a pair of locally made sisal sandals. She knew that Morgan must have gone out to a local shop or across to the mall to pick these things up. How considerate.

Felicity gathered the clothes and returned to the bathroom. Getting dressed provided another surprise. The jeans fit perfectly, although they were a little tight. She preferred them that way, and figured Morgan would too. The shirt was comfortable, and she decided to do without the bra for now, planning to rinse out her custom pocket-bra in the sink later. Finally, she slid her feet into the sandals, finding that even they were the right size. She would not have thought it possible.

Not until she was fully dressed did a more disturbing thought strike her. How had Morgan paid for all this? He couldn't have bought her a new wardrobe with no money. That morning he had told her he only had twenty dollars, and he spent some of that to pay for their disappointing breakfast.

She left the bathroom again to find Morgan still sleeping. Silently she shifted the bed, reached under the carpet and gathered up her bills. A quick riff through them told her she was missing about four hundred dollars. He had found her cache, but only taken pocket change, much of which he must have spent on her. She could not help but wonder how much he had left.

She stepped silently over to her sleeping roommate. After surveying him closely it appeared the only wrinkle out of place was on his left front trouser pocket. It would be tricky to explore, especially with a mark lying down. But she knew she had the lightest touch in the business. Her hand slid smoothly into his pocket. Her two middle fingers closed on the bills. She began to withdraw them, very gradually. The paper hit the slightest snag of cloth.

Steel fingers closed on her wrist and nine-millimeter death was suddenly staring her in the face. She caught her breath and froze. Her eyes crossed as the Browning Hi-power's muzzle brushed her nose. There was a terrible moment of peak tension, then Morgan's fingers relaxed on her arm and he lowered his automatic to the floor next to its shoulder holster.

"Sorry," Morgan said with an apologetic grin. "Trigger nerves."

"No kidding."

"Well, I'm glad you're out," Morgan said, standing and stretching as if the incident had never happened. "Are you about ready to get on the road? I think I got everything we need."

Felicity found his casual demeanor, after sticking a gun in her face, a little disconcerting. She backed away, trying to push her brain into the new conversation.

"I appreciate the gesture, and this stuff is nice, but you don't really think you can shop for me, do you?"

"Why not?" Morgan answered, pulling dresser drawers open. "Look. Jeans, tee shirt, shoes, two purses, skirt, blouse, sunglasses, a bra and panties, plus what you're wearing. Let's see, comb, brush, toothbrushes and a suitcase. My clothes are in the closet."

"Wait a minute," Felicity said. "A bra? You think you can look at me and..."

"Thirty-seven C," interrupted Morgan calmly. "Waist twenty-five. Hips thirty-eight. Ankles about seven. I never miss when it comes to judging distances. In any form."

He had stopped her. Felicity stood with her mouth partially open, unsure how she should react. Not only did he hit every measurement exactly, but she could not think of anything else she needed.

# -11-

Marlene Seagrave sat in front of her vanity mirror, dressed only in a full-length slip, brushing her shoulder length blonde hair. She wasn't pleased with what Anton had done with her hair this time, but that was only the leading edge of her unhappiness. Her image in the mirror was certainly not ugly, but it did not please her.

They used to say she had soft brown eyes, like a fawn, but now narrow lines were growing under them. Just thirty-two years old, and she was already considering botox shots. And she had just found her first gray hair. Why that should move her close to tears, she did not really understand.

Her arm movements became more and more forceful, although she knew no amount of brushing would make that gray hair go away. Besides, it was just one indicator of what was happening to her entire body. Six years ago she did calisthenics or aerobics almost every day, swam twice a week, and watched her diet very carefully. Then she married Adrian and all that changed. She went from starving model and Hollywood hopeful to society lady. Because of Adrian's money she dined at the finest restaurants and drank the best liquor. Life was so much fun when it all began. She was the belle of the ball, and Cinderella never had it better. How she loved him then.

Then?

Now, the best clothes, the best hair stylists, manicurists and makeup could not make her the woman she was before. And with time, her view of the man she loved had only become clearer. Her luxurious apartment seemed cold to her now, as did their king size bed. For this Cinderella, happily ever after was the hard part.

The bedroom door whooshed against the deep burgundy carpet as it opened. She turned, an automatic smile brightening her face.

"Adrian. I didn't know if I should expect you home tonight. That business meeting..."

"Life isn't all business, baby," Seagrave said with a slight slur. He approached her wearing only a silk robe that was too long for his squat form. After six years of marriage, she could tell by his walk how many drinks he had gotten under his belt. Seeing him standing there at the edge of drunkenness, she could not help but compare him to her six-year-old mental picture of him. His complexion was rougher now and his brown hair thinner, but that was all superficial. More importantly, his eyes had grown harder. In them she could see that he looked at her less as a lover and more as a thing, a possession.

Still, she stood as he reached out to put an arm around her. She wanted to give him the love he deserved. He was, after all, her husband.

"Take a look at this, baby," Seagrave said as he pulled a large velvet jewel box from his robe pocket. Her smile became more genuine as she accepted this unexpected gift.

"Oh, Adrian, what is it? What's this for? I mean, it's not my birthday or anything."

"Open it," he said, giving her a crooked smile. "You'll know."

Her eyes widened to saucers as light glanced off her new prize. "It's magnificent," she breathed. Her heart pounded with a flush of renewed love. He was trying to make things better, and she would try too. She knew they could make it like it used to be.

Her moment of euphoria passed a moment later as she recognized the brooch. That perfectly facetted diamond with its halo of matched pearls set in its marbled green base was unmistakable. It was the brooch she had casually targeted weeks ago at a party as part of an absurd negotiation. Her eyes dropped to meet his, showing only a hint of suspicion.

"Honey, how did you ever get this? I can't imagine any woman being willing to part with such a beautiful piece of jewelry once she had it. Besides, it must be worth a fortune."

"Don't you worry about how I got it," Seagrave said. "You just get ready to wear it to that party Saturday night. You've earned it. Or you will."

"Whatever do you mean?" she asked, not really wanting the answer.

"I told you, baby." There was an edge on his tenderness now. "Whatever you want, you get it. As long as I get what I want." His stubby fingers slid up her thigh, around the curve of the hips she had begun to think of as too full. His breathing deepened as hers became shallower.

"Oh, yes. We were talking about starting a family, weren't we?" she said, backing away slightly. "I wasn't sure you were serious, dear. Why don't you get us a drink and we'll talk about it now."

"Had a drink," he muttered low in his throat. "In fact, had a few. And we already talked. We're going to have a son. And we're going to start on it right now."

His strength always surprised her. Gripping her upper arms he pulled her in to a hard, rough kiss. Before she could regain her balance he had spun her around and pushed her toward the king size bed that dominated the room.

Marlene stumbled on the carpet. Her thighs smacked the edge of the mattress and she felt her nipples scrape across the chenille bedspread. Her fingers curled into the spread as she heard his knees thump to the floor behind her and felt her slip roughly pushed up around her waist. She was staring at their ornate walnut headboard and, above it, the cheap velvet painting of a matador she had always hated. She clamped her eyes shut, trying hard to call up a more romantic image and relax so it would not hurt so much when he entered her.

## -12-

Morgan awoke at an elbow nudge from Felicity. He had warned her that he generally made it a habit to fall asleep whenever his attention was not needed for anything. He knew she'd wake him at the end of the flight. He leaned forward to look past her. The view out the window told him that their 747 had gone into its holding pattern over Los Angeles International Airport.

At the airport in Merida, Morgan had been pleasantly surprised at the efficiency of the customs personnel. They were even fairly pleasant once he made it clear that he was more familiar with the applicable statutes than they were. No one at the airport questioned his international security officer credentials or his redundant multinational carry permits. Of course, he still had to endure an ungodly amount of hassle to get his working tools to travel with him. It was worth it, he supposed, for his machete and knives to be stored in the baggage compartment. Customs officials also forced him to pack his pistol in three separate cases, which naturally they provided, for a price. One case carried all his ammunition. Another contained the bolt from his pistol, while he packed the remaining harmless receiver and barrel in a third. All in all, he imagined it was less of a hassle than the hotel maid would go through when she found the bits of his disassembled submachine gun under his pillows.

After landing, he walked ahead of Felicity through the buzzing beehive of LAX. He hoped he looked like any traveling businessman in his lightweight sky blue suit, white shirt and maroon tie. He still wore combat boots, but he had shined them to a high gloss. He brushed a determined red cap aside, taking their two suitcases and the three small gun cases by himself. Felicity followed, now dressed in the full tan skirt, plush brown blouse and rope sandals he picked up for her. Yes, they were a convincing tourist couple.

The automatic doors opened before him, and he stepped out into air as hot and humid as the atmosphere he left behind in Mexico. Not the same though, because the air there carried a hint of sweetness from the foliage, whereas Los Angeles air, even this far outside the city, was thick with the petroleum and ash stench of smog. The heat seemed worse too, but only because he was wearing a tie now.

Between jets taking off and automobile engines running he could barely hear his own thoughts. Felicity pointed to the long line of taxis waited at the curb, and he marched toward the lead cab. The taxi pulled forward to stop in front of them before they reached the street. They slid into the air-conditioned back seat and the slim black man up front jerked the car out into the dense traffic. Felicity leaned forward to give him an address in the Manhattan Beach area.

For scenery, their trip rivaled the average hospital wall. The view was of one continuous freeway choked with cars, each mile looking suspiciously like the last. Morgan was oblivious to his surroundings, and figured Felicity would be too. After all, she had seen it all a million times before and, like his, her mind was surely occupied with other things.

Morgan did not recover from his personal reverie until their cab stopped in front of a huge, contemporary structure that had been built as close to the coastline as such a building could stand without sliding into the ocean. Felicity thanked the driver when she paid him, and Morgan noticed that she was a generous tipper. Grabbing the small suitcase and one gun case before Morgan could, she led the way into the lush, luxurious building. The lobby was appointed in stainless steel with gold accents. A uniformed security guard sat behind a marble counter. While Felicity stopped to chat with the guard Morgan read the wall-mounted directory. Most of the building, he learned, was devoted to professional offices. The top three stories held apartments.

The velvety decor mildly affected him, but other things impressed him much more. The building and its uniformed employees were quiet. A woman wearing a jumpsuit and apron was polishing a table at the side of the lobby, although the place already looked clean. A repairman stepped out of the elevator, maybe the reason Morgan saw no sign of maintenance needed anywhere. The place emanated efficiency.

Morgan and Felicity stepped past the maintenance man just before the doors slid closed. Even the elevator moved silently. At the end of the rocket ride, the elevator whispered open at the top floor, the twentieth. Two apartment doors faced each other there, separated by a central tropical garden that was illuminated from a wide skylight above. He could not remember ever seeing the bird of paradise plants indoors before. Their blues and reds and yellows and oranges glowed as brightly as they ever did in their natural setting, their petals yawning like the birds' beaks that gave them their names.

Felicity strode to the door marked "number two" in fancy scrollwork. Next to the doorknob, an electronic cipher lock presented three rows of four numbers each. Felicity pushed eight buttons in a certain pattern, much like dialing a telephone number on a touchtone telephone. After the subtle click sounded, she turned the knob and opened the door.

Morgan followed her into a cavernous space. Felicity touched a light switch revealing a huge, sparsely furnished, sunken living room. He judged the room to be twenty-one feet wide by twenty-eight feet deep. The marble tiled mezzanine under his feet continued around three sides of the room. He stepped down three steps into deep plush carpet that matched the walls. The color wasn't really pink, but not quite red either. He thought he may have seen it on a paint pallet in a hardware store with a name like dusty rose or something of the sort. He couldn't imagine anything more feminine. The furniture was plush, a velour texture that added to the feeling of softness the room exuded. Directly to his right stood a round oak table with three nicely padded chairs. In front of him, a hand rubbed oak cube filled in as a coffee table. Beyond it stood a very long and inviting sofa. Some searching of his memory produced a name for the color of the furniture. Mauve. Maybe. Ordinarily he would just call it tan, but in this case the specific shade seemed to matter. Behind the sofa, up on the mezzanine level, an array of stereo equipment looked out from behind glass doors. While he stood rooted, three steps past the door, Felicity crossed the room and stepped up to the bar beside the stereo cabinet. She reached into one of the upper cabinets, rattling glasses.

The kitchen area was to the right of the sofa, and an overstuffed easy chair stood off to it's left, almost in the corner. He continued to pan left to take in the wall on that side, and as he did his eyes widened in wonder. To his surprise, there was no wall to his left.

On closer inspection, that wall was a series of glass panels, running from floor to ceiling, each three feet wide. Sheer curtains hung at each end. Morgan was staring out at a twenty-one foot vista of the Pacific Ocean. Rarely nonplused, Morgan had to admit that the view totally overawed him. For the first time in years, he was reminded of just what money can buy.

"Isn't it lovely?" Felicity asked. "I get all the light. And I practically own the sunset." Felicity's voice had taken on a slightly Californian, almost valley girl accent that mixed oddly with the Irish tones he had detected before. She was pouring something over ice while he continued his turn around the room. Landscapes and still life paintings in a variety of sizes hung on the wall behind him in a random pattern. The huge centerpiece, an oil painting of windmills, unexpectedly changed to a field of pansies. On closer inspection, what looked at first like a huge painting was in fact a forty-two inch plasma television screen. Someone had programmed it to display a rotating collection of art, probably from a disc in the DVD player below it.

"By the way, Morgan, do we have a business deal?" Felicity asked, bouncing down the steps back into the living room. She extended her hand, with a drink for him.

"I'm still deciding."

"Oh come on," Felicity prompted, seizing a cellular telephone lying on the floor of the deck behind the couch. She walked around in front of the glass wall, sipping slowly. Watching her there, dwarfed before the Goliath moving mural, he thought this woman must be in love with the sunset.

"Oh, I don't know, Red," he said, sipping from his own glass, and reacting to the sweetness of its contents. Bailey's Irish Crème over ice was not one of his regular choices. "Maybe I can help you recover your fee if it requires any rough stuff. How about fifteen percent of what we collect, plus my expenses?"

"Fine," Felicity replied, "but don't call me Red." While she dialed the telephone, he dropped the suitcases and bounded easily up to the marble level behind her to stare out at the boundless view. He felt as if he had landed on top of some private mountain. The sky was infinite in all directions, with only one small bank of cotton ball clouds over on the left. There was no hint of the city behind them. In the distance a gull slid across the wind lazily, banking and playing the currents like a seasoned hang glider. Below, foam swirled around a body surfer as he was caught in what looked like a giant washing machine.

In the background, he could hear the beginnings of Felicity's conversation. Her voice was rising and falling as rhythmically as the hypnotic ocean swell before him. It became white noise, as if he could hear the waves below. None of her words caught his attention until a demand broke through.

"If I don't have the cash within seventy-two hours I'll come and get it. And don't be thinking I won't."

Morgan spun and leaped to her side in one long bound.

"Red! What are you doing?"

"I have friends, you know," Felicity snapped into the telephone, ignoring Morgan. "You won't get away with this."

"Don't tell them we're coming," Morgan said in a harsh whisper. "You're throwing away the advantage of surprise, you idiot."

"I won't take it, Stone," Felicity shouted, waving him to be quiet. "It's my money or it's your arse."

When she slammed the telephone down, Felicity looked up as if she was expecting an argument, but Morgan reacted with neither rage nor resignation. His initial response to her conversation was a dumbfounded silence. Slowly he moved to sit on the edge of her plush sofa, which turned out to be real velvet, not just velour as he had assumed.

"Did you just say Stone?" he asked after a moment. Felicity nodded her head.

"Tall dude? White hair? Kind of pale eyes?"

"You know him?" she asked.

"We've done business in the past," he said, settling into the deep, totally comfortable couch.

"Well that's a bit of luck," Felicity said, perching on her oak cube. "What do you know about the man?"

"He's an old pro. Sort of a general contractor." Felicity's puzzled look prompted him to continue. "Say for example, somebody has the dollars and wants a dirty job done. He contacts Stone. Now, Stone doesn't actually do stuff, but he knows how to find the people who do. He's connected. You need mercenaries, a hit man, a bodyguard, a courier..."

"A thief," Felicity added.

"Yeah, or maybe some Mafia muscle. He can get them. All for a fee or a percentage, of course, and no risk to himself. As a matter of fact, he was the contact man for this last raid I executed. This raid I didn't get paid for in Central America. You and me, we got some things to discuss." He tossed back what remained of his drink. "By the way, you got any real liquor in here?"

With a thoughtful expression, Felicity picked up the remote control unit resting in a space apparently cut into the oak block for just that purpose. She thumbed a button, and suddenly Brahms filled the room, seemingly from everywhere.

Morgan was no lover of classical music, but he considered himself a connoisseur of fine stereo equipment, and the quality of the sound reproduction impressed him. Glancing around, he spotted four of the tiny but powerful Bose jewel cube speakers. There would be an Acoustimass module hidden someplace for the base. .

Felicity had wandered back to the bar and when she returned she held a glass of amber liquid at his eye level.

"Chivas Regal okay?" she asked.

"More like it." He gratefully tipped the glass to his lips. Felicity stretched out catlike on the couch, her skirt rising high on her shapely thighs. This was not the hyperactive feline he'd met on the trail. She was completely relaxed there on her own home ground, too relaxed for his tastes. Now that he had signed on for a job, he felt he needed to take command. The tactical situation, mostly unknown, was growing worse.

"Tell me what you know about the opposition," he said, sitting up straight. "Who'd Stone hire you for? Where's your real client? What kind of backing and resources does he have?" From his jacket pocket he produced a small note pad and the sharp stub of a pencil he always carried. Felicity examined the ceiling for several seconds and took a long pull on her drink before she spoke.

"Wish I could tell you. I worked blind for Stone. That phone number I just called? It's in Denver, but from the time lapse and the clicks on the line, I think it's transferred through to another city. I really have no idea who I was actually doing the job for, or what kind of organization he might have at his base, or even where his base is for that matter. Had no reason to want to know at the time. I guess we'll have to find out somehow."

"Yeah, well, good luck," Morgan said, getting to his feet. "I figure either this guy couldn't afford to pay you, or he's so rich he don't have to bother paying you. If he's small time, he'll just drop out of sight, fade into the woodwork. On the other hand, if he's big time, he could have a dozen thugs on our necks in a couple of days."

"So what do you suggest we do?"

"We?" Morgan said with a smile. "I think you mean you. You better get busy trying to trace that number. I'm a mercenary, not a private eye. I'll hang around here for three days. You've got seventy-two hours to get a line on this mystery man. After that I'm splitting. I've got my own snake to find. Even though that job came through Stone too, I can probably find the client easier than the flunky. I'll get after him if your job falls through, and my trail starts south of the border."

## -13-

The beautiful blonde bent forward to help Adrian Seagrave out of his hot tub. Ashleigh was completely naked, and bending that way put her most prominent features very close to Seagrave's face. She had no trouble concealing the distaste she felt when she was with him. After all, she was a professional. She had been with plenty of short, pear shaped men before, as pockmarked as this one, with the same dull lifeless eyes and brown straggly hair.

She had a more difficult time disguising her fear. She had never been intimate with a known killer before. It took a lot of money to attract her to so deadly a meal ticket, but for what this man paid for her company, she would have slept with Al Capone. Besides, he had probably never killed anyone with his own hands. The rich and powerful seldom do.

Smiling broadly, she rubbed Seagrave's body dry with a thick terry cloth towel. That done, she helped him into a black oriental silk robe and silk slippers. Cool air chilled her as they left the room dedicated to the hot tub and walked across the wide contemporary study. Against the far wall stood what looked like a gilt edged cage. At the push of a button the cage doors opened like the petals of a golden blossom and folded into the wall.

"See you soon," Seagrave said, pinching her hard on the rump before stepping into the cage. Ashleigh watched the silent doors slide closed and the cage descend in slow motion. After she heard the elevator car stop at its destination she turned to return to the bedroom.

Ashleigh gathered up her clothes, marveling anew at the rooms Seagrave lived in. Clearly a professional decorator had furnished the place. It wasn't personalized much, at least, not in any way that showed a woman's touch. The few things that clearly were not a decorator's work, like that awful velvet painting hanging over the crumpled bed, were definitely the man's work.

Halfway through getting dressed, Ashleigh stopped to make the bed. It wasn't an impulse of neatness, but rather an act of respect. When she thought about what she did to make money, she had to admit that her own life sucked. Still, all things considered, she pitied the wife.

* * * * *

One floor below Seagrave's apartment, the elevator opened. When Seagrave stepped out, he faced a long conference table. Beyond it, the oak paneled room widened out. The room was laid out in a "T" shape, with the long table aligned with its base. From Seagrave's left, sunlight filtered in through two huge picture windows behind the head of the table. Rich maroon velvet drapes muted the sun.

Seagrave turned to his right, and walked past the foot of the table into the reception area, which represented the top cross bar of the "T." A wet bar filled the side of the room to his left, and a desk and office setting took up the space on his right. Seagrave focused on the two remarkable men sitting at the bar. Right then, the thinner man held his gaze.

He was tall, perhaps six feet four or five inches, but as thin as a cattail reed. His hair was stark white, yet no wrinkles showed on his face. What really captured Seagrave's attention were his eyes. They were pale, almost entirely colorless, as if someone had streaked a thin blue wash across his irises. Those cold orbs betrayed no emotion as he filled his companion's glass.

By most measures, the other drinker was even more exceptional. Not only was he an inch taller than his well dressed partner, but he seemed three times as wide. He certainly tipped the scales at something over three hundred pounds, but there was hardly an ounce of fat on him. His suit, although tailor made, still strained to contain his bulging muscles. He had uncommonly long arms, with fingers hanging halfway to his knees. His knuckles were rounded and hair ran rampant on the backs of his hands. His head was the bullet shape of the pure Saxon, connected to his body by what looked like a set of braided steel cables running down his neck and out to his shoulders. One glance at his simian form reminded Seagrave how he had acquired the nickname "Monk". He served his purposes, but Seagrave had more use for the thinner man right then.

"Give me a report, Stone," Seagrave said, his hands in his bathrobe pockets. "What's the story on that South American commodities deal?"

"It should be quite profitable," the white haired man responded. "The politician we supported in Belize will be successfully maneuvering to increase sugar prices now that he is in control of that key export in his country. He is also quite influential with his opposites in other sugar producing nations. He is presently instigating for an OPEC style sugar cartel across South and Central America. He is an excellent spokesman for the advantages of capitalist power politics, pointing to the Middle East as his example. In some cases, the fate of our man's late predecessor, this Carlos Abrigo, is being used to intimidate reluctant officials. Your accountants assure me that your sugar futures should more than double in value within the next eighteen months or so."

"Study history, Stone," Seagrave said. "More recent conquerors have been brought down by their own military than any other force. I don't want soldiers sitting around who know what I've done. They might start thinking they deserve a piece of my success."

"Yes sir." Stone waited until his employer was finished scanning a business letter before speaking again. "There is one other unrelated item. Not really business."

"Yes?"

"We've been contacted by the O'Brian girl." Stone paused, but Seagrave continued shuffling papers on his desk. Considering this a good sign, Stone continued. "She apparently intends to press her claim for her fee. We do owe her for that little robbery she performed for us."

"Robbery?" Seagrave said. "Oh yes, that brooch that Marlene wanted so badly." He broke into an unexpected smile. "She's out right now, shopping for something special to wear it with when we go to that fancy ball on Saturday."

"Quite," Stone said. "This woman could become, er, an inconvenience. Ignoring her will not resolve this issue. She will continue to make demands, perhaps drawing attention to areas of your activities that may not bear close scrutiny. Will you authorize payment? Or, shall I have the problem neutralized?"

"Yes, yes," Seagrave muttered, waving the question off without looking up. "Kill her."

## -14-

Morgan took a quick shower before stowing his gear in the guestroom. Clothes and personal items went into the closet and dresser drawers. He hated living out of a suitcase, even if he was only going to be in one place for a couple of days. After refreshing the shine on his boots with a polish kit he picked up at the airport, he pulled on a blue tee shirt and black denims. Out of habit his jeans were bloused, tucked into his combat boots. Adding a lightweight black windbreaker, zipped up a couple of inches, he grabbed one of the gun cases and returned to the living room. Felicity waited for him there, relaxed on the sofa. The flat screen that had imitated a painting earlier now displayed CNBC.

"About time," Felicity said with a smile. "I need a long soak."

Morgan fought shaking his head. "Got some business," he muttered. "Need some expense money."

"Where to?" Felicity asked. After the briefest hesitation, she drew a handful of bills from her purse and handed them to him.

"Just want to get ready for the trouble I know is going to come looking for me," Morgan said, stuffing the money into a pocket. "How about you? After your bath, that is."

"Well, I know I might have some nasty enemies out there," Felicity said, "and I ought to do something about it. But then I think about the fact that I haven't been in town for weeks, I've got a houseguest, and my refrigerator's empty. Guess I'll just follow my own motto. When the going gets tough, the tough go shopping."

Morgan wanted to shout at her to take their situation more seriously. Instead he just mumbled, "Okay, see you," and headed out. After another high-speed elevator ride he asked the security man to call a cab for him. He stepped out into the late morning sun and took a moment to settle his mind. Returning to the States was always a joy, even after a short trip away. He enjoyed watching the young girls wandering, seemingly aimlessly, and appreciated the current style in shorts. That sport lasted only a couple of minutes, until his taxi arrived. He gave an address he had found in the yellow pages and settled back for the ride.

Morgan had been away from the West Coast for a couple of years and was surprised at how much had changed. There was little he saw on the ride that distinguished Los Angeles from the rest of the vast country he labeled "Generica" in his own mind. The whole concept of the neighborhood seemed to be dying, and he found the loss of local identity depressing.

After much longer than the drive should have taken, the taxi swerved to the curb on a side street in the area between Gardena and Torrence that was and yet was not a part of Los Angeles. A painted wooden sign above the gunsmith shop's door claimed it was owned by someone named "Pop." Years ago, Morgan had chosen this shop purely based on its name. He figured the owner must have been in business for a while. He paid the fare, up quite a bit since his last visit to California, and entered the shop.

A tiny bell hanging over the door rang as he opened the door, and he knew he had chosen well. It was an old-fashioned shop run by a white haired, soft bellied fellow who smelled of gunpowder. Shotguns and hunting rifles hung on the wall behind the glass counter. Inside the counter Morgan scanned a collection of military handguns, a couple tricked out with compensators and tritium sights. Nothing had changed since the last time Morgan pushed that door open.

"How you doing, Pop?" Morgan asked the man behind the counter.

"Morgan! How the hell are you, son?" Pop moved around the counter to embrace Morgan, clapping him on the back. "Been a long time since you dropped by the old shop, my boy. What can I do for you today?"

Since no one else was around, Morgan got right to the point. "Actually, I'm hoping to use your back room for a while. I just got back in country and I need to take care of my tools."

Pop glanced out the shop's front window, his demeanor cooling a bit. "I don't know, young fellow. It's been a while since you came around, and California's gun laws have gotten worse. And there's all this talk about terrorists. Every time a professional like you asks to work in my shop it's another risk to my license."

"Aw, come on, Pop. You don't have to go through that routine with me." Morgan leaned casually against the counter and pulled a few bills out of his pocket. "Will this compensate you for the risk to your livelihood?"

"Oh, hell," Pop said, sweeping the money off the counter. "I like you, son. Come on back. Just don't make too much noise if you hear anybody come in."

Morgan grinned as he followed Pop into the back. Some things never changed and, even in laid back Southern California, money talks. Once he was out of sight of the public part of the shop Morgan unzipped his jacket and settled onto a stool at Pop's workbench. He pulled his pistol from the gun case and dropped the magazine out. Pop was watching him closely when he broke down his weapon and started to clean it.

"Relax, old man," Morgan said without taking his eyes away from his work. "Like you said, I'm a professional. I know what I'm doing here."

Pop nodded. "Don't see youngsters who know how to treat a gun these days, except for some of the target shooters that come in here. But those are stunt guns with expensive doodads."

"A craftsman's got to respect his tools," Morgan said. "This particular Browning Hi-power's like an old friend. She's been with me through four armed conflicts without a single stoppage. She's real reliable, but I know, just like any other nine millimeter, she'll jam up on me in a heartbeat if I don't keep her clean."

Pop turned his attention to inventory while Morgan completed the weapon's disassembly. Morgan inspected each part carefully and lubed it with a light coat of CLP. He paid particular attention to the sear to make sure the tiny surfaces that make the trigger-sear connection were not worn. It would waste a lot of ammunition if his pistol decided to go full auto on him in the middle of a fight.

After reassembling the weapon, he ran a full safety check and a complete function check. After some self-debate, he also decided to replace the magazine spring.

When he was finished, Morgan slipped out of his windbreaker, revealing a side draw shoulder holster of stiff saddle leather under his left arm. He slid his pistol into place, giving a final light tug to make sure the steel spring would prevent its slipping free.

"Hey, that's a beauty," Pop said. "Bianchi?"

"Yep. Custom made. Just like the knife." What hung under Morgan's right shoulder was not a holster, but the sheath holding his fighting knife. With a firm downward tug he drew his blade, a Randall model number one pattern with a black micarta handle and brass fillets.

"In the field I can slip the sheath onto my belt," Morgan said, sliding a carborundum stone toward himself. "That way it lays flat with the handle pointed to the side, so I can reach back and grab it with my right hand. That carry's a little too visible on the street." Morgan lovingly honed his seven-inch blade. When he was satisfied with the main edge, he turned it to sharpen the long "false edge" as well.

For him, weapons maintenance was almost a Zen activity, to which he gave total concentration. His left boot knife, a five-inch double-edged dagger, received the same close attention. By now, Pop was looking over his shoulder.

"Don't recognize that one," Pop said, "but it looks custom too."

"Yeah," Morgan said with a smile. "Ground it myself. This is my own work too." He pulled and began to sharpen the throwing knife he kept in his right boot. "This one I forged and as you can see, Parkerized so it won't reflect the light when I throw it."

"You keep them well," Pop said. To Morgan's surprise, the older man dropped a bottle of beer in front of him. It was the kind of amber flip-top bottle people refill at microbreweries.

"John Wayne Imperial Stout?" Morgan asked, twisting off the cap. "I take it this is local?"

"Yep, from the Newport Beach Brewing Company," Pop said, opening a matching bottle. "If you like a real stout, you'll like this. And now, if I remember your last visit, you'll be moving over to the loading bench."

"You've got me figured out, old man," Morgan said, tipping his bottle up to take a swallow, and pulling it down with a grin. "Well, I guess they can do something right around here. That's a big, bad brew. But I better go slow until I'm done with the focus work. So I guess I'll need some supplies. Some hundred twenty-five grain Remington jacketed hollowpoint bullets, and Remington cases. I like the Bullseye powder, and CCI primers."

Pop's stool was on wheels, so Morgan rolled himself over to the loading bench. The bell rang out front, and Pop hustled out to greet the incoming customer while Morgan assembled the components to create his nine-millimeter cartridges.

Morgan hardly noticed when Pop returned to the back room a few minutes later. He was focused too closely on the repetitive action of pulling the big handle down on the reloader, and placing his new ammunition in neat rows beside it. Pop observed this tricky process for a moment before he started asking questions.

"Can't help but notice you load your shells with less powder than usual."

"You've been doing this too long," Morgan said, grinning. "Yeah, I started using light loads back when I used to carry a Colt forty-five auto, to reduce the noise. Sometimes stealth is more important than power." While maintaining the conversation, Morgan kept a meticulous eye on the number of grains of powder going into the shells. "I hate silencers on handguns. Sometimes I needed to keep the volume down, but silencers are just too unreliable and clumsy in my line of work."

"Your line of work," Pop said. When Morgan failed to elaborate, he added, "Well, either way you're going to lose a few feet per second on the muzzle velocity."

Morgan brushed a couple of stubborn cartridges into the hopper. "You're right about the velocity, but if you're at all accurate with the forty-five caliber, it isn't enough to make any difference. But I was having trouble getting ammo in some of the places I was working, so I decided to switch to the nine millimeter round which is more popular overseas."

"But the nine has less mass," Pop said. "Less stopping power."

"True, but I still wanted the quieter blast. So I decided to cheat. Now here comes the tricky part." Morgan continued to narrate his actions. "I start with these common Remington nine-millimeter hollowpoints. I down load the cartridges just like I used to. Now, I put the complete cartridge in a vise, nose up, and I add just a touch of fulminate of mercury, there, right in the tip. Now I'll seal it over with a little solder. Like so. Now, when the shot's fired, she might leave the muzzle a little slow. But by the time that baby hits the target, that load in the nose is hot enough to go bang. Aside from the little explosion on impact, the hollow point spreads out all the way. Talk about stopping power. These babies always put 'em down with one hit."

Business was slow, so Pop decided to become involved in the loading process. The two veterans swapped war stories for a while, and time slid past unnoticed. Four hours later Morgan left Pop's shop with eight full magazines, one cleaned and serviced automatic pistol, three very sharp knives and a renewed friendship. In the process of chatting with Pop he had mentioned his new female acquaintance. While talking about her he realized that his attitude had shifted. He decided that if the O'Brian girl didn't come up with a lead to Stone by his deadline he would ask her to travel with him for a while. Some indefinable quality about her drew him like steel to a magnet. She was just so, well, comfortable. They connected, as if he had known her all his life. He thought that maybe they should team up on a long-term basis.

Maybe he would tell her so.

\* \* \* \* \*

With thoughts of a more settled future going through his mind, Morgan was relaxed during his short taxi ride back to Felicity's building. But he was feeling a little tension when he entered the building, and a bit more when the elevator stopped. By the time he reached Felicity's floor, he stepped out of the elevator on tiptoe. He did not know why. The flowers were still as fragrant as they were on his first visit, and the little landing was just as quiet. As he approached the door his old familiar feeling was there again, stronger than ever. He put down his small gun case beside Felicity's door, already beginning to plot his next move.

He had leaped behind the center island of foliage before he realized he had heard the elevator door open. From his vantage point he saw the lone occupant emerge from the car. It was Felicity, carting a collection of bundles and shopping bags that she could barely manage. She wore a green and white pinstripe cotton dress and her hair, he noticed, was now tied back with a wide green ribbon. It matched her eyes, which wandered warily, worry showing on her face. He stepped into the open and their eyes locked for one intense moment. He opened his mouth but Felicity spoke first.

"You felt it too," she said, more a surprised statement than a question.

"Yes," Morgan said. "I've got kind of an instinct, a sense of danger. But I didn't know you..."

"Yes. All my life." With no further explanation, Felicity put down the bundles and pointed to her cipher lock. "Look at this."

"What do you mean?"

"Right here," Felicity said. "On the edge of the button plate. See these marks? It's been pried off. Someone's broken in, someone who knows these locks but got sloppy."

"A thief friend stop by to surprise you?" Morgan asked.

Felicity shook her head. "I don't have sloppy friends. So now what do we do?"

"Several options if they're waiting inside," Morgan said. He was annoyed with himself for not noticing the lock had been tampered with, and was happy for a chance to take the lead. "As usual, there's a safe way, an easy way and a best way."

"Well, what's the best way?" Felicity asked.

"Let me teach you the cross door maneuver."

# -15-

Inside Felicity's apartment a pair of dangerous animals in cheap suits waited. Pearson sat on the couch half turned, gazing aimlessly out the window with his gun hand resting on his thigh. By shifting his eyes he could see Shaw, who had pulled the big chair forward and pointed it toward the door. Shaw looked relaxed but alert, with his Smith & Wesson .38 pointed toward the apartment's only entrance. Pearson's ears perked up as he heard buttons being pushed and saw the doorknob slowly turning. The pigeon had come home at last. This was too easy a job for a pair of experienced killers, but they got the assignment because they had been in the neighborhood. Stone said to kill the girl ASAP. It would be a nice change to receive an assignment and complete it the same day. Shaw took careful aim at the door and Pearson returned his smile as he thumbed the hammer back on his own pistol.

With an air of relaxation Felicity pushed the door open and entered, crossing to her left, toward the occupied chair. She was staring into a grinning face and a gun barrel. Her hands opened, and her packages began their fall to the floor.

Before her eyes finished widening, Morgan came in fast and low, crossing behind her in the opposite direction. His gun barked once before Felicity's packages reached the carpet. The man in the chair didn't move, but his chest burst open like a blossoming scarlet flower before Felicity's startled eyes.

Morgan continued his charge, driving his shoulder hard into the second man's midsection before the killer could quite get his pistol aimed at the new target. As the two men grappled on the sofa, the revolver bounced across the carpet. An unthinking reflex drove Felicity to snatch it up.

"Stop it!" she shouted. The killer froze, staring into his own gun's muzzle. Morgan stood calmly, straightening his clothes.

"I'll keep him in line," he said, leveling his automatic on the other man's eyes. "Got any wire or twine around?"

Felicity nodded, looked down at her hands and gingerly placed the revolver on the coffee table cube. Then she backtracked to close and lock the front door before running down the hall to the second room. It was small, but sufficient as a storage room. She spent only seconds rooting through the climbing gear arrayed neatly in the closet. She sprinted back to the living room with a five-foot length of nylon cord. Morgan hadn't moved, and she was surprised to see no expression of anger on his face.

"You know the drill," Morgan said, accepting the rope. "Turn around, on your knees, hands behind your back."

Morgan held the rope in his right hand with his pistol, while he drew his big knife from under his jacket. He cut a ten-inch bit from the cord, dropped the rest, and tied the other man's thumbs together behind him. It was a simple bind, but Felicity could see that it would be far more effective than big clumsy knots around the wrists and arms. Once the big man was secured, Morgan turned to Felicity.

"Stay here, Red," he said. Morgan walked his charge to the bathroom between the two bedrooms. The gunman was built like a college halfback, but Morgan had no trouble alternately pushing and pulling him, keeping him off balance. Once they were in the bathroom, Felicity saw the man's shoes fly out into the hall, followed by his socks, trousers and underwear. The she heard a loud thump that could only be the shooter's beefy form slamming down into her deep bathtub.

"Come out, and you'll join your partner in hell," Morgan said. Then he walked out, closed the door, and jogged to the living room.

Felicity had not moved and now stood facing him. Her eyes were brimming with tears. She glanced furtively at the corpse in her armchair, the chair she had spent weeks selecting. Blood dripped rhythmically onto her light colored, hand dyed deep pile carpet. Lit by the approaching sunset, the dead man looked like some bizarre, macabre statue melting in a wax museum. Her lips trembled and a barely audible whisper slipped through them. Morgan stepped forward and put an arm around her, cradling her head in his own massive shoulder.

"Take it easy, Red. I know it's kind of a shock but, well, death's really a natural thing, I mean in nature, you know? And if it's you or them, sometimes you just got to go all the way."

"It's not that," Felicity stammered. "I've seen death before. And don't call me..." she stopped in mid-sentence. Somehow, for the first time in her life, it seemed okay for someone to call her "Red."

He was such an enigma, this great black bear of a man. Only seconds ago, she had seen him show total ferocity, killing with ice cold efficiency. Yet now he was able to exhibit unexpected tenderness. It seemed perversely symbolic that his shoulder felt so soft and warm and comforting to her face, even as her right breast was crushed against the hard outline of his shoulder holster.

"It isn't the death, not really," she murmured. "It's just, he wanted to, he was going to, to kill me." She put a shaky emphasis on the last word.

"Yes," Morgan said slowly, "Let's go find out about that."

\* \* \* \* \*

With a gentle tug, Morgan eased Felicity toward the bathroom. When they opened the door, their tough guy prisoner was sitting on the floor trying to look belligerent. He was built like a linebacker, but now Morgan could see a bit of softness around his waist. His nose had been broken and a scar was visible just below the line of his short brown hair.

Morgan thought he recognized that kind of scar. It was probably a legacy from the less glamorous days of professional wrestling. In those days guys used to go flying out of the ring and they'd always come up bloody. Morgan knew they often cut themselves with razor blades in their hairline for the effect. If this guy was a veteran of the small-time professional wrestling circuit, he was probably pretty tough. Morgan considered what little he knew of this man for a moment before deciding how he should proceed. He decided to use a reasonable, uncaring approach.

"You know, we were kind of lucky out there," Morgan said, drawing his big knife out of its sheath again. He pulled his prisoner to his feet and sat him back in the bathtub. "If anyone heard that gunshot, they must have assumed it was something else, like a car backfiring. As usual in any big city, nobody wants to hear a gunshot so they just don't. Now, turn over." The thug glared at Felicity for a moment, then squirmed over onto his stomach. Morgan put his pistol to his prisoner's head while he cut the cord, freeing the killer's hands.

"You won't be able to get out of that slippery tub too quickly," he said. "I'll ask the lady here to keep the gun on you all the same. Now turn back over."

While Morgan gave Felicity the pistol, Pearson slowly squirmed around into an upright position. Morgan held out his hand, and his captive handed over his jacket, his tie and finally his shirt. Morgan tossed them all past Felicity, out the door. The gunman hunched over, hatred glaring from his eyes. Felicity held the pistol in two hands at arms' length, staring down the sights. It pleased Morgan to see a deep blush on the killer's face as he tried to hide his nakedness. Embarrassment was a good start for questioning. He did not enjoy torture, but he definitely would get certain information from this man.

"Now pull up your feet, please." When Pearson did not respond to the request, Morgan opened the hot water tap. First cold, then warm and finally hot water gushed out. By hugging his knees the nude man could just keep his feet from being scalded. Felicity smiled in spite of herself. Morgan sat on the edge of the tub at the faucet end, facing his prisoner. He took a deep breath. It was time to demoralize his subject.

"Now I need to know who sent you to kill the lady."

"You go to hell, nig..." The thug interrupted himself with a scream louder than Morgan's earlier gunshot had been. Felicity gasped in surprise. Morgan had flipped the knob that shifted the water flow to the shower spout. The steaming water was only on the hired killer's body for a single second, but his dripping body was glowing red. His breath was a series of rapid gasps.

"First rule, no profanity," Morgan said casually. "It upsets the lady. And you call me by my name. Mister Stark. Now again. Who sent you here?"

The silence lasted for three long seconds before Morgan gave his captive another second of heat. Now the red body quivered with each short, panting breath.

"Look, I don't like doing this." Morgan maintained his relaxed smile. "However, I need these three bits of data, see? And after trying to shoot us, I figure you owe me. So tell me, who sent you?"

The thug gritted his teeth. Felicity clamped her eyes shut. Morgan, relaxed, waited four seconds this time, before giving the killer two seconds of steaming pain. After that he imagined he could smell broiled meat. He saw Felicity's stomach heave. He knew she wanted to run from the room, but this strange ritual held her mesmerized.

After all, a grown man, stripped naked, was flopping around in her bathtub like a beached whale. He was moaning and whimpering, probably knowing he would eventually talk. Yet he went on. Morgan understood. This was part of his business, and he feared he would be seen as a coward if he spoke too soon. Morgan carried on with his distasteful duty in a businesslike manner, because he knew this was the way the game was played.

"Look, pal..." Morgan paused for a second, then asked, "What's your name?" A tense five seconds passed. Sweat mixed with the water on the prisoner's face. His eyes were locked onto Morgan's hand. As the muscles on the corded brown forearm tensed to turn the knob he blurted out "Pearson" louder than necessary.

"Much better," Morgan said. He noticed Felicity had been holding her breath since the last question, and she released it as he watched. She was still holding the big pistol with her arms fully extended toward the tub and, even with a two-handed grip, her arms were starting to shake. Morgan reached back to push down on the top of his gun with two fingers.

"Relax a bit, Red. He's not going anywhere." She lowered the pistol, but kept her eyes on Pearson's. "Look, Pearson," Morgan continued, "You can't take too much more of this pain. Besides, if this keeps up there's going to be permanent skin damage soon. When I see your boss I'll tell him you held out to the last like a good troop. Now give me a name." Four long seconds passed before Pearson replied in a voice just loud enough Morgan to hear.

"Stone."

"Now we're moving along," Morgan said, smiling. "Now for step two. Naturally I'd like to discuss this situation with Stone face to face. To do that, I need an address." He waited three seconds this time. His fingers curled around the knob.

"He'll kill me!" Pearson shouted.

"Are you so sure I won't?" Morgan asked. "Have you forgotten your friend in the living room?"

"Look, I don't really remember," Pearson said. "I only been there once. I'm just a stringer, man. I do all my work on the West Coast. The man's in midtown Manhattan. A big skyscraper, you know? You can see ground zero from the window. You know, where the World Trade Center used to be. That's all I remember, honest. Jesus, I only been once."

Pearson's eyes were pleading. Morgan glanced quickly at Felicity. Her eyes were pleading too. As much as he hated this, she was liking it much less. And he doubted this hireling knew much more. Still he had to press on.

"I guess we'll accept that," he said. "Now for the biggie. Who's Stone working for now?"

"You know I don't know that," Pearson screeched, then added, "Mister Stark" when Morgan reached for the shower knob.

"You know something." Morgan's voice became much sterner now. Pearson stared into Morgan's hard eyes. When he couldn't stand it any longer he looked around the room nervously and huffed out a blast of air.

"Okay, look. I've done work for Stone before, but things are different these days. He's a captive agent now."

"A what?" Felicity asked, confused.

"No longer freelance," Morgan explained. "Stone's always been an independent contractor. He still does the same thing, I guess, only now he's working for somebody on salary. Probably means you and me got suckered by the same guy."

"Some businessman," Pearson added, eager to please his captives. "That place in New York is his office, and he lives in the same building too. He's richer than shi...I mean, he's real rich and he's got this huge bodyguard. One thing for sure. You find Stone, you'll find this guy. Stone's like his right hand man now."

Morgan and Felicity exchanged glances. They seemed to silently agree that they had gotten all they could expect from this one. She tugged at his sleeve, getting him to lean toward her.

"Will you be killing him now?" she whispered. "I mean, do you have to?" His only answer was a sly smile.

"Throw Pearson a towel, Red," Morgan said. When she did, Pearson snatched it out of the air and spread it over his groin.

"Thank you, eh..." Pearson looked at Morgan nervously.

"Miss O'Brian." Then Morgan turned to Felicity. "Give me my pistol, will you? And I need you to go pack for the two of us. We've got to move, and soon. Pearson and I are going to be busy for a while. And you might want to stay out of the living room for a few minutes, okay?"

\* \* \* \* \*

Felicity headed for her bedroom, happy to be freed of the weight of the gun. In a lifetime of crime she had rarely been involved with firearms and wanted to keep it that way. She had also rarely taken direction from anyone, and this was a new feeling for her. She had decided she was boss of this team long ago. After all, she was paying him for his services. Still, she realized it made sense for him to lead while they played the game in which he was the expert.

Her room, in the corner of the building, had huge windows on both outer walls. The sunset melded with her décor, which was layers of blue: carpet, drapes, bedding, walls and ceiling in progressively lighter shades. Her furniture was all hand worked oak. Her big, four-poster bed stood to the side of the door, turned so she would face the beach when lying down. She quickly tossed a few things into an overnight bag. She wouldn't need to carry much for a trip to New York. Next, she figured she would go to the guestroom and gather everything Morgan had there. It should all fit nicely into a single suitcase.

But when she left her bedroom, Felicity stopped. She could hear the sound of fabric being cut. When it ended, she stepped lightly to the guestroom door. Morgan stood on one side of the floor with all the room's furniture. Pearson, once again dressed, was rolling up the other half of the carpet at gunpoint.

"What the hell are you doing?" Felicity asked, her hands on her hips.

"Cleaning up the mess we made," Morgan said. "Believe me, you don't want to watch this."

"No, I believe I do."

Morgan shrugged his shoulders as if to say, "suit yourself," and by waving his pistol directed Pearson to carry the piece of carpet into the living room. There he laid it out flat in front of the corpse-laden chair. She felt Morgan's eyes on her as he bent and grasped the dead man's ankles. She gagged, but kept it down and never turned her eyes away. Morgan's facial expression told her he was impressed and for some reason that made her inordinately proud of herself.

Pearson lifted his dead partner under the armpits. The two men stretched the body out on the cut carpet. Morgan removed the dead man's wallet, tossing it to Pearson. They rolled the carpet up, around the body. Morgan cut the cord Felicity had brought out earlier into two even pieces. With them, Pearson tied the ends of the rug roll with practiced skill.

"Be ready to leave in fifteen minutes," Morgan said. He slipped his automatic into his jacket pocket, keeping the muzzle pointed at Pearson. He lifted the back end of the bundle easily onto his left arm and Pearson, on cue, hefted the other end. Without being asked, Felicity opened the door and the men filed out.

\* \* \* \* \*

Pearson stood quietly through an uneventful ride in the freight elevator, but by the time they reached the street, he could no longer conceal his tension. The sound of kids playing in the street and the blare of horns in traffic made him jumpy. Behind him, Stark's steps made no sound at all, but Pearson was very conscious of the gun pointed at his back and he knew his usefulness would soon end. This Stark character was just too relaxed. He had even started whistling.

On the street Pearson took cues from Stark, walking at the front end of their bundle, careful to hold his end up so no blood dripped out the opening. It wasn't his first time carrying a rolled body, but he had never done this with an enemy before. The eyes of passers-by seemed more menacing for some reason. He could smell the cupric odor of his partner's blood coming from the end of the carpet roll and wondered how passersby could miss it.

After a long six block walk, they found what Stark apparently had been looking for. Every city has them. It was a deep, narrow alley. Garbage lined the sides. Some of it was even in cans and bags. The walls on all three sides were tall brick barriers, interrupted only by an occasional window. Claustrophobia now added its effects to Pearson's already ragged mental state.

They laid the carpet coffin down behind a row of trashcans. Pearson stood up, stoically facing the wall. If their positions were reversed, this was when he would do it. One quick shot in the back of the head. Why make a man build up fear in his last moments? He was ready now. He had been the man behind the gun often enough. Now it was his turn to stand in front of it. It was all part of the game.

"Turn around," Morgan said.

"Aw, shit," Pearson said.

"Look, dude," Morgan continued, "I really, really don't like for people to point guns at me or my friends. On the other hand, I don't like to leave unnecessary messes lying around, so I'm prepared to offer you a deal." Pearson looked into his eyes, trying to see there some clue to what would come next. "It's a one time offer." Morgan raised the nine-millimeter for emphasis. "If I ever see you again in life, you're dead meat. You follow? For right now, if you can be out of my sight in forty-five seconds, you can walk away from this job." Pearson stared in disbelief. "Forty seconds left," Morgan said.

That was all Pearson needed. After taking three steps backward he turned and sprinted down the alley toward sunlight and freedom.

\* \* \* \* \*

When Morgan reached the sidewalk, the hired hit man was indeed out of sight. Morgan grinned, holstered his pistol, and began a slow jog back to Felicity's apartment. It was a beautiful summer day and Morgan wasn't even bothered by the fact that he was filling his lungs with smog.

His mood darkened a bit as he approached Felicity's door. He was worried a little about Felicity's emotional state. Without warning, her life had been threatened, she had witnessed a messy death, sat in on a torture interrogation, and watched him roll up a body and cart it away. He wasn't sure what he expected when he opened the door.

"How do I look?"

Felicity sat on the couch, her legs stretched out and crossed at the ankles. She had washed her hair and it tumbled across her shoulders in rolling crimson waves. Her eyes sparkled like emeralds set in a china doll's face. An inviting smile danced across her moist lips. Her makeup was subtle but perfect. She had changed into a light fawn colored sundress and suede low-heeled shoes. A gold braid bracelet on her right wrist was her only jewelry.

"Red, you are gorgeous."

"Well, you said to be ready," Felicity said in a breathy voice.

"And are you?"

"I'm ready," she sighed, "for anything." He made a conscious effort to control his breathing. He walked over to her and took her gently by the arms, lifting her effortlessly to her feet.

"Lady, I would surely love to relax with you here for an hour or two, but we need to be out of here now. Some very nasty people know where we are."

"All right," Felicity said, somehow both energetic and breathless. "I keep a flat in New York. If we go there, it'll put us closer to Stone. Meanwhile, we'll consider your last remark a promise to be fulfilled there. And just to release some of this electricity..."

Felicity gripped Morgan's jacket with both hands and pulled him to herself. The kiss that followed was the hottest, most passionate one Morgan could remember.

## -16-

"So you're a native New Yorker." Felicity leaned against the door in the back of the limousine. "Well, now you're home. Did you miss the city?"

"Not even a little bit," Morgan said. "New York's a big, dirty town. Always has been. I spent my first fifteen hard years here, fighting just to stay alive."

"And then?"

Morgan shared a bittersweet smile. "Then I lied about my age and escaped into the United States Army. I wasn't what you'd call well educated, but back then recruiters weren't looking for computer programmers. What the Army needed was tough, vicious killers. The South Bronx was a perfect training ground."

"You're nothing like I expected a killer to be," Felicity said, almost in a whisper. "What's it like? Killing a man, I mean."

"You saw it."

"No." Felicity tried to find his eyes in the darkness. "I meant what does it feel like."

Morgan glanced at the back of the driver's head and, seeing no reaction, shifted his gaze to stare out into the dark sky. "Can we change the subject?" he asked the window.

"Okay." Felicity slid closer to him on the seat. "Tell me this, then. Why do you suppose it is that you can smell a dangerous situation coming your way? What is it makes us different..."

"I ain't different," he said, low but hard. "I'm just a damned good soldier. Damned good, and real lucky."

"But aren't you curious at all about..."

"No!" Morgan's eyes snapped toward her. "I ain't curious and I don't want to talk about it either."

To shut out the disturbing thoughts of his own uniqueness, he focused on the thin strips of night sky, which appeared between buildings as they rolled through the city. There was no shortage of light there, but not a star was visible. After almost two decades of wandering the world, his hometown seemed more alien to him than the jungle he so recently left.

Of course, when he lived there he had spent precious little time in this part of upper Manhattan. Knowing Felicity was wealthy, her having a second apartment on the East Coast should not have startled him. Despite his own six figure savings, he had never used his money this way.

Morgan slumped into his corner of the airport limo, glancing over at Felicity on the opposite side. Crossing three time zones and a four hour easterly flight combined to put Felicity and Morgan into J.F.K. Airport in the middle of the night. The long ride in from Long Island affected them like a slow motion sedative. In Morgan's mind, the Van Wyck Expressway became an endless vibrator bed shaking them past shopping centers and mini-malls. Lights flashed like hypnotic strobes between the cables of the Queensboro Bridge, or as Morgan knew it in his youth, the 59th Street Bridge. Simon and Garfunkel had immortalized the bridge in song, back when Morgan was crawling through Southeast Asian tunnels for his country. Slow down, you move too fast, his mind was chanting as they joined with the traffic coming out of Long Island City and dropping onto the East Side.

Finally, the limo rolled past the Park Avenue street sign, turned a corner and stopped in front of Felicity's New York address. A building somewhat taller than the one they left in Los Angeles loomed above them. A doorman rushed to the door to let them out and take their luggage. Felicity handed him a bill and ushered Morgan into a lobby that felt more businesslike but cooler than the one in California. A minute later, in the whisper quiet elevator, Felicity took Morgan's arm and leaned against him.

"You look a little drowsy," he said as the elevator eased to a stop. "I think you ate too much of that awful food on the plane."

"You know," Felicity said as she punched in the door combination of her penthouse apartment, "this is as close to home as I can get in the States." The door swung open and when Felicity flipped the light switch, the room Morgan stepped into left him stunned into silence for a moment. The view was different, of course. From this point on Fifth Avenue, the lake he was looking at would be the reservoir in Central Park. Aside from that unavoidable difference, this apartment was identical to the one in Los Angeles. He scanned the same layout, the same furniture, the same stereo, the same everything. He half expected to see blood on the big overstuffed chair to his left.

So much hit him at once. This woman had gone to enormous trouble and expense to have two places, a continent apart, in which she could be equally at home. She must be quite a successful thief to be able to foot the bill. But there was more to her apartment choices than money, and he considered what she said just before they walked in.

"You know, this town is home to me," Morgan said, carrying their suitcases to the sofa, "but you talk and act like you're from another country."

"I am," Felicity said, kicking off her shoes. "I'm a real Colleen from the old country, born right outside of Belfast." She dropped onto the couch.

"I think the shock of the last twenty-four hours has finally hit you."

"I'm very much afraid you might be right," Felicity said through a yawn. "Help me with this, will you?" She stood and turned her back to him. It took him a second to realize she wanted him to pull her dress zipper down. He unzipped her, then watched, shaking his head, as she walked silently and sluggishly off to her bedroom.

How do you figure a girl like that? Morgan wondered. She spent her life in a nerve shattering way, as a professional jewel thief. What could be scarier? Yet now she showed all the symptoms he had seen in combat veterans. He knew she was reacting to that chilling shock a person gets when they first realize that someone would really, really try to kill them.

"Morgan."

It was Felicity. Had he heard a tremble in her voice? One thing was certain. Now that he listened for it, her brogue was definitely more pronounced when she was tired. Well, what the hell. He marched off to her room, peeling off his windbreaker, shoulder holster and shirt along the way. As he passed the guest room, his room in his mind, he tossed them in.

When he reached Felicity's door he slowly pushed it open and stepped in. The city lights struck him head on and splashed around the blue room. The room held a slight scent of vanilla. Felicity lay face up, a deep blue handmade patchwork comforter covering her to the waist. Her bare breasts stood proudly alert, even though her head was propped wearily on two large, puffy pillows. Long red tresses lay splayed in all directions.

"Aren't you going to tuck me in?" she asked meekly. He could feel her loneliness reaching out of those deep green eyes, trying to capture his. He had never seen anyone so defenseless. He hated himself for thinking it, but this was not the way he wanted this woman.

"I know just what you need, Red." He stepped closer to her. "Turn over." After Felicity numbly obeyed, he sat down on the bed. Carefully he removed his boots and turned to kneel on the bed. Poised above her, he caught the scent of a perfume that carried more drama than beauty. With strong, sure fingers he began to knead the knotted muscles in Felicity's neck and shoulders. When he entered he had noted with interest the upsweep of her breasts. Now the firmness of the rest of her body intrigued him.

"Hey, lady, are you a body builder or something?"

"No," Felicity mumbled. "Do a lot of gymnastics. Of course, I've been kind of busy these last couple of days. I usually work out three times a week. And I run. Three or four miles, three times a week. When you're climbing into tenth floor windows and going hand over hand on a wire from one building to the next you've got to be...oooh, that feels good!"

He had worked his way down to her legs. It took all his strength to unknot those long, smooth thigh muscles.

By the time he had worked his way back up to her neck, Felicity's breathing had fallen into the steady pattern of sleep. He stood beside the bed for a moment, staring down at her perfect naked form. How like a renaissance statue, he thought, with perfect innocence on her face. The lights of the grand city glinted off her alabaster form as he gently pulled the comforter up to her shoulders and padded silently toward the door.

"Please." It was a child's voice that called to him. Her green eyes sparkled with moisture in her bed's field of blue. "You can do what you want, or you don't have to do anything," Felicity said. "Just don't go." Morgan was not sure why he should care so much for this girl he had known only days, but his affection won out over his common sense.

Feeling just a bit silly, he pulled off his pants and slid into the bed behind her. Her body was cool and soft to the touch. Awkwardly he wrapped his arm around her. The sound she made as she snuggled back into him was difficult to classify. It was clearly a kind of "mmmmmm" sound, made from behind a smile. Perhaps it was the sound a cat would make if it were somehow converted to human form and somebody rubbed its tummy.

Within a minute she dropped into a deep sleep. He figured he could probably use some sleep too. Besides, there was not much else to do, so he closed his eyes and began the process of shutting down his physical and mental systems.

"Good night, Red," he mumbled.

# -17-

Pearson shifted his weight from one foot to the other, eyes wandering around the brightly lighted room. He stood nervously in the quiet boardroom, surrounded by people whose power was beyond his understanding. The man behind him, Monk, had the bone crushing power of a giant mountain gorilla. Pearson had killed for money, but from the stories he had heard, Monk liked to kill men just for fun. The guy standing beside Pearson was cool and indifferent. Yet he had the power to move men and women like pieces on a chessboard, trading what they wanted for what they were able, and willing to do. Stone was no fighter, but he had a history of toppling governments and creating wars.

Each of them was dangerous in his own way, but only the man behind the desk gave Pearson chills. He was short, with thick stubby fingers and a pockmarked face, yet a pulsing aura of power surrounded him. Here, in Pearson's eyes, was a prime mover, a basic elemental force. He had the ultimate power, the kind that comes from wealth and position. He could have anyone in the room killed with a snap of his fingers. Pearson saw nothing in his eyes but greed. This was Adrian Seagrave, and his kind of power you just did not fool with.

"So, tell Mister Seagrave what you told me over the phone," Stone said. "Explain to your benefactor just why it was that you failed him."

"Well, sir," Pearson began, pausing to clear his throat. "We were sent on a simple hit, Shaw and me, to take care of a girl thief. Stone told me she was a loner. We set it up real easy, waiting for her in her apartment. Figured to make it a clean hit, look like a burglary, right? Then, all of a sudden, there's this big black guy comes crashing in, blasting away like a goddam war was going on. He blew Shaw away, just like that. I was lucky to get out alive. This Stark character, he's crazy. I figured I wasn't getting paid to deal with that kind of action. So I thought I ought to call in for instructions. Stone told me to get here on the double."

"And well he did," Seagrave said. "Very good." Despite his words of praise, Seagrave's face remained completely neutral. He leaned back in his desk chair, forming a tent with his fingers. "Please step over to the bar, Mister Pearson. Help yourself to whatever you like." Pearson nodded, forced a smile, and gratefully slipped over to the other side of the room. He tried to listen in on the conversation behind him. Seagrave seemed relaxed and seemed to have forgotten Pearson existed, his attention now focused on Stone.

"You have a reason for bothering me with this detail?"

"I thought you should hear it first hand, from the source," Stone said.

"Is this a problem?"

"In my opinion, yes," Stone answered.

"Why?"

"The woman is determined," Stone said. "And somehow, she has found herself some very effective assistance."

"So it would appear. Who is this man?"

"Morgan Stark. It is a name you should remember," Stone said, daring to lock eyes with his superior. "He led the team on that Belize mission for you. As you will recall, we left him in the jungle, without transportation, surrounded by a hostile army, hundreds of miles from any kind of support."

Seagrave's brows knitted over his tiny eyes. "And he survived?"

"Let me tell you about this man Stark." Stone paused for emphasis, closing his eyes as if he were searched his mental files, composing words in order to say a great deal as briefly as possible. "He's strong, tough and fast. Tactically sharp and experienced. An agile, quick thinking professional soldier, with great endurance, a high level of skill and seemingly infallible instincts."

"You are impressed by this man." Seagrave pulled a cigarette from a gold case.

"I've been dealing with mercenaries, professional killers and hired muscle for a long time," Stone said. "I can verify that Shaw and Pearson were definitely overmatched. This man is the best survivor I've ever seen. And he just might be the most dangerous man I know."

"Second most dangerous," Monk said, his low, raspy voice coming from behind Stone.

"Perhaps," Stone said, not turning around.

"And the girl?" Seagrave asked, lighting his cigarette with a large standing lighter from the desk.

"About the girl, little is known," Stone said. "However, I can tell you that she has amassed a sizable fortune as a jewel and art thief without ever once being arrested. And if Stark respects her, then so do I."

Seagrave shrugged and blew a thick cloud of smoke at the ceiling. "These people are both for sale. Pay them off."

"I don't think so, sir. They will want full payment for their jobs, plus an additional settlement for the attempt on the girl's life. Even if you considered that price acceptable, you expose yourself to future extortion from contractors if you submit."

Seagrave lowered his eyes and nodded. "Recommendation?"

"In my opinion," Stone said, "these people should be eliminated with all possible dispatch. One dangerous man and one determined woman have been enough to topple empires in the past."

"Well put, Stone." Seagrave stood, and paced for a moment behind his desk with his hands locked behind his back. On one circuit he glanced at Pearson, who smiled back and downed his drink quickly. "Surely they've left the girl's apartment by now," he told Stone in a quiet voice. "Based on your input they must both have secure hiding places. How are we to find them?"

"Based on my knowledge of them, we probably won't, now that they've been alerted. However, they'll certainly be looking for me. I was the contractor who hired them both. And I'm quite sure that worm at the bar traded our location for his life."

"Hey, I didn't tell them anything," Pearson said, sliding off his bar stool. Seagrave and Stone turned as if they had forgotten he was there. Monk's hand thumped down on Pearson's shoulder, locking him in place.

"I could alert the people on the street to look out for anyone who is looking for me," Stone continued, ignoring Pearson's outburst. "Perhaps place a bounty on their heads, thereby turning every tout and petty gunsel in town into a walking death trap, a gantlet to be run on the way to me."

"Excellent, Stone." Seagrave beamed at his lieutenant. "I'll offer, what do you think, fifty? All right, fifty thousand dollars to whoever takes care of this little problem for me. Get to it right away. Now call my secretary back in. And finalize the details for our end of the month meeting. And Monk..."

"Yes sir?" Monk grated out.

"Take our guest downstairs and show him the way out," Seagrave said with a smile.

Monk prompted Pearson with a shove. By the time they reached the door, Seagrave was back at work at his desk. Stone was at the conference table end of the suite, using the telephone. Monk escorted Pearson down the hall and into the elevator.

Two stories below, the elevator stopped. Wordlessly, Monk shoved Pearson out of the elevator car and into the room directly across the hall. Pearson was about to ask what was going on. When Monk entered, locking the door behind him, all doubt was eliminated.

Pearson glanced around the room. It was dimly lit, maybe fifteen by twenty feet. The room had no windows, no other doors and no furniture. The single door had no knob or lever, just a slot in the lock plate to accept an electronic pass card. The silence implied a soundproof room, although Pearson's footsteps echoed coldly around him in it. The stains on the cinder block walls looked like dried blood, and the air carried the musty smell of the crypt. A horizontal bar on the wall to the far left looked like it could be the handle to open a small chute, like the incinerator door in his first apartment.

A most vicious terror seized his heart. He had expected to be roughed up for his failure, maybe have a bone broken. Now he realized he had outlived his usefulness to Stone. Monk was not here to punish him, but to dispose of him. And he knew it would hardly be a fight. There was no question in his mind that this brute would certainly kill him. But maybe with luck, he could take an eye, or an ear, or something.

With a speed born of desperation, Pearson spun a powerful right cross into Monk's face. He was following it up with a claw hand blow before he realized how badly his knuckles were hurt. Monk clamped the incoming left in his own ham-like hand inches before it reached his face.

Shock dragged despair into Pearson's heart. He had expected Monk to be inhumanly strong, but who would have guessed he was so fast?

That was Pearson's last coherent thought.

Monk casually twisted Pearson's wrist until the bone splintered. Pearson battered impotently at him with his good fist until Monk slapped him on the side of his head, sending him sprawling. Pearson lay dazed until Monk reached down, wrapped a hand around Pearson's right leg just below his knee and lifted him into the air. While Pearson hung helplessly, Monk shifted his grip so he could get both hands wrapped around one thigh. He put his thumbs together, pushing out in the same direction.

Monk was not a sexual creature. He used no drugs, and rarely did he drink. He could barely read and certainly never would unless he had to. He was not perceptive enough to enjoy most television or movies. He did not even like music. There was just one thing he really enjoyed. The crack of bones breaking in a live body, that was his favorite sound.

Pearson's screams reverberated in the soundproof room, but they could not drown out the snap of his leg breaking. His screams abruptly ended as the pain overwhelmed him and he passed out.

Monk grinned at the breaking noise and shrugged when Pearson went limp. For him, this was a pretty good one. He had no bloody mess to clean up. It was too bad that Pearson fainted after only one bone. Monk would have preferred a longer experience. But, since he stayed in one piece, disposal was easy. Monk simply opened the incinerator hatch and stuffed Pearson down the chute head first.

## -18-

Some people go through layers of sleep. They drift slowly down into dark stillness. Then when morning comes, they rise from it, one layer at a time, until they open their eyes, focus through a groggy haze and slowly gain consciousness.

Felicity had never been one of them. Some days, when the nightmares came, she would walk past that same old parked car, watch it explode and see her parents splattered against a wall. She would wonder why not herself. The dream would end abruptly, and she would burst into wakefulness, panting and dripping with sweat.

Other days, like today, she would simply pop awake. Her eyes snapped open and in an instant she was alert and ready for action. First, she sent her senses around the room, confirming her location. This was her New York penthouse. It was nine thirty-seven a.m. and she was alone in her bed.

Seven minutes later she was in the hallway, her hair brushed out and her face glowing, wearing very tight jeans with an oversized white blouse unbuttoned to her breastbone. She needed no bra.

She found Morgan in the kitchen facing the stove, wearing black jeans and those ever-present boots. His black tee shirt said, "nuke 'em 'till they glow" across the back. Conspicuous to her by its absence was his shoulder rig and the weapons it carried. The crackling sound told her that he was pouring beaten eggs into a pan, filling the room with the smell of slightly burned butter.

"Well, the man's an early riser I see." She stepped up behind him, went up on her tiptoes, and placed a gentle kiss on his neck.

"Thank you," she whispered.

"For what?"

"For staying when I needed you," she said while she pulled china from a cabinet. "And for not, you know, taking advantage." She waited for a response but when she heard none she looked over at him. He was too dark to blush, but was that embarrassment she saw on his face?

While Morgan worked in the kitchen, Felicity set up a small, low table on the mezzanine at the other end of the room. When the food was ready, the pair took their scrambled eggs and toast to that table in front of the big window. Orange juice, fresh pears and cheese completed their breakfast menu. Chewing absently, Morgan settled back on the big pillow Felicity provided and got lost in the view.

"It doesn't feel like being in the world's fastest city at all, now does it?" she asked.

"You're right," Morgan said, pushing egg onto his fork with his toast. "It's kind of like I'm sitting on the edge of a tranquil crystal lake."

Felicity found her eggs scrambled hard, the way she preferred them, and quite peppery. That made them unexpected good. "Eloquent for a soldier," she said. "But that's just the feeling I get here. It's like that's New York over there, on the other side, half a mile away, while we sit here on a peaceful floating island. So. What shall we do today?"

"Business," Morgan answered. "You hired me to do a job, and I'm on the clock."

His response surprised her. It seemed that after sharing a relaxed moment in fantasy with him she had pulled him back to reality. "Oh yes," she said. "You said you'd help me find this Stone character."

"That's why I was up so early," Morgan said. "Made some phone calls. Which reminds me. I'm going to need some more spending cash because I've got a lunch date. Old contact of mine, another dude who worked for Stone in the past. We haven't been in touch much, but he might know who Stone is working for now and where to find him."

"Perhaps I should be doing the same," Felicity said, her voice cooler. It disturbed her a little for Morgan to be all business. However, she realized she had created that relationship. Not wanting to be the damsel in distress, she had hired him instead of asking him for help. On that basis he probably felt that needed to show results. "You know, I could check with some of my friends in the business," she continued. "The new owner is sure to want to wear that brooch I stole, to show it off you know, then hide it before the insurance investigators start looking this far away. A bauble that unique suddenly appearing in society will excite imaginations in my circles."

"Good idea," Morgan said, rising from the table. He took his plate and glass to the kitchen. Curiosity made her follow. She had to pry into his quietness.

"Morgan, I have to ask you something. Is it bothering you, spending my money?"

"Not at all, Red," he responded. "I could always hit a cash machine. But I'm on a mission. You pay expenses."

"And after?" she asked, hating the apprehension in her voice.

"After? If you mean about the money, I've got a couple hundred grand American dollars stashed away in a Swiss bank account. If you mean, what happens after we find Stone, well, I intend to harass his mysterious employer enough to get him to pay us both a bundle to back off." He lifted the green flap over his watch. "I've got to run."

"For a lunch date?" Felicity asked. "It isn't ten thirty."

"Yeah, but I got things to do before I talk to anybody," Morgan said. "Which means I better go suit up."

"Changing clothes?"

"No, just want my gear for this little meeting," Morgan said.

"Mind if I watch?"

Morgan shrugged and headed for the guest room with Felicity close behind. In the room she watched the ritual with rapt attention. She wondered what went on inside this man's mind as he placed a series of weapons so carefully about his person. One knife went into each boot. She watched him push on the top bullet in is magazine, confirming that it was full, and function check his pistol. After loading his automatic, he pulled back the slide and let it slam forward. He pushed a button on the side of the gun and the magazine dropped back out. Now he was able to add another bullet to the top of the column. She figured one must have stayed in the pistol.

"Aren't there enough in there?" she asked.

"Well, it's a ten round magazine in case I get stopped. Ten's the legal limit, as if that somehow makes a gun less dangerous. I like to start with one in the chamber."

"I'd think ten would be enough for anything you'd want to be doing," Felicity said.

"There's something to that, but on the other hand, that eleventh cartridge might be the one that saves my life," he said. The grip looked thick to her, but in its custom made shoulder holster it was quite invisible beneath the lightweight black windbreaker Morgan pulled on.

"Lord, it fits like it was made for you," Felicity said, trying to lighten the mood.

"The shoulder rig? It was. Wet molded and hand boned, with a hand rubbed oil finish. Got this half harness for maximum concealment, and the premium saddle leather it's made out of will last a lifetime. At least, the lifetime of anybody in this business." While he talked, Morgan pulled on a belt with a large square steel buckle.

"Won't that thing hurt you if you're moving around, like if you get in a fight?"

That brought a grin from Morgan. "Believe me, this special buckle might actually help me in a fight. I'm real careful to dress for comfort these days. I remember one time I hurt my back. In the field I wear this big knife in its sheath at the small of my back. Took a fall wrong and man, that hurt. Had to find a better way."

\* \* \* \* \*

After a final glass of juice, Morgan gave Felicity a peck on the cheek and left the apartment. When he closed the door, his mind was alive with conflicting thoughts.

He hailed a cab and pointed it downtown. In the taxi, his mind centered on Felicity. He was most uncomfortable with what he was feeling for this mysterious but beautiful redhead. He liked being in control of a situation, but he had certainly lost control of this one. Here he was, working for a woman, taking care of her business.

Or was he? Right now, he admitted to himself, he was on a self-motivated mission of revenge. The rules of the game had changed since yesterday, when Pearson and his partner had suddenly turned up. Morgan had made some nasty enemies who clearly had no qualms about killing and could set their machinery in motion in a matter of hours, cross-country. That alone implied incredible power. For his own selfish interests, he had to end that threat. He couldn't simply leave dangerous people in a position to hurt him.

And wasn't that the point? This was no time for beginning a long-term relationship, especially with an unpredictable, bullheaded, white, Irish expatriate, professional criminal with expensive tastes. Damn.

While the cab bumped down Fifth Avenue, he managed to drag his mind back to the business at hand. Hopefully, by moving to New York so quickly, he had gotten the jump on the enemy. He knew enough people in this town that, with any luck at all, he could track Stone down before Stone got him pinpointed. With luck! All in all, he liked it better stalking his enemies in the jungle.

He left the cab at Washington Square, four blocks from the small cafe in the heart of Greenwich Village at which he would meet Griffith. The sun was harsh, the sky unusually clear and the air thick and stagnant. Not the best day for a hike through New York, but he wanted to walk in and tour the area before the meeting.

For a hundred and fifty years the West Village has been the home of writers and artists of all types. Something about those twisted, narrow streets in the midst of an otherwise grid work city has traditionally made it the place where society's oddballs fit in. It has been through beatniks, hippies, heads, freaks and punks, and while the residents have changed, the area has not really changed much. It remains a good place for a meeting if you do not want people to notice you.

J.D. Griffith, Morgan's "date", was ex-Marine Recon. He served his country in Vietnam, and himself later in Rhodesia and the Congo. Morgan had worked with him briefly, and had kept in touch for professional reasons. Both men were respected team leaders when they worked, and they did not want to get in each other's way somewhere when the action got hot.

Morgan crossed the street within a block of his planned meeting place without looking toward it. He passed a storefront Thai restaurant, and its sweet and sharp aroma followed him around the next corner. Halfway down that block Morgan hopped to grasp a rusty fire escape ladder. The squeal of metal against metal set his teeth on edge, but the ladder did come all the way down and Morgan scrambled up it to the roof four stories above the street.

Standing at the edge of the roof he could see the heat rising off the black surface, and it somehow reminded him of his youth. Crouching low, he lumbered three quarters of the way across the roof before dropping to low crawl the rest of the way. The asphalt's pungent odor stung his nose. He relaxed at the end of his brief journey, absorbing the warmth from the tacky surface. Looking over the roof's edge, he was directly above Georg's Cafe, a little Greek place with umbrellas over its outdoor tables that said "Cinzano" in red and blue letters. In about twenty minutes he would meet Griffith under one of them. Now he carefully scanned the windows across the street.

There! Second floor, second window to the left. That had to be one of Griffith's men in the window. And on the near corner to the left, that dude loitering in the doorway was just a little too alert. He found another to the right across the street. The man in that telephone booth was not really talking to anyone. Griffith had covered the street quite well. Simple caution, Morgan wondered, or something more?

He backed off from his vantage point, retracing his steps down the fire escape. As he sauntered around the corner, he zipped his windbreaker halfway up. He started whistling and relaxed his pace. Morgan's normal gait was very much like marching, but now he exaggerated his walk into the inner city "bop" so many black men have, as if he were listening to some dance track no one else could hear. The impression he gave was extremely casual.

He recognized Griffith's grin as he approached the table. He was at least five years Morgan's senior, but he still retained a jocular baby face. His hair was cut in the style Marines call a "high and tight": short on top and nearly shaved to the skin on the back and sides. He wore a wrinkled corduroy suit and top quality hiking boots. A typical blond haired, blue eyed, bullet headed type, Morgan thought.

"S'happenin' my man?" Morgan called in greeting as he sat down, extending his hand.

"You know the deal," Griffith replied, adding a strong handshake to the habitual military greeting. "I took the liberty of buying you a beer. Hope you don't mind a Michelob."

"Well, I still prefer that Black Cat we used to get in the 'Nam. However..." Morgan picked up his bottle and tipped it up, putting down half of the brew. It was light, crisp, cold, and unremarkable, as Morgan found all mass-produced American beers to be. Griffith also took a strong pull from his amber bottle. Morgan figured that should take care of the opening rituals.

"So, why the meet?" Griffith asked. "You got a new contract in Africa? Want to make sure I'm not on the other side?"

"No, it's not like that," Morgan said, leaning back in his chair. "In fact I'm not working right now. I came looking for you because I need some information. A few phone calls told me you've been working out of New York for a while now, so I figured you'd be the one to ask."

"Well, I do pretty much know what's going down around town," Griffith said, lighting up a Cuban cigar. He offered one to Morgan, who declined. "I don't come cheap, but I can be had."

"You remember Stone?"

"Sure, I've worked with him," Griffith said, signaling into the cafe for a couple of refills. "Every gunfighter I know has worked with him. Everybody worth a damn, anyway. He's always been straight with me. Course, he's not an independent anymore. Took a steady contract with somebody."

"Yeah, I heard that. That's what I wanted to talk to you about. The last job I did for Stone didn't go too good. He crossed me. Who would have figured it?"

"Crossed you?" Griffith repeated, blowing cigar smoke into the sky. "Like how?"

Morgan leaned forward, bracing his elbows on the table. "Like, he pulled my transport at the end of a hot mission. Like got my men killed, and damn near got me, too. I can't let people get away with crossing me. You know that. It's bad for future business, you know." Morgan finished his beer, and tension showed in his arm as he set the empty bottle down. "I sure would like to find him."

"Well, getting to that boy could take some doing," Griffith said between gulps. As he finished his first beer, the waiter came out with the second round. All conversation ceased until he was well beyond hearing range. Once he was gone, Griffith continued. "Still, from what I've heard, it can be arranged."

"And just what did you hear?" Morgan sat up just a little straighter. The hairs on the back of his neck stirred. Damn it! He had looked it all over so carefully and still stepped square into a trap.

"Well, while you're out looking for Stone, it turns out Stone's also looking for you, old buddy," the ex-Marine said. "I'd like to get you two together."

"I see you're in a helpful mood," Morgan said, starting to rise. Griffith waved him down.

"You need to stay in your chair, old pal, so as not to make anyone nervous. I know how dangerous you are, and I guess

Stone does too. He's put quite a little price on your head. Word is, he wants you dismissed. With extreme prejudice." In the vernacular of the business they were in, Morgan and Griffith both knew that meant killed in cold blood.

That was when Morgan felt the waiter's gun barrel resting gently against his twelfth vertebrae. He was the one member of Griffith's team Morgan had not made. Not that he was a particular problem. Morgan knew that he could free himself from the waiter, even kill him, but he knew he would never get away. Griffith's men had the street too well covered. If Stone had put a price on his head, Morgan knew his old rival Griffith just might collect it.

## -19-

All Felicity got when Morgan walked out the door was a peck on the cheek. As he closed the door, her mind was alive with conflicting thoughts. She had not really wanted him to go. She suspected he was on his way to meet some dangerous contact from his mercenary past. His confidence appeared absolute when he left, but did that have any meaning? His confidence seemed total under all circumstances, no matter how dangerous.

Despite some difficulty concentrating, she made several phone calls and moved off to her room to get dressed. She moved through these motions almost unconsciously, her mind awhirl with recent happenings. Why had she fallen into such a trusting mode with this tall dark stranger? Sure, he had proved worthy of her trust last night when she was too tired to think straight, but why oh why had she taken him so to her heart in the first place?

He weighed on her mind while she flipped through her closet. He was a mass of contradictions, this Morgan Stark. Even his name conjured up different images. Morgan, as in the pirate. Stark, as in raving mad. Perhaps she found him so easy to trust because he was so open, so "up front" as he Yanks liked to say. He was certainly outspoken. There seemed to be no subtle side to this one. And so proud, he was. And yet, she had no idea who he was, and knew nothing about his life. He had revealed only the barest bones of his past.

Facing a full-length mirror, Felicity held a dress in each hand. She held one in front of herself, then the other, but was at a loss about which would be the better choice. Morgan, she reflected, seemed totally competent and never at a loss. He could be as cold as a Norwegian winter night, and then turn around and be as warm and soft as a sheepskin coat. And how could he be so intuitively intelligent, yet so socially unsophisticated? And how did she seem to have some sort of emotional connection with him, almost a psychic link? Was it some side effect of her, now their, danger sense? Was it just her romantic reaction to being rescued, protected, defended and comforted by a heroic stranger, like in those cheesy novels? Or, and this was the big question, was she falling in love with this regimented, stubborn, black, ill-mannered professional soldier? Damn!

Because the texture appealed to her fingers more that day, Felicity chose the long sleeved, cream colored, wool dress. She pulled the garment over her head, stepped back, and turned so that she could check herself out in both her wide dresser mirror and the full-length looking glass on the other side of the bedroom. She was dressed to the limits of elegance for her luncheon downtown. The dress was just this side of too tight. The back was a drape, which hung low on her tanned back, almost to the swell of her ample hips. She had put her hair up for the occasion and applied the slightest hint of makeup. She smiled at her image. This look would take her to the world's most stylish eateries.

Minutes later, she pulled her 1966 Corvette Stingray coupe out of the parking garage and slid smoothly into traffic. She hated driving in New York, but she had to admit it was better than trusting her fate to any cab driver. And if she was going to drive, it was a joy to pilot this classic bit of transportation, so she pulled it out whenever she was in the city. The day's brilliant sun would make her glossy, tuxedo black machine hard for passersby to look at, but she knew they would want to stare. Dipped in chrome and airbrushed with twelve coats of paint, the agile vehicle seemed to slip like quicksilver through traffic on the wide one-way avenue. A twist of the knob of the factory installed AM-FM radio filled her cockpit with Van Morrison's folksy blues sound. After all these years, she still found "Domino" to be great driving music. Humming along, she pulled a pair of Dragonfly sunglasses out of the glove compartment and slid them into place. Life was good.

But less than three blocks from home, she started to get fidgety. That odd, intuitive discomfort always had a cause. She glanced in the rear view mirror. Was someone following her? She switched to the far left lane, signaling for a turn. Yes. The little Fiat four cars back was jockeying to get behind her. She suddenly darted to the right lane and the Fiat nearly ran a Lexus onto the sidewalk getting to the right also.

No style, she thought. A rank beginner would have spotted him. She could see two men in the car. Were they police? She knew they put a tail on her from time to time, hoping to get lucky. Then she saw the passenger side man hold up a pistol and charged back the slide.

"Nope, you're not the police, are you?" she said softly to herself. "Who, then? Friends of the two killers I met in my apartment on the West Coast, perhaps? Well then, no time for games now."

She could find out for sure why the men in the follow car wanted her later. Now she had to shake these guys in a hurry, and she knew how. A couple of years back, Felicity took an offensive driving course. Her instructors thought she was a bodyguard in training, but in fact she needed the skills of an expert evasive driver to escape police pursuit. That was also the reason she replaced the 327 turbocharged engine the factory put into her little Corvette with the 426 blown hemi under its hood now. The same reasoning led to the button on the side of her Hurst T-shifter, but she did not need that now. Her own driving ability would do the trick, along with her knowledge of New York streets, and New York drivers.

She slowed just enough to let the Fiat gain on her. Her pursuer, predictably, pulled up next to her on her right. He rolled his window down as if to yell to her. To her surprise, the passenger leaned over the driver to point his gun at her. These guys were a lot more serious than she thought and for the first time she realized she was in real danger.

## -20-

Morgan spread his hands on the table, hoping to reassure the man holding a gun against his neck. "This is hardly a combat situation, J.D. You got your boys killing on contract now?"

"Stone wants to see your corpse, buddy, and that's a fact," Griffith said, "but I think, if your behavior is reasonable, we'll take you to him as is and let him do the dirty deed himself, if he can."

Morgan found Griffith's grin infuriating. He was too damned confident. He controlled the street, but Morgan wondered if he had covered the inside of the little cafe. He hoped not, because it was his only option. He would have to play it that way and hope something turned up. He started his ploy by grimacing and clutching his stomach in apparent pain. He rose slowly when Griffith did. The waiter/gunman began patting Morgan for weapons.

"You going to wave your hardware and mine around out here in the open?" Morgan asked.

"Good point, sport. Let's move this party into the cafe."

Morgan groaned again, and continued to reach for his gut as they walked into the small Greek luncheonette. A counter stood on the left and half a dozen tables crowded the floor, too close together. Each table was dressed in a long white tablecloth and surrounded by four chairs. The smell of burning garlic rose out of the floorboards but no lunchtime chatter greeted them. To Morgan's dismay, the place was deserted.

"Were you expecting somebody in here to use as a distraction?" Griffith asked, locking the door behind them. "I rented the place for the afternoon. You know, for a private party."

Morgan could not believe how quickly the opposition had moved. Oh well. At least the gun-toting waiter had become accustomed to Morgan reaching to his waist. Morgan was no longer getting jabbed in his back each time his arm moved. But now Griffith, facing him, pulled a forty-five caliber automatic from a side rig.

"Okay, sport," Griffith said with a smirk, "what are you carrying?"

"How long you known me, man? You know what I carry. I'm a creature of habit."

"That'll be the death of you one day," Griffith said. "Now, unzip that jacket. Tommy, there's a Hi-Power under his left arm. Grab that will you?"

The waiter reached under Morgan's windbreaker and slid the nine-millimeter out of its holster.

"I'm pretty sure that's a knife on the other side," Griffith said. Tommy nodded and pulled on Morgan's left shoulder to partially turn him. Morgan turned just enough, and Tommy reached forward awkwardly, his left hand going across the front of Morgan's body as it slid under his windbreaker. This was the moment.

"What'd you do, poison me?" Morgan asked through clenched teeth. He bent farther than before, again grasping his own waist. As he did, he gripped his belt buckle in his right hand. With a short tug, it came loose from his belt.

As the buckle came away, so did a three inch, black, razor sharp, double-edged steel blade. The belt buckle served as the square handle of a push dagger, concealed in the leather of his wide belt.

Morgan turned half way to his left, thrusting up under his own left arm into the exposed ribs of the gunman behind him. The blade slid in high enough to find Tommy's heart. The man did not even have time to moan before death took him.

Morgan knew that Griffith could not really see what was happening. Morgan's back faced him for an instant, and Morgan's jacket cloaked the action. Griffith might be staring into his accomplice's astonished face just long enough for Morgan to spin back toward him, very fast. Morgan snapped his right arm out in a wide arc, and it was a blur as it swung past Griffith's outstretched arm. Griffith's pistol dropped from nerveless fingers, and blood burst from the heel of his palm. He had time for one short grunt of pain before Morgan's left fist, powered by all the rage an old soldier can hold, crashed into his jaw, sending him tumbling over a table.

Morgan knew he had been lucky. First of all, Griffith and his backup man were guilty of unforgivable carelessness. The idiot behind Morgan had stretched out his left arm, leaving his heart side ribs wide open. And Griffith had been close enough so that, after the killing thrust, Morgan's back swing had just caught Griffith's gun hand. Morgan had continued the spin and his left cross put Griffith over the table and into dreamland for a while.

Ignoring his aching knuckles, Morgan tucked Griffith's larger automatic into his belt, then recovered his own. After wiping the push dagger on the dead man's shirt, he returned it to its belt scabbard. While Griffith was dazed, Morgan performed a quick body search, netting a twenty-five caliber pocket pistol and a big folding knife.

Tossing Griffith's backup weapons aside, he roughly yanked the ex-Marine to his feet. When his eyes snapped open, Griffith found the cold steel muzzle of Morgan's pistol resting on the tip of his nose. He raised his hands slowly, giving Morgan a half smile of respect. Morgan released his shirt and sat down on a table for two.

"So you sold me out." Morgan practically spat the words out.

"Nothing personal," Griffith said, trying for a light tone. "Strictly business. You'd have done the same thing."

Morgan let that pass. "And what was the plan, really?" Moving his pistol, he motioned Griffith into a chair. "Were you going to just kill me in here and deliver my head to Stone for a fat reward?"

"No, man," Griffith said, tying a cloth napkin around his hand and wrist as he talked. "I was just going to deliver you. Whole. I'm a soldier, not a hit man. I figured, if Stone wanted you taken out, he'd have to do it himself. He could take care of you face to face, if he's got the balls."

"Sounds like fun," Morgan said. "Why don't you just take me to him. Now, I know you've got the front covered. So we'll just go upstairs and across the roof. Then we can go have a little rendezvous with our mutual friend with the white hair."

"You know I can't do that." Griffith's face dropped into a genuine hard look. Morgan's twisted into a snarl. They stared into each other's eyes for ten long seconds. Morgan knew that he was facing a tough, hard man, a veteran of many battles and a man who, like Morgan himself, had walked with death every day for years. A bullet in the brain would hold no terror for him. But maybe, just maybe, something else would.

Without breaking eye contact, Morgan reached under his right arm an exaggerated slow motion and pulled his fighting knife free. Mindful of the distance, he switched his pistol to his left hand, the knife to his right. He held the flat of the blade toward Griffith. A light beam flashed off the steel, making the seated man blink.

"Hold out your left hand," Morgan commanded in a cold monotone. Griffith clenched his teeth and lifted his arm out straight toward his captor. One tiny bead of sweat swelled from his forehead and rolled down into his left eye. He blinked twice, his gaze brushing over the corpse lying behind Morgan. Quickly his eyes snapped back to the Morgan's grim face.

"You recognize this?" Morgan asked. "It's a Randall Number One custom made fighting knife. It's seven inches of the best steel available, high carbon 440C stainless, hand forged and hand ground, and tempered to a hardness of sixty on the Rockwell scale. I can put an inch of the tip of this blade in a vise and stand on the handle without bending or breaking it. Do you think I keep it sharp?"

He stretched out his right hand, keeping the pistol in his left centered between Griffith's eyes. He was impressed that the ex-Marine's hand remained completely steady. He rested the edge of the blade against Griffith's skin, tilted it to a sharp angle and slid the knife toward himself. The harsh scraping sound filled the otherwise silent diner. With one long slow stroke, Morgan removed all the hair from the offered arm starting two inches above the white wrist. Tiny red dots rose from the razor burn of a dry shave. While he wiped his blade clean on Griffith's pants, Morgan again made strong eye contact.

"Now we can go to the meeting place you had arranged with Stone," Morgan said, "or, I can drag you upstairs and gag you and tie you up real tight. You friends out front would assume you were working me over in here. Or maybe they'd think I escaped and you followed me. Eventually they'll knock that door open and find Tommy over there. Eventually they'd just leave. Then I could spend the next three or four hours making one inch cuts, an eighth of an inch deep everywhere on your body. Everywhere. When I got through you'd be covered with blood. Hands, feet, genitals would become useless. You'd hurt like hell. For months. But you know what? You wouldn't die. You'd never walk or work or fuck again. But you wouldn't die. Now. Shall we go?"

For the next several seconds Griffith's eyes wandered the room, as if he was considering his options. Morgan waited patiently until Griffith slowly rose from his chair.

"I didn't like the food here anyway," he said.

\* \* \* \* \*

A door at the top of the stairs provided easy access to the roof. No one paid any attention to them trotting down the fire escape stairs. Once on the street, Morgan pocketed his gun. He put his left arm around Griffith's waist, with the Browning in his right side pocket pointed at the Marine across the front of his body. Then he ordered his captive to hail a taxi. He did not worry about their appearance. Hacks cruising the village would think nothing of a couple of guys looking for a ride who were embracing, or even holding hands. When a cab pulled to the curb in front of them, Morgan was confident he would soon meet with his betrayer.

Apart from an unduly talkative driver, Morgan's taxi ride was uneventful. They took the local route, up through midtown Manhattan. Griffith began to relax a little, which Morgan took as a bow to his own professionalism. The tense moments of capture had passed. Now Morgan wanted Griffith to know he was in no danger as long as he didn't try anything stupid. So they sat in silence, watching the busy city go by.

New York passed in an even flow of images, through clean and dirty neighborhoods. By moving at exactly thirty-two miles per hour, the streetwise driver approached each traffic light just as it turned green. He dodged around jaywalkers, cursing them in Armenian as he sprinted past. A local bus briefly barred their way, but by swerving around and past it, between the bus and a little Honda, the taxi freed itself. Morgan was thinking that the little stores and shops, so boldly ethnic, were the same in every major city in the world.

Traffic filled in as they left Manhattan and suddenly, they were in the Bronx. Morgan had seen the results of urban guerrilla warfare up close many times. Here, in the world's richest city, was an area that bore an unpleasant resemblance to downtown Beirut. He knew those crumbling tenements he was riding past had spawned some of the most hardened fighters civilization had to offer. The broken windows were empty eyes staring out of pockmarked stucco faces.

The people here were black or Hispanic. They walked quickly, alert as any jungle animal, ready for an attack. When they moved around the neighborhood, they traveled in packs. They roamed these mean streets as warily as if there was a war on.

The driver lapsed into silence as he pulled the cab over to the curb. Morgan paid him, and the two passengers, captor and captive, stepped into the littered street. The men locked eyes as the taxi pulled away.

"I recognize this feeling, this emptiness," Griffith said in hushed tones.

"Yeah," Morgan said. "It's that feeling, like when the choppers take off and you're left in that LZ, inches from the forward battle line, unprotected."

Griffith nodded, pointing a little up the narrow avenue. The empty lot directly across the street was covered with broken glass, broken bricks, broken bottles, broken boards. To its right stood a crumbling four story tenement building filled with broken windows, broken doors, and, Morgan imagined, broken dreams. Beyond the building was yet another empty lot.

The building stood like a single tooth, sticking up out of a rotting mouth. The number 1313 was painted on the door.

"So this is the rendezvous point," Morgan said, his voice invading the silence. "Good thing I'm not superstitious."

"This is where I was to bring you. Second floor left."

"Well, let's not disappoint him." Morgan pulled out Griffith's pistol, dropped the magazine and pulled the slide back, popping out the chambered round. As that lone bullet spun to the asphalt he extended the gun toward its owner. "Now take this. I'll holster my gun. You walk me in like I'm a prisoner. Once I make contact with Stone or his representative, you're free to go. Right?"

Griffith seemed to consider the situation for a moment. "You know, even if I lay off you, even if Stone don't get you, my men will be after you," he said. "They're very good and very loyal."

"I'll take my chances," Morgan said. "You in?"

"Okay. I'll play," Griffith said, reaching to accept the empty automatic.

Morgan wondered if any of the local citizens were watching as a military looking white man marched one of their black brothers across a pothole-covered street in the South Bronx. As they stepped through the rickety front door, he noticed a junkie crouched in the far corner of the unlighted hall. The junkie ignored the two intruders. They ignored him.

The odor of urine almost overpowered them. Morgan led the way up the stairs, stepping over the broken ones. On the second floor landing, Griffith thrust the impotent gun barrel into Morgan's back and nodded toward a door.

"Good-bye and good luck," he muttered. Morgan thought he might mean it. Griffith reached around Morgan and hit the door with three fast knocks and two slow ones.

A bolt shot back, a latch turned, and the door swung inward. Morgan expected to see Stone or an underling, seated comfortably, waiting to take him to some unknown Big Man. Instead, he stepped forward into a room even darker than the hallway. On the left, he made out a couch canted away from the wall. To his right sat a big torn up chair and a small table. As his eyes became accustomed to the deeper gloom he thought he saw a doorway about twenty feet ahead, perhaps leading into the kitchen.

Almost too late, all of his internal warning lights went on. A short, squat figure appeared in the far doorway. A flash of light glinted off of something as he swung it up. Morgan had just enough time to realize that Griffith was in the line of fire. These bastards would toss him out to get Morgan.

"Jesus!" Morgan said through clenched teeth as he dived desperately to the left. The blast coincided with his leap. Two or three stray shotgun pellets raked his right side ribs. His left shoulder crashed into the wall and he slid down behind the sofa. He had time to catch only a glimpse of J.D. Griffith pointing his useless forty-five before a swarm of angry twelve gage hornets blasted him into, and all over, the hall.

For Morgan, there was no way out. The couch provided some concealment, making it tough for anyone to pin down his exact position. But concealment is not the same thing as cover. He knew that riot gun in the kitchen would find him before too long. Twenty feet away, against the opposite wall, the backup man lay prone under the small table. He fired his small caliber pistol occasionally into the sofa. The crossfire was simple, smart, and inescapable. To stand and get a shot at one, he would have to expose himself to the other.

What an ugly place to die, Morgan thought, and gave pragmatic consideration to which of these killers he would take with him.

## -21-

Felicity tore her eyes away from the gun pointed at her. Ahead, she saw that the tarnished pole on the corner held a green light. At the intersection she pulled hard on the wheel and slid around to her left. The Fiat also managed to corner, accompanied by a blare of horns. The cross street was short. She hit her left signaler, indicating a turn up Third Avenue, back the way she had come. She knew the big avenues were one way in alternating directions, and she figured her followers did too.

At the corner the Fiat was right behind her, trying to squeeze onto her right side, to get on the outside of the turn. She looked up and sighed in frustration. The light was already yellow. She would never reach the corner before it turned red. Well, tough. She leaned back, put on her best "dumb broad" face, down shifted, cranked the wheel and tapped her brakes.

The racing change gave her just enough of a fish tail to slide between lanes of oncoming traffic as she cocked the wheel to the right, against the one-way flow of traffic. Surprise caused the river of cars to part for her. There were raised fists and horns sounding in all possible tones and keys. From every car arose a chorus of "dumb broad", "out-of-towner" and other dirty names New Yorkers call people.

Felicity smiled, affected a look of fear, embarrassment and apology, and wound through a block of impatient but obliging drivers. She had long believed the world's most skillful drivers outside Paris, lived in New York. They could not survive otherwise. She made it to the next intersection feeling the impact of much cursing and swearing, but no collisions.

The driver of the Fiat was less fortunate. New York drivers might adjust for one idiot, but not two in a row. The hole that had opened up for the Corvette closed immediately behind it. A Lincoln was stopped, grill to grill with the Fiat. Its engine growled menacingly. In her rear view mirror Felicity saw the drivers of the facing cars get out. The Lincoln's driver, in a chauffeur's uniform, was noticeably larger than the other.

Then she was on the cross street, on her way back to Fifth Avenue. A part of her wished she could see the result of the massive traffic snarl she had caused, but she did not want to arrive late for lunch at the Waldorf.

\* \* \* \* \*

The magnificent structure known as the Waldorf-Astoria Hotel has occupied the same prestigious corner of Park Avenue and 49th Street for more than seventy years. She chose this place for lunch, not because the guests were frequently film stars and big name politicians, but because she would face less of a crowd there than would be present at some other famous spots. New Yorkers often forget that hotel restaurants offer some of the finest eating in the city.

Actually, the Waldorf offered three very different restaurants. Inagiku was probably the first upscale gourmet Japanese restaurant in midtown Manhattan. Oscar's was perhaps the most gracious coffee shop on the East Coast. For that day, she had chosen the third alternative, the Bull and Bear.

Over the years, Felicity had learned the advantages of style over substance. The Bull and Bear Restaurant had style to spare. She loved the warm wood paneling and soft, discreet lighting. The decor was rich with antiques, so carefully matched and selected, that to walk through the door was to be plunged into another era.

She chose a table near the nineteenth century hand carved boar's head. She always felt as if she had invaded a private men's club there. After turning away the offered glass of water, she tried to settle into some people watching. A head of state or two caught her eye, but as always the place held her attention more than the patrons. Her eyes were drawn to an English catchpole and a matched pair of three hundred year old French rapiers behind them. This activity kept her serene until her date, and his escort, joined her.

"You are even lovelier today than you were on the Riviera last season, my dear," Duncan Baptiste said. He kissed the back of her left hand and took the seat opposite hers. "This magnificent decor is almost a sufficient backdrop for your beauty."

She flashed Baptiste her most dazzling smile. "You are most gracious," she said. Bullshit, she thought. Duncan Baptiste was a jewel thief with few rivals. The product of a French peasant girl and a visiting Scottish soldier just after the end of World War Two, he was obviously named after his father. He started stealing to live while still in his childhood. His reputation came partly from being successful in his chosen field for twenty years before Felicity ever began. The rest of his name came from a half dozen truly spectacular heists in the nineteen seventies.

A waiter brought a plate of sandwiches, which Duncan must have ordered. The other, bigger man who joined the table reached for a half sandwich and pushed half of it into his mouth.

"Who's this big fellow?" She asked.

"James is an associate of mine," Duncan said. "As he matures, a man finds he needs assistance for the more physical bits of business."

As their cocktails arrived, she checked her seatmates. While Baptiste's dark brown hair was styled, James' was barber cut. Baptiste wore a hand made and tailored wool suit with Italian hand made shoes. His companion wore a Sears polyester suit and penny loafers. Obviously a flunky, but with none of the panache she would expect to see in a thief Baptiste would accept as an apprentice. A bodyguard, then? Was Baptiste losing his confidence in his old age?

"Now, my dear, exactly what was it you wanted to discuss with your old rival, eh?" Baptiste asked through the smoke from his Dunhill cigarette.

"Well, Duncan dear, I'm afraid it's business."

"I had hoped for a more social reason," Duncan said. "Oh, well, what will it be then? Some professional advice, perhaps?"

"Well, sort of." Her eyes wandered nervously as she answered, while her fingers fidgeted with the pepper shaker in front of her. "A few days ago, you see, I was casing a particular bauble that caught my eye down in Mexico. Fact is, I had invested a lot in this score. Not money, but a lot of time and planning. I was all set to make the touch when the mark up and moves to New York. Well, followed the boy here, I did, but then I hear the bauble changed hands. Now this is a particularly nice piece, it is, a real prime target for sure. I know you've been making New York your base for a while. If this piece wandered into your bailiwick I figure you'd smell it. And I just kind of figured that out of professional courtesy and for a small consideration..."

"That I'd lead you to it?" Baptiste asked. "Well, O'Brian, when you tilt your head just so and bat those big green eyes at me like that, how can I say no? Besides, I'm not above collecting a small finder's fee. Now just what are we talking about? What does this bauble look like?"

"Oh, 'tis a honey of an antique brooch," Felicity said. "Picture a teardrop diamond set in Russian malachite, surrounded by matched pearls. It's really quite lovely." Her speech slowed because without warning, her senses had again heightened. If humans had antennae, hers would have been out. Reaching for a sandwich she dropped her napkin, apologized and bent to pick it up. While she was under the table she scanned the room. She took six precious seconds to confirm the locations of exits and to plan for trouble. When she sat up she could sense a man standing behind her. She didn't turn, but kept her eyes on Baptiste.

"All right, Duncan," she said, her voice cool but not threatening. "Why ever do you think you need two bodyguards to have lunch with me? So very dangerous, am I?"

"I don't really know, Felicity."

"Why a trap?" she asked, still not looking at the man behind her. "I'm here alone, unarmed, asking an old friend for help."

"Sorry, sweetheart," Duncan said, "but I'm afraid I had a secondary agenda for our meeting. You see, there's a gentleman, a man about town, who would like an introduction to you in the worst way. I couldn't resist the reward offered, but I couldn't be at all sure that you would agree to the meeting. My friends are here to escort you to him."

She turned finally to stare up at the big, bald man with the cavernous eyes who stood behind her chair. "But I never even had my lunch," she sighed.

"I will remain and enjoy the marvelous menu in your stead."

She bit her lower lip, and her shoulders dropped in apparent resignation. "Well, I'll travel with gruesome here if I must, but he'll at least have to be neat." With that, she twisted around in her seat, reached up and began straightening the tall man's tie. Out the corner of her eye, she watched Duncan, who was plainly amused at how nervous her attention made his hulking bodyguard. He must believe she was simply trying to make the best of a bad situation.

When she saw that Duncan and his seated assistant were relaxed, she knew the time for action had arrived. She smiled sweetly up into her standing "escort's" eyes, subtly tightening her grip on his tie, and slid herself off the edge of her chair.

Her rump smacked the floor painfully. Her guard, snapped forward by her weight, bent awkwardly at the waist. His tongue jutted out when his Adam's apple crashed into the back of her chair.

Before the tall man had slumped to the floor gagging, even before James could rise from his seat, her hand darted like a striking adder to the table. She flipped a shaker at the big man's face. The cap, which she had loosened in her assailants' full view, dropped away. A cloud of black pepper engulfed the flunky's head. Fingers that were originally headed for his shoulder holster, now clawed at wounded eyes.

She and Duncan rose to their feet simultaneously. His eyes gleamed with hatred. She tossed her scarlet locks and smoothed her dress. The agile, continental cat burglar took one step toward the girl and fell on his face. He had not noticed Felicity tying his shoelaces together during those scant seconds she spent bent under the table.

The statuesque redhead was pushing the door open before her three "dates" recovered. The entire episode, from tie tightening to darting across the room toward the door, had taken place within eight seconds.

## -22-

Felicity wasted no time getting into her Corvette and moving it into traffic. She was angry. Angry with herself for being so trusting. Angry at an old friend for being untrustworthy. Angry at a world that twisted people so easily, turning friends into enemies in a heartbeat.

Her brain spinning, she drove by reflex. As she cruised, a growing uneasiness crept into her mind. She wandered the streets, pursuing an elusive feeling. It was her usual danger warning, but then again it was not. She was confident of her own safety, but her senses were never wrong. Whatever it was, it was driving her crazy, like a hornet trapped in her ear. And something was drawing her uptown, making her turn. She wondered if Morgan ever...

That was it! Her eyes snapped wide and she squealed her tires taking the next corner. It was Morgan. He was in danger, deadly danger. Perhaps walking into a trap. She did not know how she knew, nor did she care. All she was sure about was how she cared about this man. He had saved her life and by God, she would save his if she could.

Felicity usually kept a low profile because she hated the idea of entanglement with the police under any circumstances, but this day her need for speed tossed all that out the window. She turned up the Chieftains blaring from her radio, then pressed her thumb into the button on the side of her Hurst T-shifter, releasing the nitrous oxide kicker to her engine. Her head snapped back as her car leaped forward and suddenly she was drag racing across town, aiming at the ramp onto the Henry Hudson Parkway.

The Henry Hudson, recently rebuilt, was a narrow strip along Manhattan Island's western edge. It was two lanes wide each way, with a two-foot high cement wall on either side. The lanes were wavy lines dotted with potholes. The traffic flow was fierce, hot and unforgiving.

At times like this, she did her driving on another mental plane. The union of driver and machine was nearly meditative. She flowed among the cars, weaving with the wavy lines at eighty miles per hour. Pursuit was not a concern. She knew no policeman would be insane enough to chase her on this madcap road.

While much of her consciousness focused on guiding her car, another part of her brain considered her reactions, as if she could stand outside herself as an observer. She wondered if this mad urge she felt was the same as whatever drove Morgan Stark to her, days ago in an obscure South American jungle. Where had it come from? What was the bizarre link between their minds that appeared to be functioning right then as a biological homing device?

After all, they were barely more than strangers and they could not be less alike. White and black, sophisticated and earthy, educated and not. They had nothing whatever in common. Of course, they both traveled in an underground subculture, but she moved in a world of thieves and confidence men, not professional soldiers and hardened killers like he did.

She remembered two or three people in the past telling her that she was psychic, usually after a narrow escape. She had never really accepted it. A natural skeptic, she had always figured she just had good instincts, or sharp senses. But now this had happened. There was no denying this, no explaining it away. There was no logical, rational way that she could know Morgan's location. But she also had not cared about anyone this much since she had left her family. Now her respect, affection, and perhaps something stronger she felt for this adventurer rogue was leading her right to him.

Although she was quite familiar with Manhattan's streets, she had very little experience with the rest of New York City. She somehow got onto the Franklin Delano Roosevelt Drive on the east side of the island. Soon she found herself on something called the Major Deegan Expressway. Minutes later she was smoothly shifting down through the gears in a slum neighborhood in the South Bronx. She remembered seeing Dublin after a clash between the IRA and British forces. The setting was eerily familiar.

Fear and doubt were eating their way into her mind. This was insane. She could cruise around for days looking for Morgan. She must have been crazy thinking she could find one man in a city of millions. Oh, God, she would hate to fail.

She shifted down into first gear to lose more speed just as her ebony Corvette slid past a building surrounded by vacant lots. At the moment she glanced up at the tenement, she heard the sound of a small explosion come from inside the building. A bomb? No. Too high pitched for a bomb blast, but too loud for a gunshot. It could have been a shotgun blast.

In less time than those thoughts took to form, she had pulled the 'Vette over to the curb, locked the car, engaged the anti-theft device, kicked off her high heels and started her sprint toward the door. It was Morgan. Somehow she knew he was in there, and the intermittent gunshots she heard could spell his death.

Seconds later she stood in the hall, panting as much from anxiety as breathlessness. She had lunged up the front stairs to the landing before she had time to think. People were upstairs shooting at each other and here she came to save the day with nothing but her teeth and her nails. She cast about quickly for a weapon. In a far corner lay a dirty man, slumped over in a ball. Next to him lay a broken wooden table leg. In desperation, she snatched it up. With a leap she smashed the single naked bulb illuminating the building. Now the entire hall was midnight dark.

As silently as a cat creeping through a graveyard, the girl stepped up the stairs, avoiding the broken ones. She thanked the

Lord for blessing her with almost inhuman night vision. It was an invaluable asset for a burglar. Now it was her only equalizer against men whose profession was killing.

\* \* \* \* \*

Darkness also filled the apartment on the second floor, interrupted only by the intermittent muzzle flashes of pistols and a shotgun. Morgan could smell rather than see the cloud hanging in the air. The smell, gunpowder mixed with sweat, stung his nose. His back against the sofa and gun in hand, Morgan braced to make his move. His crash into the wall had sprained his left shoulder but, aside from that minor injury, he considered himself pretty lucky so far. A half dozen bullets had ripped through the couch but none had hit him. The well-stuffed sofa had also proved solid enough to absorb two follow-up shotgun blasts, mostly because the man firing the shotgun lacked the courage to get any closer to Morgan's gun.

Morgan weighed his options during a brief lull in the firing. He had a pretty good mental fix on the riot gun user. He planned to slip around the couch on the end toward the door. He would pop up and take out the shotgun man with his automatic. Number two would fire at the bright pistol blast. He would score or he would not. If he failed to kill Morgan, Morgan would surely kill him with one shot. It was a gamble, the only one in town.

He poised on his haunches behind the end of the couch, both hands gripping his pistol. He would make his move now, following three deep breaths. One. Two. What was that? As he stared in frozen disbelief, he thought he saw two green cat's eyes enter the room, just inches from the floor. He knew those eyes. They disappeared briefly behind the big chair, but reappeared a few seconds later against the middle of the far wall, slowly rising to five and a half feet above the floor. She was standing straight up. What was she doing here?

Silence spread through darkness of the small apartment, and for one brief moment, time froze for Morgan. When things finally moved again, they seemed to do so in slow motion. Turning to face the kitchen, Morgan lifted his pistol over the edge of the arm of the couch. In the kitchen doorway, a riot gun barrel was raised. A single drop of light splashed off Morgan's automatic.

The man lying under the small table shattered the silence.

"I got you now," the killer snarled in a strong Spanish accent as he raised his revolver. He was unaware of the woman straddling his upper body but Morgan could see her eyes above him, blazing with hate.

"Paco!" Felicity shouted, bringing her makeshift club down between her ankles, and into his face, with all her strength. Simultaneous with the Mexican's squeal of pain, Morgan sprang to his feet, firing twice, quickly. One final shotgun blast exploded into the ceiling and the figure in the kitchen fell backward and crashed to the floor.

Paco bolted for the door, holding his face with both hands. Felicity followed, and two quick sets of footsteps clattered down the single flight of stairs. Morgan followed as best he could. There was no point in checking the man in the kitchen. Morgan knew with cold certainly that he was dead.

Out on the stoop, the Mexican was trying to run with a hellcat on his back. One of her hands was clenched in his grease-slicked hair. The other was raking his already bloodied face.

"I told you I'd get you, you son of a bitch," Felicity screamed, her voice thick with her native Irish brogue. Paco was also screaming, while he fought to escape this mad eyed, red headed she devil by moving across the vacant lot. He stumbled on some broken bricks and she was on him again, clawing and scratching like a maniac. It was an interesting new side of Felicity to the lone observer.

Standing at the top of the stoop, Morgan chuckled at how overdressed the woman was for this. He was not sure what it was the little man had done to deserve this furious attack, but Morgan certainly hoped he never did it himself. The guy was trying to protect a smashed-in nose by hiding his face in his arms. Felicity was pounding on him now with clenched fists. It seemed a comical sight, until Paco reached down and grabbed a broken bottle by its neck. The smile dropped from Morgan's face.

"O'Brian! Roll clear!" Morgan's voice carried piercing authority. Felicity sprang away from Paco, his broken glass weapon cleaving empty air. Forty-five meters away, Morgan raised his nine millimeter one handed, at arm's length, aligned the three dots of the combat sights, and squeezed off a single shot. Paco had turned toward Morgan when the back of his tee shirt flared, and then blackened. He was dead before his scream stopped.

Without a hint of hesitation, Felicity dashed across the lot toward Morgan. As she approached he considered the picture he must have presented. His right side was shredded, as if some wild beast had raked his ribs with giant claws. His left arm hung limp and temporarily useless. He straightened his posture and forced a small smile onto his face. He didn't want his minor injuries to look worse than they were. Felicity stopped in front of him, with one bare foot on the bottom sandstone step. He saw a brief flash of worry crease her forehead.

"I'm thinking we'd best be going," she said. "Somebody's going to want to be asking a lot of questions about that creep. And I assume there's a dead body upstairs."

"Well, two actually, but who's counting?" Morgan replied, wincing his way down the steps. Looking up, he spotted a deep black Corvette with polished aluminum racing wheels.

"That's just got to be your ride, right? Nice wheels, Red."

Felicity hustled him across the street without a response, thumbing a fob to unlock the doors before they reached he vehicle. Once inside she reached across to open the door for Morgan. He hurried to slide into the velour seats that, like the carpet, matched her eyes. Once under his seat belt, Morgan could do little but hold on while Felicity got them several blocks from the shootings. When she slowed below thirty he thought something must be wrong.

"Morgan," she said, keeping her eyes focused ahead. "I got here but I'm not quite sure how to get back to my place. I'm afraid I don't know The Bronx."

"Well, lucky for you, I do," he said, massaging his left shoulder. "Hang a left here, and don't be in such a hurry, okay? This car will draw enough attention without speeding."

For half of the drive back Morgan watched her drive in silence, except when he gave occasional directions. He recognized all the signs of a person slowly coming down from an adrenaline rush. He also noticed her complete lack of nervous habits. That is, she did not play with her hair or drum her fingers on the steering wheel or anything like that. She seemed to be just peacefully enjoying that deep calm that comes after a successful mission. When he thought she was completely relaxed, he broke the silence.

"So, you had history with the Spanish guy, huh?"

"You could say that," Felicity responded. "He was one of the boys who gave me that Safariland tour."

"Well I got to hand it to his boss. Whoever set up that trap was a real pro. Of course, I guess that deal in Mexico gave you a good reason to hate these guys."

"Damned right," Felicity said. "And on top of that, the Mexican made improper advances. I told him I'd see him off, too. Of course, I didn't really expect to watch him die."

She lapsed into quiet long enough to draw a deep breath and slowly release it in a long sigh. He accepted her pensive silence without feeling a need to rush in and fill it with words. Powering down his window, he leaned his elbow out, inviting the air in. They had reached Manhattan and were on a wide southward street, moving slowly enough to let an occasional car pass them. After a moment Felicity looked over at him and smiled.

"You know, this feels pretty good," she said. "I mean, I've been on some pretty hairy capers in my time, but I never had anyone to share the letdown period with."

Morgan nodded. "I think I know what you mean. After a good mission, or even after a shambles like today, it's nice to get with the guys and tip a couple of brews and just enjoy that relaxation. And refine the stories you'll tell. Man, I can't believe I walked into a trap like that. And the poor slob who led me in, he didn't even know the setup. They blew him away trying to get at me. By the way, you were great in there. Quiet as a pro."

"Well, I am a cat burglar," Felicity said.

"Yeah, I guess. Can you really see in the dark?" He stared into her face.

"Better than anyone I know," Felicity said, smiling. "Born with it."

"Pretty handy in your line of work. By the way, how did you find me?"

They were in front of Felicity's building and she let the question pass. The Corvette purred down the ramp into the parking garage.

## -23-

Felicity wanted to feel useful but Morgan wasn't making that easy. He winced when she grabbed him around the waist and bellowed in pain when she tried to support him by gripping his left arm. He politely declined assistance on his way across the parking garage, but by the time they reached the elevator she was squeezing his hand.

Once in the apartment, he headed straight for the bathroom. On the way, he shed his light windbreaker, shoulder holster and shirt in a trail along the floor. Felicity gave one brief huff of exasperation and followed, picking up garments as she went. By the time she reached his shirt, Morgan was washing his side. Felicity's eyes widened as she watched blood flow into the sink with the soapy water.

"Ow! I didn't realize," she said. "That's a lot worse than it looked with your jacket on. What's the damage report?"

Morgan grimaced. "Less than I deserve. Some bruised knuckles. Sprained left shoulder. This flesh wound here, where some shotgun pellets scraped me. Don't seem to have any in the skin. Sure hurts though. You got any gauze and maybe some surgical tape laying around?"

"Wait a minute," Felicity said. "What I have is a doctor who won't be asking any questions. Let me get him on the phone."

Felicity was in the living room and had punched the first four numbers when Morgan said, "No thanks. I'd just as soon handle this myself." After only a moment's hesitation, Felicity put the telephone down and joined him in the bathroom. He was rummaging around in the medicine cabinet. Felicity went to the shelves behind sliding doors, which stood to the left of the sink. A quick scan across those shelves revealed everything he needed, and she gathered up the armload of supplies as he pointed them out.

Wrapping his side in a towel, he moved to the living room and settled onto the couch. With Felicity's help, he applied an antiseptic and covered his wound. Felicity fumbled with the bandages, while he was obviously an expert in first aid.

"Lord, you're so stoic about this," she said while taping him up. "Led a rather active, dangerous life, haven't you? I have to wonder how many times you've done this for yourself."

"Maybe just a couple more times than I care to remember." When they finished bandaging him, he leaned back on the sofa, almost chuckling at his situation. It was the first moment she accepted that he really was all right.

"You know, I'm not used to seeing you smile," Felicity said, "but I love it when you do. Drink?"

\* \* \* \* \*

Morgan closed his eyes for a second to relax his muscles and quiet the niggling voices of angry nerve endings on his side and in his shoulder. He opened them just as Felicity brought his scotch and her Bailey's to the couch and settled in. He gratefully accepted the glass and they lapsed into silence again. He didn't expect to, but he found himself looking into her deep emerald eyes and realized that he had something to tell her. As if it was the natural thing to do, he reached out and took her hand.

"By the way, you ought to know I'm off your payroll now."

"What?" Felicity was startled.

"You saved my life. Cancels all debts. Besides, it's personal now. I'm doing this for me. And you. I'll make sure you get what's owed you, but I won't take your money, okay? We'll just work together. And by the way," he softened his voice, "how did you find me?"

Felicity stared into the plush carpet, her hair flipped down, hiding her face.

"I., well, I don't know. I just, er, just knew you were heading into danger. Almost like the feeling I get when there's trouble ahead for me. I just feel it. But this time it was almost like a panic coming over me, like an anxiety attack. You know?" Her head snapped around and she stared into his face, as if she expected to find signs of skepticism, laughter or derision. He felt none of that.

"I know," he said. "I've felt it. Couple of days ago. In Belize. It steered me right to you. And it scared me. I guess I resented feeling that way about somebody else. At least, that's how I felt at the time."

"And now?"

"Well now it's different," Morgan said, glad to see the brief look of worry pass from her face. "It's kind of good to know it's mutual. Almost like having someone else inside my head. My instincts have saved my life lots of times. I'm guessing the same is true of you. Now we've saved each other's lives thanks to that same weird, er, whatever it is." He closed his eyes again for a second and licked his lips, preparing himself to take a big step into open space. "Look, I'm rambling and you're just listening. What I wanted to say is...well, we share a peculiar closeness. I'd kind of like to get a bit closer."

Felicity's eyes laughed at him, all tension drained from them. "Now did you go through all that malarkey just to be saying you want to get laid?" She smothered his startled response with an intense kiss. After a brief hesitation, Morgan put his right arm under her long legs. She locked her arms behind his neck and he lifted her effortlessly.

He couldn't fail to notice Felicity was partially covered with brick dust from a vacant lot in the Bronx. Nor could she have missed the dirt and perspiration and hint of blood smell on him. Instead, their earthy condition heightened their lust, calling back memories their first meeting.

"My goodness," Felicity chuckled. "We've already spent the night together, and this happens at three-eleven in the afternoon."

She clung tightly to him until they reached her bedroom, where Morgan gently lowered his lovely bundle onto the down comforter and watched, fascinated, while she squirmed the once expensive dress up over her head. It took only seconds for him to shed his remaining garments.

He stood for a moment, drinking in the richness of her naked form. How like a Greek statue, he thought. Classically beautiful, her skin was that same uniform creamy color everywhere, like marble. She was flawless, without blemish. He wondered how she reacted to his body, swathed in white around the middle, his legs and arms scattered with scar tissue from near misses in past conflicts.

She lay back and her hair became a scarlet whirlwind on the pillow. Here scent was sweet citrus and he could feel her body heat despite the distance between them. Her lips pouted. Her fingers implored. He could stand no more.

Morgan descended on her, and this time the kiss was hard and cruel, his breathing tight, labored. Felicity's legs rose, locking him hard in a velvet vice.

Morgan's hands excited her like no one had before, and his hands were everywhere on her, exploring, coaxing, drawing her on, to the very edge of orgasm. It was as if he somehow knew exactly what touch would inflame her most.

At precisely the moment she teetered on the brink, when her every nerve was screaming for release, he entered her. He throbbed within her, huge and swelling, sending shock waves throughout her body with each wonderfully slow movement. Felicity arched her back, screaming her ecstasy. She could fully feel exactly how hot he was. They would pace each other, and reach the finish line together.

And then the universe went haywire. Morgan's eyes bulged as he experienced being penetrated even as he moved into Felicity. Simultaneously, Felicity could feel herself thrusting, impossibly, with an organ that she did not, could not possess.

Their two bodies snapped apart, like magnets of the same polarity. Morgan found himself on his back, panting, his fingers digging into the bed. He turned to see Felicity in similar condition, a look of pure horror on her face.

"I...you..." Felicity's mouth moved but she clearly had little control of what came out.

"What the hell?" Morgan asked, staring straight up. "I could feel everything you felt. I...Jesus, is that what it feels like?"

"Lordy, my thoughts exactly," Felicity said. She focused on the ceiling until the room stopped spinning and her breathing returned to a normal pace. Thoughts ran around the inside of her head too quickly for her to keep them from spilling out.

"Guess we must be mentally closer than we thought," Felicity babbled. "My God, I've never felt so, so violated. Must be our brains are on the same wavelength or...hey." While she talked, Morgan sat up and swung his feet to the floor. Felicity rose behind him and gripped his shoulders. "Hey. Please. Don't go away. Not now. Maybe we can't have it all for some weird reason, but we can still, you know, I mean, stay together. That really shook me. I need holding." His shoulders felt like two smooth stones in her hands. Thick cords stood out on his neck. Because she was chilled to the bone, she had only seen her own needs. Now she suddenly realized how devastating it had all been for him. In a way, she realized, the experience tapped into every man's deepest fears.

\* \* \* \* \*

Hearing the odd tone in Felicity's voice, Morgan began to consciously relax. It was finally striking him how rattled she must be. He turned, clumsily wrapping his arms around her.

"Sorry, Red," Morgan whispered. "Guess I didn't understand what was happening in your head. Look, why don't we just get some rest?" More relaxed, the two bodies squirmed under the comforter. Felicity snuggled into the safety of Morgan's shoulder, enjoying the rough dryness of his skin, absorbing the man scent of him.

"I could love you," Felicity whispered shyly. "You could be the brother I never had."

"Well, I never wanted to be your brother exactly, but I guess I'll settle for a friend. I can always use one of those."

## -24-

Just before dusk, the tall thin man with the ice blue eyes stooped under the yellow police tape. Stumbling over broken brick pieces, he walked up to the detective standing over the body. The detective looked at his neatly pressed white shirt, tie, and light blue suit, and accepted his card. After reading it he smirked and shrugged his shoulders.

"Okay, so no surprise, you're an attorney," the detective said in a nasal Yonkers accent. "But the name don't ring any bells."

"No reason it should," Paul said in his even, accent-free voice. "I represent the owner of this building. When he hears about violence in the South Bronx, he gets curious. When he heard it happened next to his building, he asked me to check it out."

"Tell him he better either relax or buy property in a better neighborhood," the detective said. "Actually, this one looks pretty routine. Spanish guy, around thirty. Took a good shot in the face. Broke his nose. Some scratches too. Then I guess they got sick of playing around and shot him. Probably over drug territory. Either that or a jealous girl friend. Believe me, there's nothing odd or special about that."

"How many times?"

"Eh?" The detective's mind was already elsewhere.

"You said he was shot," Paul said, keeping his voice polite. "How many times?"

"Oh." The detective lifted a note pad and scanned, as if looking for some nonessential bit of information. "One bullet. Nine millimeter. Through the heart, low and inside."

"Powder burns?" Paul stared down at the corpse's face, showing no emotion.

"Nope. Wasn't that close."

"But he wasn't running I see," Paul said, squatting down. "That's an entry wound in his chest."

"Hey, who are you, Columbo? Why don't you go chase an ambulance or something?"

Paul responded to the policeman's ire with a smile. "You've been very helpful, detective. Mind if I check the inside of the building while I'm here?"

"Help yourself. Just stay out of my people's way."

"Oh, I always try to do that," Paul muttered under his breath. He stepped up the outside stairs and entered the darkened hall. He noticed the broken light bulb hanging above him. With his automatic held close to his right thigh he climbed the stairs, avoiding the broken ones. At the top he examined the body in the hall, sitting up against the wall. It was J.D. Griffith, a merc and a gunfighter. He knew the man only by reputation, but that reputation was excellent.

The apartment door was ajar. He pushed it just enough to slip through and pushed it almost closed behind himself. Once inside he drew a penlight from his jacket pocket and quickly checked the room. To his seasoned eyes, scattered shell casings and bullet holes in and around the tattered couch told a story. Not far away he found a splotch of blood on the floor behind the easy chair. It was too red to be the result of a bullet wound. Blood from a shallow cut, he thought, or from someone's mouth or nose after a blow. Further in he found the fat man Stone had saddled him with. No need to touch him to know what had happened. The left side of his neck was torn, and a hole above his left eye was crusted over with dried blood.

"Amateurs," Paul muttered. His contempt for them was so often justified. Pocketing his light, he slipped out of the flat and down the stairs into daylight. Across the street he got into his brown, two door mid sized Chevrolet and pulled away. He would let the police discover the mess upstairs on their own.

A block away, he was still shaking his head at the incompetents who turned up in his profession. He had offered the fat man and his Mexican friend a chance to step up, to play in the big leagues. An error, certainly, but perhaps not a waste. Natural selection had cleared the field of two men who did not belong there.

And he learned that he had certainly underestimated this Morgan Stark.

## -25-

What a wild nightmare, Morgan thought. He had been trapped in a circuit of sensory overload. He had experienced the sex act both as a man and as a woman does, simultaneously. For a man who had not known fear in years, it was as close to terror as he could come. Thank God it was over.

But when his eyes popped open he realized his dream had been reality. His cheek was pressed into a soft stomach. His right hand rested on a creamy thigh. The rest of the visible world was varying shades of blue. The sheet he was on, the comforter he was under, the walls, the ceiling, the carpet, all blue. Images of the rest of the previous evening returned, and he remembered where he was.

"Finally awake, sleepy head? About time. Must be a couple of minutes after six." Felicity was sitting up, propped against two pillows. His head was in her lap and the fingers of her right hand were in his hair. With her left she scanned the Sunday New York Times. A pot of coffee sat on her nightstand, next to a plate of Danish pastries.

"Morning," Morgan smiled up at her. "Do you ever look at a watch?"

"Never," Felicity said, holding a Danish to his face. "I just have this weird time sense. Now bite this."

The smell of fresh baked pastry awakened his hunger. He filled his mouth with the Danish, which was warm and just short of too sweet. He sat up and Felicity handed him coffee. It was hot, black and strong. Perfect. How did she know?

He could not remember the last time he had just sat in bed with a woman. She looked so comfortable and relaxed - comfortable with her nakedness, comfortable with him. He had to admit that he was pretty relaxed too.

"So you have a clock in your head and can see in the dark?" Morgan said, playing with her hair.

"Yep. I think the time thing's a side effect of my photographic memory."

"Jesus, you really are some kind of freak." He meant it as a joke, but regretted the words as they came out.

"This from a man who tells me he can find north without a compass and judge distances down to the centimeter. And let's not forget that danger sense. You must have been designed to be a soldier."

"And you to be a cat burglar," Morgan said, reaching over to snare a chunk of newspaper.

"Looking for the sports section?" Felicity asked.

"Actually, I always start with the international news. Got to keep up, you know. That's how I know where my next job opportunity's likely to be." He looked up, noticing Felicity was deep in the fashion news and the society section. The significance of their choices was not lost on him and, he guessed, not on her either.

After being shot at and shot, ambushed, lured and captured, set up and pursued over the last three days, exhaustion had kept him asleep through nearly fifteen hours. Morgan had slept for the first time in years without a gun within easy reach. Now, fully rested and relaxed, his mind started wandering around the present situation, peeking at it from all different angles.

"Morgan?" Felicity's voice shook him out of his reverie.

"Yeah, Red?"

"You know, I didn't think a person in your line of work would be so literate. What made you become a mercenary?" she asked, not looking up. He thought for a moment, sipping his coffee. He could never remember anyone asking him that question before.

"Well, you know, when I was in the Army, crawling through tunnels, killing commies, I guess I felt like I'd come home. After Vietnam ended, I was discharged, but the idea of coming back to New York after that, it just didn't feel right. So, I wandered for a few years, trying to see everything, do everything I could think of. After a while I just started picking up merc work because it seemed like a way to go back to doing what I figured I did best. It hasn't been a bad life, really. Got to admit, I still envy you, though."

"Me?" Felicity's emerald eyes glinted with surprise. "Why on earth?"

"You might not guess it, but I've done a lot more than fight in my time," Morgan said, ticking off the list on his fingers. "I've conducted safaris in the Congo, dived for sunken treasure off the coast of Mexico, climbed mountains in Switzerland, hustled pool in Philly, raced motorcycles in France, even flown photo surveys for prospectors in Canada. Been around a lot, but I still can't do what you do."

"What do you mean?" she asked. "You've got the moves to be a great thief."

"Not that stuff," he said. "What I mean is, I can get by in a couple different languages, but I can't order properly in a French restaurant, you know? I can choose gear for combat, but I can't dress myself for a night out at a fancy ballroom. What you got, lady, is class. Maybe I just need to hang around somebody who could teach me that stuff."

"What I've got," mused Felicity, "is a lifetime of shoehorning my way into upper crust society. You know, I've never told anyone about those times. I was seventeen when I made my first big heist. One rich lady's jewels can go a long way." Her eyes drifted off into the past, and Morgan stretched his arms behind his head. He was drifting off with her.

"Before that I was ragged, living hand to mouth, travelling with some friends all over the Irish countryside. I could have stayed there and probably lived off that one score for months. Instead I sold that jewelry to a fence and bought some decent clothes and a ticket to Monte Carlo. Lord, I wanted to meet the beautiful people, the people who had real money. I figured I'd just look around and go home when I ran out of cash. But the rich turned out to be the easiest pickings. It was like walking up on money lying in the street. I couldn't just leave it there. Anyhow, now I'm one of the people who's got real money, but sometimes I wish I'd never left my old friends behind. I've built a great life for myself, but I must admit I miss having people to share it all with. It's hard in my business to have people who are really close. I'm not talking about a lover, mind you, but a real mate. Someone special."

"Well, we ought to talk about doing some travelling together or something," Morgan said. "I mean, after we get our money. And that means we need to get moving on finding your precious brooch."

"Well, that's no problem, my lad," Felicity said. "I reasoned that no one would hunt out a piece of jewelry so unusual just to sell it. And no man would want to keep it. On the other hand, no woman would want to hide it. So, I looked in the most obvious place."

"And just where was that, Sherlock?" Morgan asked.

Felicity raised an eyebrow. "Was that skepticism I heard in your voice? For shame, lad. That place would be right here, in the society page." He followed Felicity's long index finger down to a grainy black and white photograph in the newspaper. It was a party scene as far as he could tell. The kind of thing that passes for fun among the cocktails and hors d'oeuvres set. One member of the tuxedo-draped crowd was a short, portly man with pockmarked cheeks. A slightly taller, heavyset woman in a dark evening gown hung on his arm. Morgan could see that at one time the woman must have had fabulous legs. An oval piece of jewelry sat at her throat. He figured it to be less than two inches long, and a little more than an inch wide. A large teardrop diamond dominated the center of the piece. Pearls surrounded the gem, ranging from the smallest at the top to the largest at the bottom. The pearls were perfectly symmetrical.

"The woman's a little past it," Morgan said.

"Never mind her," Felicity said, playfully slapping his head. "That's the brooch."

"Pretty," Morgan said.

"Pretty? Why it's one of the most beautiful pieces I've seen in an entire life of crime."

"Well anyway, at least we know we're in the right city," Morgan said.

"Yes, and this party was big news," Felicity said. "I'll know that brooch's address by tonight. And then, I'm going to go claim it."

"I thought you wanted your money?"

"After this guy tried to have us killed, don't you think we ought to be getting both?" Felicity asked.

"I guess that's reasonable, Red. But we don't need to rush out and get it today, do we?"

"You're right, I suppose," Felicity said. "No point pursuing it on a Sunday. So I guess we have a whole day. What say we see the city?"

\* \* \* \* \*

An hour later, Morgan and Felicity were walking slowly down Fifth Avenue, with only a steady stream of traffic separating them from Central Park. They had decided to dress casually and show each other New York. The oaks were shedding their summer covering, and Morgan realized he missed the swirling eddies of multicolored confetti that whipped through the gutters. Felicity turned her face away as a bus pulled past, belching carbon monoxide.

"You know, I can't remember the last time I used public transportation," Felicity said when she could face him again. "This could be an adventure."

"Yeah, well I think driving would have been a lot more exciting," Morgan said, "considering that whoever's looking for us knows your car. I don't think there's much danger of anybody coming after us on foot."

They had only to walk a couple of blocks to leave the area Felicity was familiar with, and this wasn't an area of the city Morgan knew well either. But with traffic adding a white noise background they meandered at a gentle pace, enjoying the sun on their faces on a cool, cloudless day. A few blocks south of Felicity's apartment, Morgan stopped to stare up at a group of tiny hooded cherubs carved into a column beside an ornate wrought iron gate.

"What the hell's behind there?"

"Actually, it's a French Gothic chateau, believe it or not, right in the middle of New York City," Felicity said. "Used to be some wealthy fellow's house. Now it's the Ukrainian Institute of America."

"You're kidding."

"Who could make something like that up?" she asked with a smile. "And, by the way, your prediction was a little off. We've picked up some company. A lot smoother than the idiots who followed me yesterday. About a half a block back."

"Damn. Must have been watching the door, waiting for us to come out," Morgan replied. He casually looked back and zeroed in on a short black man in jacket and tie who worked at not looking back at him. "I've got him. Doesn't look like a shooter. Probably bird dogging for somebody else. That his back up across the street, a block back, in the leather coat?"

"Uh huh," Felicity said, leading him to the curb. "There's a third man a block behind number one on our side. Let's screw them up and cross the street."

As they stepped into the street Felicity looked back, appearing to check traffic. On the other side she stopped, pretending to examine the route map at a bus stop. She nodded her appreciation, speaking to Morgan without looking at him.

"Very good. Number two moved up. Number three crossed the street back there. You know, the FBI uses a three man team just like this."

"If they're tracking us for somebody else, they'll do anything not to be made, even if it means losing us," Morgan said as they resumed their walk. "Did you say you run?"

"For exercise, yes. Why?"

Without warning, he turned and started jogging into Central Park. Felicity tucked her purse under her arm and followed. They trotted cross-country where anyone following them would be very obvious. When their aimless run again brought them to a street, he stopped and they both burst out laughing. They were still chuckling a little when a bus stopped in front of them. They boarded without being sure where this bus would take them, not that it mattered. Having shaken their shadows, their tour of New York could now begin.

Felicity pulled Morgan off the bus before he had time to get comfortable, and walked him down to Seventy-ninth Street and the Museum of Natural History. They wandered the dinosaur halls for a while, followed by a visit to the Rose Center, which looks like a gigantic blue marble encased in a Lucite cube. They got comfortable inside the darkened sphere and sat through the show in the Planetarium. After a short bus ride from Central Park West to Central Park South she lunched him at Trader Vic's in the Plaza. Morgan glanced around at the Pacific island decor while he sipped from a syrupy, colorful, rum-based drink whose name he had already forgotten. Paper lanterns hung from the bamboo and woven rush ceiling.

"So, it's not too much?" Felicity asked, picking up her club sandwich, prodding a bacon strip back under the bread.

"No, it's kind of cool," Morgan said. "Even though that totem pole in the corner is Polynesian, not Japanese. You picked a good one. And I've got to admit I dug the museum too."

Felicity nodded. "Yes. At first I thought I might overawe you with the planetarium, but you sure showed me. Do you know all the constellations?"

"I've spent a lot of nights under the stars. Hey, here's a nice surprise," he added as a slice of cheesecake arrived. It was the dense, golden-topped kind only found in New York, despite what restaurants in other cities advertise. "You're just full of good surprises."

"I'm thinking maybe I can pop another one," Felicity said. "A museum uptown you're sure to be liking."

*****

Preferring trains to buses, Morgan insisted they take the subway to their next destination. They walked down the steps into the tunnel on Eighth Avenue and took the fabled A train as far as 190th Street. That still left them a short bus ride up to Fort Tyron Park and The Cloisters. Just approaching the building cast Morgan back into medieval times. He gazed at the square tower ahead, taking in the four quadrangles, the nearest topped by a vaulted passageway. A few seconds passed before he noticed Felicity's stare.

"I knew you'd love it," she said. "Takes the mind back to more romantic times, doesn't it?"

Morgan turned to take in the view of the gray Hudson below, and the sheer Palisades across the river. "Romantic? I don't know. A time when warriors were for real, I can tell you that."

"Myself, I love the gardens here," Felicity said, taking Morgan's arm, "but the really cool stuff is inside."

*****

After basking in the beauty of the great treasures of the Middle Ages, Felicity agreed to turn the reins over to Morgan. They were at the very northern edge of Manhattan, but Morgan insisted they board the train again and travel almost to the other end of the island. Their destination was just north of Greenwich Village, but south of Little Italy.

Through the market-choked streets of Chinatown, Morgan led her to an obscure little second floor restaurant on Mott Street that he had discovered years ago. Felicity grinned at the more garish nods to tourism in front of the restaurant, like the telephone booths, each wearing a red pagoda roof. The restaurant's neon sign, hanging over the sidewalk, was partially covered with Chinese characters. In English, it advertised "Real Chinese Food," and that it was air-conditioned. The roast duckling was superb, and it delighted Felicity to learn that Morgan could converse with the employees, albeit a little roughly, in Chinese.

After their meal, Morgan walked her a few blocks south to a dark, smoky jazz club in Greenwich Village. This was one of the few places left where cigarettes were accepted, and a wispy haze hung a few feet off the floor, highlighted around the performers by stage lights. Felicity loved the music and spent the entire evening analyzing it riff by riff, even making comparisons to classical works. Morgan just sat back and mellowed out.

\* \* \* \* \*

Felicity knew it was after four in the morning when they ended their leisurely stroll in the dark across the street from her apartment building. It was hard for her to classify her own mood. She was tired but energized. Perhaps dreamy was the word she was looking for.

"I don't know when I've been so comfortable in a man's company," she told Morgan, scuffing a toe along the line between two of the hexagonal cement tiles that made up the path out of the park. "Even walking through Central Park in the wee hours, I've never felt safer."

"Don't you always feel safe?" Morgan asked. "Your instincts seem as good as mine. No chance there were ever any watchers lurking in the shadows."

"True, true. And I've got to admit I'm a bit surprised at how much I enjoyed taking a look at a familiar city from another person's viewpoint."

"Me too," Morgan said. "A great day. And I'm not going to let that asshole behind the bushes spoil it."

Felicity smiled up into his dark eyes. They weren't hard, like they had been in that Mexican hotel. She was glad. "Do you suppose we can just talk to him? I'm not feeling like he's a threat to our lives or anything."

"You want to chat? Stay here." Morgan stepped to the low wall that separates the park from the street, crouched, and seemed to disappear. Felicity moved back a few steps, thinking that the sliver of a crescent moon would give her a view of the events. She focused on a certain group of bushes and waited in silence. After twenty-seven seconds by her flawless reckoning, she heard a rustle of leaves followed by a short, low grunt. After a brief silence, Morgan stood up and stepped out of the bushes, hauling a smaller man by the back of his collar. Arms crossed, Felicity left the path to lean against a nearby tree. The lights of the city formed a corona around her world, yet she knew they would be invisible to passers-by.

Morgan's charge seemed to struggle briefly as he was dragged toward her, but she saw Morgan's free hand dart into the man's midsection. There was another grunt and the struggling stopped. Morgan drew himself to attention in front of Felicity, holding the smaller man so that his toes barely reached the ground.

"Sergeant Stark reporting," he said in a deep voice. "So, what did you want to talk about?"

Up close, Felicity recognized the man's face, despite its being distorted by fear. She held her left elbow, her left index finger pointing at their captive. "You were tailing us this morning. You were originally across the street." The man's eyes widened to silver dollars circles.

"You don't sleep much, do you?" Felicity asked quietly. "But you're no gunman. They just left you staked out for us, right?" Morgan shook his prisoner by the neck, and the man nodded his head.

"Glory, does everyone in the city know where I live?" Felicity asked. Her brows knit as she faced Morgan, "We may have to find another place to stay."

Morgan's sigh was more exasperation than anger. He pulled his fighting knife free of its scabbard and held it in front of his charge, making sure the blade caught the moonlight. "Who else knows?"

The captive shook his head. "When I found out about the price on your heads I found the girl's place, but I didn't tell anybody but my own posse. Willy and Joe won't tell anybody else, on account of they know somebody else will get you."

"Willy and Joe," Felicity said. "That would be the other two following us this morning? You guys are pretty good. But you don't look particularly dangerous. Now my friend here, now he is. Particularly dangerous, I mean. Were you really thinking of butting heads with him?"

The little man's eyes moved from Felicity's face to the knife blade to Morgan's face. "I don't know what we were thinking."

Morgan looked at Felicity, waving his knife under his captive's nose as if it were a fragrant flower. "What happens if I kill him?"

"Questions. Hassles. Big pain in the arse."

Morgan turned his charge's head toward himself, as if the man were a ventriloquist's dummy. "What happens if I let you go?"

The smaller man took a few seconds to think, as if he realized the importance of giving the right answer. "I go away?" he asked tentatively. Morgan stared. "I go away and tell Willie and Joe to disappear too." Felicity waved her hand as if she were trying to draw more out of him. "Oh, and we don't tell anybody where you at."

"What do you think?" Felicity asked Morgan.

"Well, I'm in such a good mood and, like I said, I don't want to spoil the day. We can go catch and release with the small fry I guess."

"That's me," their captive said. "Small fry. Not worth the hassle. And I been thinking of taking a long vacation. Florida maybe."

Morgan grinned and dropped the man to his feet. "Get the hell out of here."

\* \* \* \* \*

Approaching the door of Felicity's apartment gave Morgan a small flash of déjà vu, but this time his natural senses told him that no ambushers lay in wait for them. Once inside, Morgan dropped his jacket and holster rig on the guest room bed and pulled off his boots. He sat for just a minute, testing the idea of going to bed and finding it wrong. He wandered down the hall to watch Felicity, pouring herself a glass of wine in the kitchen. He wasn't sure what she was thinking about, but he was pretty sure it wasn't lying down with him. He was equally surprised to find he had no sexual urges toward this woman with whom he had spent such a glorious day.

Still, he wasn't ready to be alone. It was an awkward moment for him. If he even mentioned going to bed, would they go together or alone?

"You don't look tired yet," Felicity said over her shoulder. Was she shielding her eyes from him?

"Thought I might see what's on TV," he vamped. He dropped onto the velvet couch and fired the remote toward the screen. He was flipping through the choices without really seeing them, until Felicity called out.

"Hey! Isn't that the opening music to The Magnificent Seven? Now there's a classic film."

"One of the great action flicks," Morgan said, turning it up.

Before Steve McQueen stopped the coach at boot hill Felicity was seated beside Morgan with a bottle of white wine, some cheese, sausage and crackers. Within minutes she was snuggled up under his arm and he could hear her breathing drop to the steady pattern of sleep just before his own eyes slid shut.

# -26-

"I can't believe I slept to one o'clock," Morgan muttered as they stepped down from the bus.

"One-twelve, actually," Felicity said. "I was only up a few minutes before you, lad."

"Yeah, but you made good use of the time."

"Just doing what comes naturally," she said as they strolled down the short block toward Bryant Park, backyard of the New York City Public Library. What came natural to her in this case was making connections. She had made phone calls to two society friends and a fellow thief who traveled in those circles. Those calls had led to an enjoyable conversation with her contact at the hall of records.

"So you're sure your pals gave you the right address?"

"Morgan, this is what I do for a living," she said. "The mark's name is Adrian Seagrave, and there's no doubt about the building he lives in. And guess what? His view of the river is a lot clearer today than it used to be. You could see the World Trade Center from his windows before 9-11."

"So that killer Pearson didn't lie. Glad I let him go."

Felicity glanced at him, and looked away trying to hide her surprise, but Morgan saw her smile. "Now Mick's agreed to meet me at the library with copies of the official blueprints, diagrams, building history, the lot," she said. "With them in hand, I'll be having no trouble getting in and getting our just due."

They started up the long gray stairway to the front door of the New York Public Library's central building, walking at the far right edge of the steps. About halfway up, Morgan stopped to look fondly at one of the gigantic marble lions that guard that depository of knowledge.

"Remember when you asked me why I became a merc?"

"Don't tell me it has something to do with lions." Felicity started to laugh but stifled it when she saw the serious expression on his face.

"Not lions, Red. These lions. I think maybe it all started here. This was the first library I ever went in, and it was the lions that made me want to go in."

Felicity took a seat on the steps. "Okay, you're saying it was reading that set you on the soldier's path."

Morgan's eyes went upward, and his brow knit as he realized how implausible that sounded. "Red, this town is a tough place to grow up in. One day I wandered in here looking for an escape, I guess. I wanted far away places. A smart librarian handed me Tarzan of the Apes."

"You're kidding," she said. "You mean she hands you that book, with the great white hunters and all those daft natives running around?"

Morgan smiled. "Black people are treated a lot better in the book than in the movies they made later. Anyway, I ended up reading the Tarzan novels straight through, all twenty-four of them. Then, just about when I outgrew them, I discovered Hemingway. That's how I found out how much world there is out there. So, I set out to see it all, to get as much experience as I could."

Felicity nodded her understanding. "So all the time since then you've just been, what, living?"

"Yeah, I guess. That and killing commies. Course, I'm starting to run out of them. But it's been a good life, at least for me."

They entered, and Morgan was pleased to see how little had changed. The library still had the kind of solid, metal-clad doors that imply that the books inside are a treasure worth guarding. Inside, both light and sound were muted. It seemed cooler, but

Morgan thought that might be an illusion caused by the cave like surroundings. He wondered if the air really was thicker here than outside, and if he really could smell the dust of yellowed, crumbling pages of type.

"Just where in this huge place are you supposed to meet your friend?" he whispered.

"The most public place," Felicity answered in equally soft tones. "The main reading room."

This was what Morgan had thought castles must be like when he was a child. The library's main reading room was so vast that its long row of twenty-foot tables did not appear at all crowded in. The ceiling was so high, its collection of electric chandeliers could only provide atmosphere. For reading, each long table held four evenly spaced lamps. A mezzanine wound around the room, bordered by a three-foot high wrought iron railing.

Felicity moved directly to the middle of the fourth table, her pleated skirt swinging around her thighs as she walked, making a subtle sound, like quiet breathing, which could not be heard anyplace else. The man she sat next to was clearly familiar. They would chat for a few minutes and when they were both comfortable Felicity would exchange a previously agreed upon amount of cash for a cardboard tube containing the blueprints.

As the girl had this bit under control, Morgan wandered into the stacks. Of course, that misleading library term really indicates the most orderly arrangement of information humanity has been able to achieve, ruled by the Dewey decimal system.

His wanderings took him into the history section. In the narrow aisle between the tall shelves, his hand dragged along the spines of a series of books he wished he had time to read. He was halfway down it when his pulse speeded up, his blood pressure rose slightly, and adrenalin poured out into his bloodstream. Somehow he knew something was about to threaten his life.

Keeping his eyes on the books in front of him, he inched forward. The sense of danger increased. He took a few steps back. Same reaction. Whatever the danger was, it waited at both ends of the aisle.

Whoever had set these traps was smart enough to track them to the library without him or Felicity noticing. He had to expect professionalism from this crew. To go to either cross aisle would mean unnecessary risk. The best solution was to wait for it.

He pulled Jervis Anderson's "This Was Harlem" off the rack, turned to lean his left shoulder against the shelf and began to turn pages. But he was not reading. His senses were spread like a radio net, waiting for an attack. He did not think even a silenced pistol could be fired in there without being heard, and no one could escape the stacks without being seen. If his enemy wanted to dispatch him quietly, he would have to do it up close and personal. That was the way Morgan wanted things.

Two minutes later he could feel the danger getting closer. His attacker was completely silent, which in this case did him little good, but spoke volumes about his ability. Morgan's mouth went dry while he held still, allowing death to approach.

Then, an unexpected distraction gripped him. His teeth began to ache with the intensity of his danger warning. It wasn't just him.

Felicity!

\* \* \* \* \*

"I think we've already agreed on the price, Mick." Felicity's smile hardened a degree. "Don't be killing the golden goose now, lad."

"That was before I found out half the city's been out looking for you, darling." Mick was a broad, squat man with a ruddy complexion and the wild eyes of his Celtic ancestors. "Don't I deserve something for the added risk of meeting with you under those circumstances?"

"Well, I'm thinking I'm getting hustled here, but..." Felicity's head suddenly snapped up, her eyes widening. With her gaze focused on an imaginary spot in space, she gently slid the tube out of Mick's hands.

"Mick, do you trust me?" she asked in a whisper.

"Well, of course. We're countrymen, and..."

"Fine." She forced her smile back into place. "Believe me when I say, you'll get the price you're asking for the research assistance, but I'll have to get it to you later."

"Your credit's good with me."

"Good." Felicity slid the cardboard tube under her chair. "Now, stand up, and move away from me as quickly as you can." Mick started to protest, but her eyes focused on him with a new intensity, letting him know that debate would be foolish. With a nod he got to his feet and slipped away.

Felicity's body was vibrating with the drive to take flight. She was in very real danger from something at a distance. Slowly she brought her instinctive sense into focus, narrowing the feeling by direction. Her eyes, glazed over in concentration, slowly focused on the wall straight ahead. Was that the source of her danger? No, it was not the wall of books, but above it. The mezzanine.

Just as she brought the man lying on the floor of the mezzanine into focus, her body won control from her mind and flung itself hard left. Before she hit the floor, she heard a sound like a loud cough, and something hard hit and splintered the table where she had been sitting.

A woman screamed, but too far away to have been hit. Felicity jumped to her feet and spotted the sniper in less than a second. He had been prone, aiming a long barreled, silenced rifle. Now he was scrambling toward a window.

Felicity shouted "Up there!" focusing the whole room on his location. She was about to follow the security guard when a wave of perception sent her reeling.

"Morgan!" She turned and ran to the nearest bookshelves. Springing upward, she hooked both arms on the tops of facing shelves and, like a gymnast on the parallel bars, swung herself up to the top.

\* \* \* \* \*

Morgan's hands were clammy from waiting. He heard what sounded like a silenced rifle shot, but he dared not react. He could see his assailant in his mind's eye, creeping up on him. He imagined the other man close enough to touch him. When he heard the rustle of an arm being drawn back, he knew it was time to move.

The book closed as Morgan spun around to his right. It's spine cracked into the attacker's arm just below his elbow. His knife ripped Morgan's windbreaker as it was slammed into the wall of books. Then Morgan shoved the book forward, jamming its top edge into the other man's throat. Gagging, he dropped to his knees. Morgan did also, grabbing the man by his shirt.

"Who the hell are you?" he demanded.

"Griffith," the man wheezed. "You killed Griffith."

"Wrong," Morgan said, "but it hardly matters now."

"True." The new voice came from the other end of the aisle. The man there barely fit between the bookshelves. He must have decided the chaos in the rest of the library was sufficient to disguise another shot. He held a silenced automatic, its muzzle aimed at Morgan's head.

The man Morgan held passed out, his head dropping backward. He was no shield against nine-millimeter shells. There was no room to dodge left or right, no time to get to the other end of the aisle, or draw a weapon. The man only advanced three steps, still much too far away to dive for.

Morgan could see in his enemy's eyes that he had followed Morgan's thought process. "You're all out of options, asshole." He raised his gun to arm's length.

Felicity's knees landed on either side of the killer's neck, her weight slamming him to the floor. She quickly rolled as far to the side as space allowed. A bullet tore into a shelved book's spine just before Morgan's foot landed on the shooter's hand. He kicked forward hard, surely costing the man several teeth and sending him into unconsciousness.

"I owe you again, Red," Morgan said, helping her to her feet.

"Later. There's another one out there and he's probably getting away."

Felicity pointed out the sniper's original position, and the window he opened. While both security guards and patrons rushed outside to try to follow him, Morgan led her up to the mezzanine.

"I want a better look at that rifle," he said.

Above the now deserted reading room, he squatted on his haunches to examine the weapon closely. "Very nice. This is a custom job, Red, built on an old Krag action. A very personal piece. Sure must have hurt to leave this beauty behind."

"Maybe he didn't." Felicity was looking out the window, watching the crowd down in the park. Morgan joined her at the window. Judging from the confusion below, the sniper had not been found.

"How could he make that drop?" Morgan asked.

"I know how I'd have done it," Felicity said in a soft tone. "It's easy with a rope and pulley system, but I don't see any signs of the clamps that would have held the system in place."

"He could have rappelled" Morgan said. "If you're good, it can get you down real fast."

"True enough, but it doesn't seem likely he could have slipped down from this window without being seen, especially if he took the time to retrieve his rope." Morgan looked into her eyes and thought for a moment that he could see her mind working the situation. When she took his arm he let her ease him back away from the window. She turned toward him and leaned toward his ear.

"You know, if I was stealing something in this kind of situation, I wouldn't be down there," she mumbled for his hearing alone. "I'd be up here somewhere." With a wink, she headed downstairs.

Morgan waited a moment before starting down the stairs, to avoid looking like he had a plan. When he reached them he walked down six steps, turned quietly, and lay down on the stairs. He could just see over the top step.

He had only a two minute wait before the sniper appeared from his hiding place and looked over the rail to make sure he could leave unseen. He looked at his rifle like it was an old friend, and stared to reach for it.

"Don't try it." Morgan stood with his gun drawn. The sniper hesitated, then turned and ran for the stairs at the opposite end of the mezzanine. Morgan slid his pistol back into its holster and ran after him. He had hoped to bluff the sniper, but a shot now would surely bring the police and he did not want that kind of involvement.

The sniper had a lead, and desperation helped him widen it. Morgan moved as quickly as he could but he was still on the stairs when the sniper reached the bottom and sprinted across the right side of the reading room toward the door. Morgan followed, but he knew he had no chance of catching the sniper before he went out the door and disappeared.

Felicity surprised him when she emerged from under the left end of one of the last tables and shoved with all her strength. The table slid out, blocking the path. The sniper, running full tilt, smashed his thighs into the table and flew over it, landing hard on the other side. Morgan leaped over the table and was on him in a second, pressing a knee into his chest. It was unnecessary. He felt a damp spot at the back of the sniper's head, and his hand came away red. The fall had put his head into the floor hard enough to knock him unconscious.

"Leave him." Felicity pulled on Morgan's sleeve. "They'll find him, and his fingerprints will tie him nicely to the rifle. We need to get to a secondary exit. I don't want any complications with the police."

"We're on the same sheet of music there, but you need to go back and get those diagrams, or this was all for nothing."

"Right," she said, recovering her package. "This has got to stop, Morgan. I can't live like this, with people gunning for me every minute. It's time to take some kind of action for sure."

## -27-

Steaming mugs of coffee, flavored with amaretto, flanked a set of blueprints on the oak cube in Felicity's living room when she and Morgan sat down to make their evening plans. One of Bach's organ works filled the room. Morgan stretched forward from the right side easy chair to pick up his coffee, savoring the almond smell of the liquor in it while he listened to Felicity.

"Here's where the brooch, and its present owner live." Felicity, kneeling on the sofa, leaned forward to point at the diagram. "This particular building's inhabited by a variety of limiteds, private companies with obscure names. A lot of them are holding companies and shell operations or dummy corporations assembled for tax purposes. A couple of them are mail order fronts. The top five stories belong to Seagrave Incorporated, a closely held corporation whose patriarch is one Adrian T. Seagrave. He and his wife Marlene were the stars of that newspaper photograph I showed you. Officially his business is import and export. He is also heavily invested in the commodities market, and street talk has it that he has taken some extreme measures to influence the market."

"Extreme measures," Morgan said, sipping his coffee. "Like maybe having foreign officials assassinated. Nice guy. So I take it you intend to go in and get your jewelry. What's security like?"

"Well, the building's top floor is a warehouse," Felicity said. "Why he'd store whatever he's importing and exporting on the top floor is kind of a good question, but there it is and it looks to be pretty well guarded. Right beneath that is Seagrave's luxury flat."

"How do you move stuff in and out of a that top floor warehouse?" Morgan asked. "I'll bet you money that top floor's empty. It's just an excuse to maintain security up there. Our boy's too nervous to enjoy the penthouse suite."

"Perhaps, and he likes to be insulated too," Felicity said. "The next three stories down hold his administrative offices, and that lowest level is also pretty heavily guarded."

Morgan nodded slowly. "Are we talking electric eyes and stuff?"

"Not a lot of electronics, but that's understandable. In these older buildings, rewiring is expensive. Instead, he's got a pretty hefty staff of human guards. I've marked on the blueprint where they are. Or at least, where my information says they patrol."

Morgan rubbed the back of his neck and shook his head. "He's not worried about getting robbed. That's a setup for personal protection. Either the man's made some nasty enemies before, or he's a raving paranoid. You got all this background stuff out of just three phone calls?"

"Most of it," Felicity said, picking up a piece of biscotti and handing another to Morgan. "The rest is public knowledge, all down in the hall of records. Now look. According to the building plans filed with the city, the main elevator only stops at the lower forty-one floors, those below Seagrave's block of offices. See, a second elevator serves the top five floors, and you need a computerized pass card to make it work. The stairs are blocked off at the forty-first floor with a door that takes the same kind of card. Pretty good security, as far as it goes."

"Sounds pretty solid to me," Morgan said, dunking his biscotti. "But you don't sound like you think so. So where's the flaw?"

"The flaw, my boy, is that little housing right there on the roof. Fire stairs, lad. The stairs were blocked off at the forty-first level, in violation of all fire safety codes I might add, but they look to be clear above that. I don't see any problem with just going in from the roof, going down the stairs and right into any of Seagrave's levels."

Morgan smiled broadly, like a ball player anticipating a good game. "If this drawing is right, the building on the right's only separated by a narrow alley, about five feet from his. And it's the same number of stories, although this makes it look a few feet taller."

"Now you're getting it," Felicity said. "That one's also got stairs to the roof. No guards posted there, I'm betting. See what that leaves us?"

"Yeah, a very simple operation," Morgan said. "You walk up next door, jump over, take the roof door to the stairs to get in, get your objective, and get out the same way." He munched his biscotti, also almond flavored.

"Yes," Felicity said, leaning back and sipping her coffee. "And if you can be quiet about it, I'll even let you come along."

\* \* \* \* \*

That led them, by nine o'clock that evening, to the building next door to Seagrave's. A uniformed security guard sat at an imposing desk just inside the main door. After Felicity parked, Morgan got out of the car and closed the door as quietly as he could. He was a little nervous about entering.

"I don't know, Red. If I saw people dressed like us coming, I wouldn't let us in."

He wore all black: jeans, boots, and a windbreaker over a pullover. Thin black leather gloves completed the outfit. Felicity wore identical clothes, except for the modified carpenter's tool belt around her waist. It was smaller than most, and, naturally, dyed black. Her hair was banded back with a wide, dark green ribbon. So it swayed back and forth across the back of her pullover. Unlike Morgan, she wore no windbreaker.

"You know, I'm not just wearing this thing to cover my weapons," Morgan said, staring up at a threatening sky while she opened the trunk of her car. He was watching a bank of clouds sliding in like a huge dark amoeba trying to envelop and eat the moon. "It's going to get cool out here, and we might get a drop or two of rain."

"I might get a little chilly," Felicity said, lifting a large canister out of the trunk, "but I find garments like that binding in my line of work."

Felicity pulled a metal spray canister, much like he would have called an Indian tank, out of the trunk and handed it to Morgan. After he helped her get the tank strapped on he pulled another onto his own back.

Felicity led the way into the building and walked directly to the reception desk. Following his instructions, Morgan went straight to the elevators.

Felicity leaned over the reception desk, offering the guard a plastic identification card. "Exterminators. Got a call..."

"Yeah, yeah," the guard interrupted her, not even glancing at the I.D. "Sign in here, then go on up. Check in when you leave."

Seconds later Morgan and Felicity were riding upward. At the top floor they left the elevator and climbed stairs to the roof. Morgan had run the roofs of the projects when he was a kid, so he was at home with the air conditioner housings and the tarpaper beneath his feet. The street noises seemed a world away, like a radio broadcast from some distant planet whose language was indecipherable yet familiar. Leaving their empty insect poison canisters behind, they walked to the edge of the roof. The gap looked wider than it was, and the black chasm seemed endlessly deep. After giving each other a smile, they stepped back ten paces in unison. Morgan watched Felicity's breathing and when her head snapped forward they both raced forward and jumped together across the five feet and down a few more to the adjoining roof. After a few seconds of seeming weightlessness, they landed side-by-side, tucked and rolled, and came up to their feet easily.

"Perfect PLF, Red," Morgan said as they started toward the roof door.

"PLF?"

"Parachute landing fall," he answered. "What you just did is exactly what they teach in jump school."

His smile faded because he saw hers disappear. She was staring at the roof entrance. It was not a regular door, but twin sliding panels without a handle or knob.

"The blueprints don't show this," she said slowly.

"What's wrong?"

"The blueprints didn't show this." Her hands became fists, vibrating at her sides. "It's a bleeding elevator door. They must have demolished the stairs. The private elevator isn't next to the stairwell. They put it in place of the stairwell. It's the only roof access, and the doors are computer locked, just like inside. Bloody hell!"

Radiating frustration, Felicity stalked over to the street side edge of the roof. Morgan leaned against an air conditioning fan, staring around the roof of that old office building in midtown Manhattan. When it was built, he knew, they had called it a skyscraper. Now, newer, far more gargantuan towers dwarfed it. It still looked plenty tall to him.

Felicity was bent over the edge of the roof, looking down. Against the black tar background she was lost to sight except for her hair, moving in the evening breeze.

The silence was as thick as quicksand and Morgan knew that if he struggled against it he would merely sink deeper. Felicity was focused on the present problem to the exclusion of all else. Morgan imagined he could almost hear the wheels whirring and clicking inside her head. He had no fear that she might back away from the problem. Her determination appeared to be unshakable, and that was a trait he was coming to truly admire about her.

After a short time, Felicity said, "I'm going down. I'll let you in."

A moment passed before he realized exactly what she was saying. He leaped forward, but by the time he grabbed her arm, Felicity had one leg over the short parapet at the edge of the roof. Unhindered by his grip, she swung her other leg over. She seemed so fragile, suspended by her slender limbs into black space.

"What in God's name are you doing?" Morgan asked.

"It's called a deadfall," Felicity replied calmly. "I'll drop down three stories, go in a window and come up the elevator."

Morgan's mouth hung open for a second before he spoke again. "What are you talking about? Drop down. You've got no rappelling equipment, no grapnel hook, nothing."

"Look, this is something I can do." Felicity's reply was steel and ice. "No sweat. Now just back off and let me do my job."

He took two slow steps back, holding eye contact as long as he could. When her head was below his level of vision, his eyes never left her hands. He was watching an unfamiliar, fascinating mystique. He thought he already knew this woman, this stranger, pretty well. But now he was seeing her from a new angle. This was the lady in her own world, a narrow subculture most people only saw portrayed in the movies. He was involved, yet totally excluded.

And he wondered if she had felt this way when he burst into her apartment not long ago to gun down two men waiting in ambush.

\* \* \* \* \*

Hanging over the edge, Felicity had withdrawn herself from the world, leaving a vacuum around her. Slowly she allowed the darkness to surround her. The gentle breeze caressed her lithe form. As she relaxed, she hung at arms length, suspended from the edge of the roof by only her eight fingertips. Bit by bit, she surrendered to gravity's loving tug. The warmth of her breath reflected back from the sandstone into her face. Perspiration broke from her shirt, chilling her arms. Remote traffic noises brushed her ears, carried on the cooling evening breeze.

When fear tried to intrude on her mind, she squeezed it into a tiny ball and forced it down into the pit of her stomach. In the following seconds she relaxed completely, starting with her toes and working her way upward. Last to relax were her fingers.

She slipped through the atmosphere as a dolphin through the surf. Her lungs froze during her decent, neither filling nor pushing air out. A window flew by. A second. A third and her hands snapped out, grasping the windowsill. The greedy hand of gravity gave her one bone-jarring yank, stretching her spine.

Then it was over. She hung for a moment, gasping for breath. She neither looked up nor down. Her view was stone, four inches away from her face. One tear crawled out of her left eye. She could smell her own sweat, hear her heartbeat, taste the acid fear fighting to crawl up out of her stomach.

Now for the hard part, she thought.

She gripped the wall with her fingers and toes and hung, nearly four hundred feet above the sidewalk, with her body thrust out from the wall like an arrogant spider on the face of a mountain. Her right hand released the windowsill and slid down to her belt. Without looking she selected a small jimmy.

Whoever had set up security on this place had never expected anyone to reach these windows. They were the old style with basic turn locks and no alarms. She simply popped the lock with the jimmy, raised the window and hauled herself inside.

She landed like a snowflake on an ice floe, becoming one with the darkness. As her eyes adjusted she saw she had invaded a conference room of some sort. Deserted. She moved to the door and listened. Silence.

The hallway was just as empty, but not dark. Willing herself to stand tall, she walked over to the elevator and pressed the button. Apparently the coded card was only needed to enter at the top and bottom of the shaft. On the levels in between, the private elevator operated just like any other. The door slid open within two second and she stepped in.

Morgan did not appear at all surprised when the roof doors hissed open. She was glad he didn't embarrass her by gushing with praise, but as he stepped in he wore a smile that spoke volumes. She tossed her full red hair in a gesture of triumph, pushed a button, and returned them to the floor she had just left.

"We should search the offices first, on the floor below the apartment," she said. "He might be keeping a safe down here, and it's the safest place for us to start anyway. The business should be all shut down for the night."

Nonetheless, the two intruders walked along the walls. Felicity pulled on a pair of surgical rubber gloves and tested doorknobs. The first two doors were unlocked. In each case, Morgan stood at the door prepared for trouble while Felicity searched the small offices with swift, thorough efficiency. Using a penlight barely larger than a pair of AAA batteries she moved every object in the room, yet she left everything exactly as it was before she came. No valuables came into view in either room, although she did find some interesting files in the second office.

"This looks shadier by the minute," she told Morgan when she left the room. "For an import company, they sure don't import much, but the company does seem to move a great deal of money in the commodities market. I think our boy spends his time influencing the market for profit."

Morgan shrugged. "We're talking about a guy who'd see a piece of jewelry he wants and then just steal it. That kind of person would do anything."

"You think so, eh?" Felicity said. When Morgan didn't respond she returned to the elevator and pushed the up button.

When the doors slid open Felicity froze. She hastened to the double doors on the other side of the hall. Leaning forward, she could hear voices. She eased the knob around a quarter turn and pushed the door open a quarter inch. A bright beam of light stabbed out through the crack. With her left eye, she scanned the long meeting room, past the reception area, up to the conference table. Two well-dressed men sat at each side of it. Behind each of them stood a larger, yet also well-dressed man. At the near end of the table a thin, gray haired man drew on a long cigarette. But at the far end, there sat the man from the newspaper report.

"It's him!" she hissed. As she stared into Adrian Seagrave's pockmarked face, something snapped inside her. Being so easily swindled and so carelessly disregarded had stung her pride. It short-circuited her brain. At that moment the brooch lost all meaning for her. The money was no longer the issue. Her professional pride demanded justice. It screamed in her head that Seagrave must be made to treat her with respect. Her reputation, her pride, her professional standing were her most precious possessions. Before Morgan could react, she burst through the door, hearing it slam against the wall behind her as she stalked forward.

"Seagrave!" she shouted, teeth bared. "My names O'Brian. Do you know the name? You owe me!"

Ignoring the two football player types pulling snub nosed thirty-eights from under their jackets, she surged forward into the late business meeting, carried along by her indignation.

# -28-

Just when he thought he was getting to know Felicity, Morgan watched her do something totally irrational. The door she had burst through hit the wall with so much force it bounced back toward him. He shoved the door wide again and drew his pistol as Stone stood, stopping Felicity's charge with a hand on her stomach. Her eyes were locked on Seagrave's. He and she were in their own world, with her launching ice darts from her eyes. Judging from Seagrave's face, he had no idea who she was or why she had invaded his meeting with talk of some forgotten debt.

Morgan had drawn Stone's attention away from that conflict when he entered behind the girl. His gun was drawn but he was out in the open, facing two pistols. He had to protect Felicity, yet he knew it was impossible. His only hope was that Stone would stop the other two from opening fire.

"Tell your boys to drop their guns," Morgan snarled with all the arrogance he could muster. "You're the only one here who knows what I can do, Stone. We can avoid a bloodbath if you stop them now."

"Is he mad?" Seagrave broke away from Felicity's gaze to find Stone's face.

Stone's eyes shone with fear, but his voice was tightly controlled. "I assure you he is sane, but not rational. No doubt if one of these men were to open fire, he would fight. Based on his previous record, he could well take out the whole room full of us, and to hell with himself when he finally went down."

"I'm getting nervous over here." Morgan stepped closer, madness in his eyes. "I might start shooting anyway if they don't drop those pieces."

"Please don't," Stone said firmly. "There is a third gun on your back. You must surrender."

Stone's limpid blue eyes and hypnotists voice had been just enough of a distraction. Before he could react, Morgan felt two fleshy vices clamp onto his upper arms. The grating voice behind him said, "I don't need my gun."

Morgan's hands went numb and his pistol dropped with a muted clunk into the carpet. Monk's fingers bit into his biceps, cutting off the circulation. Monk lifted him off the floor, holding him at arms' length. Morgan swung a booted heel into one of the brute's thighs with no visible effect. He hung helplessly in the air as Stone stepped majestically toward him.

"I believe some introductions are in order," Stone began, picking up Morgan's automatic. "The lovely lady with the rather confused expression on her face is Miss Felicity O'Brian, jewel thief extraordinaire, obviously quite skilled in breaking and entering. The black gentleman is Morgan Stark, the mercenary soldier we've discussed before. Our business companions at the table and their protectors had best remain nameless. Paul?"

Another tall, neatly dressed man stepped from behind the desk to Morgan's left. He expertly searched Morgan, removing all three of his knives in the process. His ice blue eyes stared into Morgan's appraisingly.

"So you're Stark. No surprises."

"This gentleman is Paul," Stone continued. "He and Miss O'Brian have met."

"I'd guess you set up that ambush in the Bronx," Morgan said. "Very professional."

While Morgan spoke, Paul body searched Felicity as well. He nodded acknowledgment of Morgan's remarks while, in a cool, detached manner, he removed her tools and explored her entire body for weapons.

"Just two days ago," Stone went on, "Mister Stark escaped a trap rather carefully laid on by Paul, killing two of his closer associates in the process. Oh, and the genetic anomaly which stepped from behind the bar to detain Mister Stark is known as Monk. You may put him down now, Monk."

Monk tossed his captive to the floor as if he were a broken doll. Morgan sprang to his feet immediately and Felicity moved to his side. They both followed Stone's gaze across the room.

"And this gentleman, whom you have both dealt with but never met, is Adrian Seagrave."

Seagrave stood, and Morgan stared hard into that face of granite. Yes, the body was soft, but the eyes were as hard as marble. In that face, he could see the strength and ruthlessness a man needs to be a dictator. Behind Seagrave's eyes he saw the coldness of a man who would kill casually for what he wanted, a man completely devoid of conscience. A man strong enough to control a huge financial empire, control a man like Stone, and even the apelike man now guarding the door.

Morgan had been momentarily captivated by Seagrave's ugly aura. Felicity broke the silence and the spell.

"You don't know who you're messing with," she snapped, her accent drifting to a stronger brogue. "I want that brooch and I want it now. And I want the money you owe me to cover for the mess your boys made in my home before Morgan took care of them. We had a deal, damn it, a contract. And you just plain cheated me. You can't just go around doing stuff like that and expect to be getting away with it."

"She's right about one thing," Morgan added, his calm tones standing out in sharp contrast to Felicity's anger. "You can't keep doing business this way. Stone must have told you that. Without a reputation to lean on, nobody worth having will work for you for long. And someone will bring you down. If not me, then somebody like me later on."

"You're out of your league, boy," Seagrave said with a smirk. "I have broken most of the men who have stood in my way. The others I have had killed."

"Maybe," Morgan said, sneering back. "But I've killed every man who's crossed me. And I did it with my own hands. Face to face."

"I suggest we handcuff this dangerous pair," Stone said. "They can be placed in the detention room until our meeting is completed, then Monk can have his fun with them."

"Why wait?" Morgan asked, turning to face the giant. "Put the guns away and let the girl go, and gruesome and I can settle this thing right here and now." He dropped into a low fighting stance and put on his best hard look. Felicity just stared at him. Everything about him, body language, facial expression, vocal tone, said he really believed he could take this monster. He projected his confidence purposely at Monk, who hesitated for a moment, and Morgan saw a wave of doubt pass ever-so-briefly across his simian face.

Stone had seen it too. "No!" he snapped. "Later. Paul, handcuff these intruders."

Looking at two pistols focused on his head, Morgan consciously relaxed, and slowly moved his hands behind his back. He decided he had judged this Paul correctly. The man was a pro. He held his pistol close to his right side, and expertly locked the cuffs around Morgan's wrists with his left hand. As he reached for Felicity, she turned defiantly, jabbing her index finger into Paul's face.

"I told your little helper Paco he was a dead man the day he slapped me," Felicity said through clenched teeth. "You ought to know we left him lying in a vacant lot in the Bronx. And I'm willing to bet that your other chubby friend is up in a certain tenement building up there with one of my partner's bullets in his head. And now I'm telling you, mister, you're going down next. You won't hold me."

She sprang for the door like a scalded cat, diving into space as if she might clear the human wall blocking her way. Her agility startled even Morgan. The sole of her left foot hit Monk's chest, her right landed on his shoulder and it looked as if she would simply climb over him until Monk grasped her lower legs. For a moment Morgan thought she might squirm free, but Monk's grip was just too strong.

Monk dragged her back over his shoulder, hand over hand, reaching higher on her leg each time. Felicity clawed and pounded madly at Monk's face and chest in apparent desperation. Monk merely grinned at the assault and tossed the girl casually to the floor. Felicity's face was pressed into the carpet as Paul's knee dropped into the small of her back. He had handcuffs locked on her wrists before she could move.

"I do remember some of what Stone told me about you, girl," Seagrave said. "I must say, you failed to live up to your reputation. That was stupid. Monk, get them out of here. But return immediately. We have business to conclude, and I need you here."

Monk grabbed each of his charges by an arm and tossed them roughly into the hall. The jarring impact with the wall stunned them both. Unasked, Paul followed into the hall, his pistol held close, but always on Morgan. When the elevator came, Felicity followed Morgan's lead and remained docile as she entered. He was sure they were in no immediate danger, and attacking Monk while his hands were locked behind his back would be sure suicide. Paul slipped into the elevator just before the doors closed.

"What's the matter," Felicity asked. "Don't you trust the ape here to handle us?"

"I just don't want you taking off in different directions when the doors slide open."

Morgan nodded at the compliment and stayed relaxed as he stepped out of the elevator. Monk opened a door across from the elevator. Morgan grimaced and approached the door with caution until a hulking arm shoved him and Felicity unceremoniously into the small room and slammed the door.

Morgan rolled forward and sat up on the cold cement floor, scanning his surroundings. One naked light bulb cast crude shadows against the cinder block walls, and in its pale light, he saw nothing he liked. The room was about fifteen by twenty feet. Big for a bedroom, maybe, but it didn't offer much space to maneuver and nowhere to hide. In other words, Monk's perfect fighting environment. The faint smell of dried blood told him that past fights in this room had gotten ugly. There was no window, no furniture, not even a molding along the ceiling or baseboards. He saw nothing that he could turn into a makeshift weapon. There was no inside door handle. And on the far wall, he spotted the ominous down-swinging door of an incinerator. Disgusted, he turned and looked into Felicity's face, shaking his head.

"Before I die, would you please share with me just why you decided to charge into the enemy camp, unarmed and outnumbered. I hate being handcuffed."

"I guess I got carried away," Felicity said. He could see that she was chilled by the room's temperature and maybe by the coolness of his anger as well. "I can't very well take it back now, can I? The cuffs, on the other hand, we can do something about." With a short hop, she pulled her legs up and swung her arms forward, so her feet slipped through her arms. Now her hands were in front of her. From her hair band she pulled a small slip of spring steel. With casual ease she used it to remove first her shackles, then his. "Better?"

"Better." He rubbed his wrists to regain circulation. "Now at least we have a chance. Sure hate to fight that monster in here, that's for sure. It's too close."

"You're thinking of fighting that fellow?"

Morgan nodded, his hands on his hips. "I'll have to hit him as soon as he opens the door and hope for the best. I think I can maybe bowl him over. He'll expect us to be handcuffed and helpless. If we can get past him, we can get out."

"Could be. But we're not going to play it that way. I got us into this, after all, and I'll get us out."

"Yeah? How?" Morgan asked. "With no weapons, locked in here..."

"Slow down," Felicity said in a soothing tone. From under her shirt she produced a small revolver.

"Where did you...?"

"Remember when I made that 'stupid' attack on Monk?" Felicity asked. "I could have taken that clod's boxers and he'd never have known it. He said he didn't need his gun, but I figured you could use it. It is a wee thing, but I'm hoping it's enough if we meet him in the hall."

"It's only a thirty-two," Morgan said, accepting the revolver. "But I can kill any man with a thirty-two. You just have to hit the right spot."

"Good," Felicity said with a smile. "Now for the door." She crouched in front of the door for a closer examination. Morgan stood behind her, hands on knees, watching her work. A steel plate had been screwed on where a lock and doorknob would normally be. There was a slot for a coded card like the one on the elevator door on the roof.

Felicity's hair band yielded a flat steel rectangle, one inch by two inches, about as thick as a dime. She used this as a screwdriver and seconds later the plate was gone. Next Felicity chose two springy lock picks, one slightly longer than the other. It required exactly twelve seconds for her to open the door.

Morgan held the gun forward in a two-handed grip as they stepped out of the room. A menacing gesture, he figured, but unnecessary. The hallway was vacant. It seemed too easy to simply push the button and summon the elevator. In fact, he was just wondering if his luck could get any better when the elevator doors slid open.

There stood one of the bodyguards from the conference room, all alone, holding Morgan's big fighting knife. He stared down the barrel of Morgan's pistol, actually following the sights in reverse until he was looked up into Morgan's laughing eyes. Slowly he licked his lips and extended his arm, presenting the knife like a peace offering. A few drops of sweat slid down his forehead making him blink when they hit his eyes.

Morgan accepted the knife. He and Felicity stepped into the elevator and Morgan pushed the "one" button. Felicity crossed her arms and stared up at the guard.

"So where's my tool belt?" she asked. "And his gun?"

"Upstairs, somewhere," the prisoner said. His eyes never left the handgun pointing at him. "Stone gave me this knife as a gift."

"So you came from upstairs?" Morgan asked. When the man nodded Morgan added, "He's just the advance man. He's supposed to make sure the coast is clear before the big wigs come down."

The trio rode the elevator to the bottom of its shaft, disembarking on the level below Seagrave's lowest floor. Felicity reached to ring for the other elevator and turned back just in time to see Morgan bring the gun down across the captive bodyguard's head. Grinning, Morgan reached under the guard's sport coat to pull his gun from its holster before stepping over the broad shouldered form into their escape car.

The skies were dark with thick clouds the color of dirty paste when the two black clad escapees left the building in silence and briskly trotted three blocks to Felicity's black Corvette. Felicity roughly threw the heavy-duty synchromesh transmission into gear and shot into traffic, heading for home. Morgan turned in his seat to face her. A soft smile lit his face. He was looking at the stern expression that his lovely driver wore. How familiar it was from his own past. He listened to the engine's purr, settling into the plush emerald seat. She was taking an indirect route, weaving down small streets, likely trying to get some of the emotion out in her driving. He hoped conversation would wait until they reached her apartment.

"Sure and the girl can certainly be an arse, can't she?" Felicity asked without preamble.

"Before you say anything else," he began, "I want you to listen, okay? You're frustrated. You're disappointed. You set out to achieve a goal and you failed. And you're not used to failure, are you?"

"Is this going to be a pep talk you're giving me?"

"Sort of," he replied. "You made a mistake. You confronted the enemy prematurely. Okay. All I'm saying is, you learn from your mistakes and you go on. Don't beat yourself up too much about it. Turns out these are some extremely dangerous men we're dealing with."

"Well, that's the Lord's truth," Felicity said. "Dangerous and ruthless. So what do you suggest? Should we be running away?"

Felicity stopped at a red light and Morgan turned to face her. "I suggest a late supper, then a good night's sleep. And then we hit them again, soon, because they'll think we feel lucky to just get away with our skins. We take the brooch and whatever else is worth having on the premises." The light changed and as Felicity pulled away Morgan faced the windshield again. In his mind he was cursing the inevitability of the situation. "Of course, we'll have to finish it."

"Meaning?" Felicity glanced toward him, but Morgan was watching the lights change as they approached, green lighting their progress. "This guy Seagrave, he won't let it go, Red. If we hit him he'll send out his dogs and they'll stay on us until they get us. If we're ever to have any peace in life, I'll have to sign him off."

"You mean you're going to top him? Kill him?"

When she looked at him, Morgan shrugged grimly. "Hey, he tried to kill me first, Red. And you know what they say. Payback is a bitch."

## -29-

Morgan stretched hard, listened briefly for activity in the apartment before swinging his feet to the floor. After an unremarkable late supper with Felicity, he had enjoyed the easy, after action rapport they seemed to share, along with a couple of beers. They had returned to Felicity's apartment and turned in pretty quickly. A two-hour nap in the guest room had been plenty for him. He could sleep more, but he had things to do, and they were things that should not include Felicity.

Getting dressed made Morgan aware of some minor soreness, residual damage from his brief meeting with Monk. Pulling on his holster rig he took another look at the pistol he seized from the man who rode with them in the elevator. It was a little Colt Commander, complete with a full magazine of eight rounds of .45 caliber ball ammunition. Not his favorite, but it would do a much better job than the little .38 revolver Felicity took from Monk. He pulled the slide back to charge the Colt, pushed the safety up, and slid it into his holster. His plans didn't include any shooting, but in his mind, it was better to have a weapon and not need it than the reverse.

In the hall he stopped long enough to tune in to Felicity's breathing. Confident that she was resting comfortably, Morgan moved quietly through the apartment and out. There were things he had to do before they even considered dealing with Seagrave in his own little fortress.

Rain met Morgan at the door. He pulled the zipper of his jacket to his chin, turned up the collar, and stepped out into the darkness. It was not a hard, driving rain, but somehow the drops felt unusually sharp as they slashed against his shoulders. New York rain didn't carry the sweet scent of a jungle shower, but it set the sidewalks aglow in a way that made him feel welcomed. Hands in pockets, he moved purposefully uptown. He thought he might be followed but frankly didn't care. He hoped whoever might be out there in the shadows would show themselves. If they did he would end their night violently. Otherwise, he would move on to the little after hour spot he remembered from the old days.

Morgan fell into a steady forced march pace, his leather boots seeping moisture in to his feet, water running off his head into his eyes. The city was relatively quiet, people moving quickly under umbrellas or wrapped in plastic, not bothering to pretend they noticed anyone else. In some indeterminate amount of time Morgan reached Forty-sixth Street, just west of Eighth Avenue. He stopped on a corner from which he could see the waterfront. He was deep in the neighborhood called Clinton, although for the better part of a century it had carried the nickname Hell's Kitchen.

Part of Forty-second Street leaked into this little area of narrow storefront restaurants and dance clubs. There were more luxury rentals and fancy condos now than when he was growing up, but he could see that there were still plenty of walkup tenement flats available. The city kept moving, shifting out from under him. There were some pretty nice places within an easy walk - the Hudson Library Bar on 58th, the Float, a hot dance club up on West 52nd Street - but his destination was old school, a nameless basement after hours spot that sort of rebelled against the new age nightlife. Stepping away from the street lamp, Morgan seemed to pull the darkness around himself like a cloak before moving quickly down a flight of stairs to the entrance of a place only people in his business would know about.

As Morgan pushed the door open, a wave of oppressive heat burst outward onto him, like the fetid breath of the desert. If a wet dog could be set afire and made to smolder, it would smell like this place. He pushed his hands back into his pockets and stepped inside, crossing the bare wood floor toward the long bar on his left. In a far corner, a jukebox boomed out a hard rock song Morgan didn't recognize, with a base line he could feel in his feet. The room was a dimly lighted square, barely big enough to hold the forty or so patrons seated at its closely packed tables. A small team of barely dressed women wove between those tables, mostly ignored as they exchanged full beer bottles for empties and collected bills from the tables.

These men were all hard cases: bush pilots, treasure hunters, fire eaters, personal protectors, and professional soldiers like himself. They would call themselves gunfighters, or runners and gunners. They were men who didn't ask many questions, and didn't pay much attention to others. So far ignored, Morgan scanned the room slowly. He was surprised to find a few women at the tables, playing cards and drinking with the others. This was an all male joint the last time he was here, but things do change. Anyway, they were females, but they were certainly nobody's dates. The girls he saw seated were hard cases too, evidence, in Morgan's mind, of equality gone wildly wrong.

Morgan spotted what he was looking for at a table almost in the center of the room. The man was short, with broad shoulders and a deep chest. He wore a blonde crewcut and a fatigue shirt with its sleeves rolled up. At the moment he was playing poker with three others but Morgan had last seen him standing in a telephone booth pretending to make a call.

Morgan got the bartender's attention and using hand signals ordered a mug of beer. He drank about half of it at the bar, then began weaving through the tables as if he was looking for an empty seat. In a moment he was standing behind the blonde poker player. He gave the man on the other side of the table a friendly nod before gripping the back of the blonde man's collar. Morgan twisted his fist hard enough to choke Blondie with his own shirt, and calmly swung his mug up against the side of the man's head. While the others stared on impassively he yanked Blondie from his chair and dragged him across the room. Just as Blondie began to regain his balance, Morgan slammed his head into the bar a couple of times as if ringing a gong.

"Can I get your attention over here," he shouted. "My name is Morgan Stark." All eyes turned to him. A few men stood with clenched fists, and he saw some hands easing toward holsters or knife scabbards. He had their attention.

## -30-

Morgan stood with his back against the bar, holding up the unconscious man by his collar. Someone unplugged the jukebox and the room suddenly seemed even closer. Morgan figured he had about forty-five seconds to make his point before it got nasty.

"Some of you know me by reputation," he said, using his drill sergeant voice, "and I see that most of the rest of you have heard my name. I understand there's a price on my head."

He was tracking one man on his right visually, and another directly ahead of him looked ready for trouble. Yet his senses told him that the real danger was behind him. The bartender must be screwing up his courage to try to end any trouble before it started.

"This guy here, he worked for Griffith," Morgan went on. "Griffith tried to earn that reward. He's dead now. His crew's been following me around though, at long distance. They even got ahead of me once and set up a trap, complete with a sniper. That guy's probably in jail now, and a couple of his friends are hanging out with Griffith in hell."

Blondie cocked a fist back but before it went anywhere, Morgan slammed a left hook into the man's midsection. He crumpled to his knees. A couple of the other men in the room stepped a bit closer. The serving girls eased to the far corners. The man Morgan had marked as a danger man, over on the right, had his right hand behind him, surely on the butt of a gun.

"Now this could go a couple of ways," Morgan said, pulling his hands out of his pockets and slowly unzipping his jacket. "You could all come rushing at me, right? I'd make a hell of a mess in here," he pulled his jacket back to show his automatic, "but I'd eventually go down. Then, you'd end up chewing each other up over who gets the money, right?"

While he spoke in a tightly modulated voice, Morgan felt his senses going crazy. The bartender must be about to make his move. Morgan had him pinpointed by the direction he expected the threat to be coming from.

"Or, you could let me walk out of here, and chase me around the city until somebody gets lucky," he went on. "Or..."

Morgan's left elbow swung up and around, as if of it's on accord, crushing the bartender's nose, causing him to drop the scotch bottle he was about to use as a club on Morgan's head. Before the bottle hit the bar, Morgan was diving to his right, his pistol thrust forward, rocking in his hand as the slide slammed back and forward, the blasts echoing in the packed room. As he slid across the floor the two men who had drawn were falling backward into their neighbors, their blood splattering the men standing behind them.

Morgan slowly stood, halfway to the door now, his gun still at arm's length toward the room. A particularly large, olive skinned man in a wifebeater and jeans stepped over to the bar, separating himself from the others.

"You got a point here?" he asked in a thick Corsican accent. "What do you want, Stark?"

Morgan nodded his recognition at the man who apparently spoke for the group. Even in a room full of alpha males, one would always surface.

"What I want is forty-eight hours of peace," Morgan said. "I know who put the price on my head, and it's nobody in the business. Not a fighter or a shooter, just some rich businessman. I'm telling you right now, he's going to be in no condition to pay up by this time tomorrow night. I just don't want to be looking over my shoulder while I'm taking care of him."

The Corsican huffed impatiently. "And if you fail?"

"Hell, if I don't put this guy down in the next two days, then I deserve to get capped by whoever thinks they can get close enough."

Morgan's mouth felt unnaturally dry, as he stood alone, gauging the crowd. It all came down to what kind of mood they were in, what kind of night it had been. He had played it the best way he knew, and now he would learn if it worked or not.

The big Corsican looked down at his table. He glared over at the two unmoving men on the floor in the middle of the room. He shook his head for a minute. He unconsciously fingered the hilt of a Kukri knife hanging from his belt. Finally, he locked eyes with Morgan.

"I come here to drink beer and play cards. That's what I want to do. Get the fuck out of here."

Morgan took a slow deep breath, nodded, and slowly holstered his automatic. The jukebox came back on as he backed toward the door. By the time he was opening it the room's occupants had already forgotten him, except for the men who were lifting the corpses for disposal.

A cold rain stung his face as he stepped outside. Not a big deal, he thought, and his remaining errands would be a lot more pleasant.

## -31-

Felicity's eyes popped open at eight-thirteen. She had slept well. A bright sun beamed into her room, the sky rinsed clean by night rain. She got up and stretched her naked form into the sunbeam, absorbing the warmth, absorbing the silence. Fully stretched, she headed for the door. She knew before she opened it that Morgan was gone.

She had no rational way to know. They had slept in separate rooms after stopping for some barbecued ribs she found both interesting and delicious. She remembered that Morgan had made her laugh by painting word pictures of their enemies, turning them into caricatures. He joked about the trouble they had with "Donkey Kong", "Stone-face" and their boss, the walking pear man. He had made her feel confident and relaxed. She had awakened only briefly in the night, with an uneasy feeling, but it had faded in seconds and she knew he was fine.

She treated herself to a hot shower, dried herself with a plush terry cloth towel, and gave her hair a hundred brush strokes. Halfway through them she knew he was back. It was eerie in a way, but also very comforting, being able to feel when someone was nearby. They had not had a chance to talk much about these strange phenomena, but she felt some experimentation would be in order as soon as she had her brooch in hand.

As she squirmed into her Calvin Kleins, Felicity heard the stereo pop on. Music filled the apartment, happy but fierce. A trumpet wandered effortlessly through lilting expository phrases. Very soothing, she thought as she pulled on a sweatshirt, pushing the sleeves halfway up. Soothing yet driving.

Morgan, standing in the living room, looked up as she approached. The overstuffed shopping bag at his feet prodded her curiosity almost as much as the man standing beside him. The stranger was shorter, with curly black hair and an olive complexion. When he spotted her he took a small step back.

"What a fox," the newcomer said, under his breath.

"I know what you mean," Morgan said. "She never just comes into a room. She always makes an entrance. I always feel grubby next to her." Felicity chuckled at that, since he had on black denims, new black running shoes he had picked up someplace and a charcoal wool blazer over a gray, Italian cut dress shirt. It was a sharp contrast to her jeans and sweatshirt. He had clearly been shopping, but the only clothing stores open at dawn were parked at the curb of certain city streets.

"Good thing I wasn't walking around starkers," she said, stepping forward to offer her hand. "Who's your friend?" She was surprised to find Morgan bringing a guest to the apartment, but figured he must have a good reason. Besides, the man was handsome in a Middle Eastern way, dressed very nicely in a conservative blue suit of obviously steep price tag.

"Felicity, this is Aaron Goldsmith. I met him in Brussels during an arms deal. Now he sells insurance."

"A very pleasant surprise," she said, smiling at Aaron.

Your boyfriend here was ringing my doorbell before the sun was up," Aaron said. "Believe me, I'm not a morning person."

"Maybe," Felicity said with a smile, "but as I've learned, Morgan can be a very persuasive person. Now, Morgan, what else did you bring me?"

"Assorted pastries for you to pop into the microwave," Morgan said, lifting a package from the top of the shopping bag.

"Well, there goes my diet," she said, accepting the little bundle. "What else?"

"Stuff."

"What kind of stuff?" she called from the kitchen.

"Stuff for tonight."

"Great," she said. "Find out what Mr. Goldsmith wants in his coffee."

"Aaron, please," Goldsmith called. "And I'll take a little cream and one sugar."

Felicity's coffee maker had automatically ground beans and brewed a fresh pot just minutes before. She reveled in the tangy aroma of her own personal blend of Costa Rican and Columbian beans while pouring three cups, Aaron's she prepared as he requested. For herself she added two sugars, a little cream, a stick of cinnamon, a drop of vanilla and a little chocolate powder. Morgan, she knew, took his straight.

She placed a tray on the oak cube in front of the sofa, next to Morgan's shopping bag. With Morgan and Aaron on the couch and Felicity in one of the overstuffed chairs, they ate warm pastries and drank hot coffee and listened serenely to the African rhythms. The cherry and cheese-filled Danish in her mouth was as sweet and relaxing as the music.

"You know, this is good stuff." She nodded toward the stereo.

"Yeah. Miles Davis," Morgan said, moving his head with the sound. "The CD is 'Bitches Brew'. The state of the art of jazz in the early seventies, and one of the best albums ever cut."

She let the music rule the room, waiting for Morgan to tell her the new scenario. After a couple of minutes, he glanced at Aaron, who nodded.

"Aaron wasn't that anxious to come over until I filled him in on the week we've had," Morgan said. "And I didn't drag his ass out this morning to sell me an insurance policy. He's also kind of an information broker, too."

Felicity's brows knit accusingly, and Aaron quickly added, "I don't deal in blackmail, miss."

"No, he just makes it a point to know things, and shares that information with interested parties," Morgan said. "For a price."

"I see," she said. "And he knows things we want to know, I take it. That's why he's here. He knows you, but he wanted to meet me to make sure I was okay. Well, do I pass?"

"That's not it at all," Aaron said around a mouthful of pastry. "I know you too, at least by reputation. I just wanted a chance to meet you in person."

"Okay," Felicity said, turning to Morgan. "I assume that you didn't bring Aaron here for a social call. What is it we're wanting to know from him?"

"I thought a little more background about Seagrave was in order."

"I checked him out," she said, sipping her coffee. "He's a ruthless businessman, made a lot of enemies, but seems to know how to handle his money. What else is there to know?"

"You checked society sources," Aaron said, leaning back. "Maybe you got his business background but nothing of the real man. That's what Morgan wanted me to give you." She sat forward as Aaron spoke. She really had seen the man from a single point of view, and realized the possible advantage of a different perspective.

"Adrian Seagrave was born forty-two years ago to a pretty well-to-do family in Bridgeport, Connecticut," Aaron began. "His father's health was poor, and at twenty Adrian was running the family car dealership. He moved from that into the import export business. My contacts tell me he was handling contraband by the time he was thirty, but nothing's been proven and no charges filed, at least so far. He went into partnership with a Greek shipping man to increase his cash flow. Two years later the partner disappeared. There was no will and no family. His half of the business went to Seagrave."

"Gee, things just seem to go this guy's way, huh?" she commented.

"It gets better. I know he's smuggling, but he's never been hassled by the police. He set up in New York about six years ago, same time he married a woman ten years his junior."

"I've seen this guy," Felicity said. "She must have done it for the money."

"Right, and he for the status," Aaron said. "She was beautiful at the time, a trophy wife."

"Sounds like he might have some heavy connections," Morgan said. "What's he into now? Anything that'll bring heavy heat if he meets with some bad luck?"

Aaron gave a short, sharp laugh. "Just the opposite. The man's got no friends. His latest gig is the commodities market. He likes to influence the market through political maneuvering. This, I believe, is how you got involved with him. He sent you after a guy in Belize, right? He wanted that man you went after taken out of office so somebody he liked could get in. I think he's losing what little respect he ever had for the law. He's branched out into outright extortion."

"Got a personality profile on this guy?" Morgan asked.

"He's a sadistic, ruthless, manipulative man overcome by greed," Aaron said, leaning forward for emphasis. "He's trying to set himself up as a private Mafia. Some scattered bits of intel lead me believe he's looking for a foreign base of operations. I think he indulges his wife in the hopes of starting a dynasty for himself. I don't know all of why you're having a run in with him, and I've no idea how the lady got involved, but I hope you've got it in for him bad."

"Why?" she asked.

Aaron leaned back in his seat and locked eyes with Morgan. "I've heard this Seagrave put a price on your head. Well, that kind of thing works both ways. It's worth twenty-five thousand dollars to me to see this man dead." Felicity stared at him, trying not to look like she was staring. When she turned her eyes to Morgan's face she saw a cold stare there that she recognized.

"Aaron you've known me for years," Morgan said in a low, guttural voice. "You know I'm not a hired gun."

"Nonsense," Aaron replied with a lopsided smile. "In fact, that's exactly what you are."

"You know what I mean," Morgan said, looking uneasy. "I'll shoot in a war situation, but I'm no hit man. When I fight with a team, there's a reason besides money. Generally politics."

"What is it this time?" Aaron asked. "Besides money."

"This time I want to help Felicity get what's owed her," Morgan said, his baritone dropping to a deeper register. "And there's also a debt involving a few friends of mine. He's responsible for their deaths." Then, Morgan surprised Felicity by suddenly standing and heading for the door. "Well, we've got some things to take care of, Aaron."

Aaron nodded to Felicity, mumbled that it was nice to meet her, and followed Morgan to the door. Once there he turned to face Morgan, his face twisted with shame.

"Look, old buddy, I didn't mean..."

"I'll talk to you later," Morgan said.

Felicity barely waited for him to close the door behind Aaron before she spoke.

"Well, that was rude."

"He insulted me," Morgan said simply, returning to his seat. "He knows the difference between a mercenary and a murderer. There are people who take money to drop a civilian. I don't do that stuff."

Felicity turned her eyes to the floor. In a soft, almost sympathetic voice she said, "You did for Seagrave."

After a pause Morgan said, "That was a mistake. A mistake I intend to erase."

"But don't you intend to..."

"Sure." Morgan took a big swallow of coffee, staring with single point concentration as if he was looking over a battlefield after the action had ended. "I'll do it. For honor. For your safety. For my team that got slaughtered in Belize. Not for Aaron. Not for money." A small smile curled the edges of his mouth. "And since I won't do it for him, Aaron's safer if he didn't hear me say I intend to do it, anyway."

Felicity felt a need to change the subject, so she returned her attention to the shopping bag that was now between them in front of the sofa.

"So, my man of mystery, what did you get this morning besides Danishes?"

"Well, for one thing, this." Morgan pulled his jacket aside, revealing a carbon copy of the Browning Hi-power he had left in Seagrave's office.

"Should I ask what was wrong with the other one?'

"I knew a guy once who was a chef," Morgan said. "He would only use a certain set of knives from a certain company, and nobody else better touch them."

"I see," Felicity said. "Boys with their personal tools. But this can't be a big bag of guns. Can it?"

When Morgan grinned and shrugged, Felicity reached into the bag herself and pulled out a small package wrapped in brown paper.

"Jewelry?" she asked, shaking the package to see if anything rattled.

"Actually, it's about two ounces of C4. High explosive."

"Oh." She gingerly returned it to the bag.

"Hopefully, I won't need it. But since we're on the subject, let's talk a little business. Can you defeat that electronic elevator somehow?"

"With ease," she said, stealing furtive glimpses into the bag. "I just need to have the right tools with me."

"Good. Let's go back tonight."

"You're serious." Felicity said, eyes narrowing.

"Sure. They won't be expecting us, not this soon. You can go in however you usually would. I'll go in on your tail. If they're asleep, I should be able to avoid any guards and sign off Seagrave without any gunplay. If they're alert, I picked up some unique hand grenades to liven things up."

He had said it so calmly she had to replay it in her mind. Sign him off? And without gunplay would mean being right up close to Seagrave. This was the man she had allied herself with. "Have you ever thought of going legit?" she asked.

"What?" Morgan face twisted as if her apparent non sequitur had completely disrupted his thought process.

"I figure I know as much about security planning and equipment as anybody. I mean, I know how a thief thinks, you know?"

"What brought all this up?" Morgan asked.

"Well, I was just thinking what great partners we'd make." Felicity was on a roll now, using her hands to frame her point.

"You know all about training men for dangerous work. You know, like bodyguard stuff."

"Slow down, girl," Morgan said. "I don't know if I'm quite ready to settle in one place. I'll admit I've done some personal protection work, and I have considered starting a business like that from time to time."

"Can we talk about it?"

"After tonight," Morgan said. "Now get me that blueprint of the target building you had yesterday."

Morgan shuffled over to sit in the center of the sofa with the blueprint spread out in front of him. Felicity stood by, waiting to hear his plan. She had done this herself a thousand times, and even laid out capers for a group from time to time, but she had never actually worked with someone this way. It felt odd. It felt good.

"Do you know what a field order is?" he asked, seemingly out of the blue.

"A what?"

"It's the way us military types plan what we're going to do," he explained. "I'll walk you through it. First, you clearly define your mission."

"Well, that's easy," Felicity said, picking up Morgan's cup and heading for the kitchen. "Find Seagrave's safe, nick the brooch and our cash if we see it, and, er, you know. Deal with the man himself."

"Right, eliminate the opposition leadership," Morgan called behind her while she refilled their coffee cups. "You're right. That's it. No side trips." She bent to place a fresh cup in front of him. He stared into her green eyes, causing Felicity an unaccustomed flash of embarrassment.

"I get the message," she said. "I really do. No side trips and no ego trips."

"Right," he said. "Thanks for that, Red. Anyway, next we outline the situation, concentrating on what we know about the enemy and the building, and what we can guess." When Felicity lowered herself into a chair he reached into his inside jacket pocket. "I've got another pencil here, and a smaller pad."

Felicity waved his offer away. "Got the memory, remember? Besides, I won't be sitting still long."

As if to prove her point, Felicity was on her feet within a minute. As the pair worked through the day, Morgan remained seated on the sofa, hunched over his steno note pad with a mechanical pencil. Again, Felicity was struck by how differently they worked. Morgan was a continuous note taker. He seemed to think best on paper, while Felicity thought best on her feet, walking in free form circles around the oak cube in front of the couch, and wandering around the room, arms crossed, head tilted to one side.

Morgan went on to outline what he called the execution paragraph of his op order, where the "operational concept" was laid out. They agreed on the need to carefully arrange how they would maneuver and coordinate with each other.

Planning was one of Felicity's strong points, and brainstorming was the fun part of that exercise. She threw out some outrageous ideas, but from her creative mind came daring and workable concepts. Together they examined obstacles they would likely meet and, one by one, planned their elimination.

The sun was casting long shadows across the room by the time they had a plan they were both comfortable with. Morgan sat barefoot with rolled-up sleeves. Smiling, Felicity squatted in front of the oak cube, tapping her hands on it to the beat of the upbeat rhythms from the CD Morgan was playing, featuring someone called Dave Koz.

"Okay, we've got a plan," she said. "In fact, a darned good plan. Simple is always best I say. Anyway, I think we deserve a break. Want to slip downstairs for a little dinner? My treat."

Morgan leaned back, releasing a long breath. "Yeah, I could eat. But we're not done. When we get back, I want a briefing on the gear you use."

"Like what, for instance?"

"Well, remember telling me how you put the dogs out on that job you did in Mexico?" Morgan asked. "I'd kind of like to know what kind of drugs you keep on hand, and how you use them. I'm also curious about what's in your safe cracking kit. What else might you use in your business?"

Felicity thought for a moment. "Well, anything and everything, from electronic safe breakers to protective masks to insulated gloves to bug and alarm detectors. But what's the point?"

Morgan sat back up, serious again. "The more I know about the tools you use, the less likely I am to get surprised. The same reason I'll tell you all about how those grenades work, and show you the basic workings of my pistol."

"Whoa," Felicity backed away, both palms toward Morgan. "I'm not planning on shooting anybody."

"And I don't plan to pick any locks, but you never know what you might have to do in a pinch. Let's face facts, Red. We're going into a dangerous place, and this time I don't want any mistakes, any chance of failure."

## -32-

Marlene just managed to get the door open before she dropped her bundles. The four large bags cascaded out of her arms before she could reach the sofa. A puff of air flipped the curl hanging over her forehead. She loved shopping, but getting the stuff home was sometimes a challenge. First she had to switch elevators at the forty-first floor, which meant finding her pass card and getting it into a slot. As if that wasn't a big enough pain, she had to fumble with the cipher lock to get into her own apartment. With all this security, you'd think someone wanted to kill them.

As her breathing quieted, she heard voices from another room. Adrian was home early. Her breath caught in her throat, and her jaw set harshly. Did he have one of his women here? She did not think she could stand for it anymore. In the last few days she had more than fulfilled her obligations as a wife, and his carnal desires had grown steadily more extreme. She would not tolerate another woman. Not now.

Straightening her spine, she marched across the carpet headed into the study. At the doorway she stopped, listening for the voices inside. She did not hear a woman's voice, but that of a man. It was the one she had heard her husband call Paul.

"No sir, just the fact that they escaped makes them a threat," he was saying. "I'm afraid we're putting ourselves in a position to underestimate these people."

"What's to underestimate?" Seagrave asked in the haughty voice he so often used toward his employees. "The woman's a flake and the man's probably terrified of tangling with Monk again. I'll bet they're still running. You're just being paranoid."

"I disagree," Paul insisted. "Besides, you pay me to be paranoid. I'm trying to protect your safety. Just let me lay on a little extra security. I'd like a few more guards at the entrances and patrolling the floors."

Marlene held her anger, but she felt she had seen enough. She strode into the room, her eyes on Paul.

"Adrian. What's he doing here?"

"Business," Seagrave said without looking at her.

"He's one of those violent men you hire," she said in an accusing, whining tone. "I can tell just looking at him. You think I don't know what you do? I do, you know. And I imagine there are lots of people out there who would wish us ill because of it. But you promised me you'd never have those people in our home."

When Seagrave turned toward her, all the frustration he had felt in the last few days showed in his eyes and she realized suddenly that she had crossed some invisible line. With unexpected strength Seagrave gripped her right arm and forced her down to her knees. His nails bit into her skin as his eyes burned into hers. Looking up at him, her lower lip began to quiver and she was close to tears.

"You listen to me, bitch. You don't care how I do business when it's buying you all those clothes, and all that jewelry, and trips to everywhere on earth. All you need to do is mind your damn business and be there when I want you."

Seagrave's voice had slowly risen to a squeaky falsetto. As the last sentence ended he drew his left hand back across his shoulder, preparing to swing his knuckles backhand across her face. Marlene gasped and stared into his face, too scared to even turn away.

"Sir!" Paul's voice froze Seagrave's swing.

"What is it?" Seagrave spun his head to see Paul's face. The tall man's ice blue eyes never wavered, his gaze both cold and hard.

"The men?"

"Yes, yes." Seagrave released his wife's arm and she backed away across the floor. "Get all you want, put them everywhere if that'll make you happy. Now get out of here."

Paul took one last long look at Marlene, as if expecting her to say something, then stepped silently out the door.

## -33-

A crisp autumn breeze cut through the stocky blond man in the doorway. He put his hands into the pockets of his black leather jacket and hugged the corner of the doorjamb. His left side was chilled by the mini-Uzi slung under his arm, beneath his coat.

He thought it was stupid, posting guards downstairs on the street entrance. Nobody would try to break into the building that housed the Seagrave Corporation. Besides, if a problem came up, fifteen people on five floors were patrolling in patterns that only looked random. Here it was, almost four in the morning and he was wasting his time out here. His two buddies inside were sleepy too, but at least they were warm. At this time in the morning there wasn't even enough traffic noise to keep him alert. The occasional taxi rolled past, but the business district was largely unmoving. Why did rich people always lay on extra protection after the action? Did they really think troublemakers would come back after barely getting away with their skins?

As the guard turned his jacket collar up, he noticed a black man rounding the corner and trudging toward him. The man showed weariness in each step, pushing a big-wheeled pretzel cart. He hugged a ragged coat around himself as he clicked down the sidewalk in worn-down shoes. The fingers were cut off his gloves. His beard was crinkly and a floppy slouch hat covered his head. He was thickening around the middle and he had the street urchin's twinkle in his eye. As he came even with the door, the mouth-watering smell of his wares reached out to the guard.

"Hey, man," the blonde at the door called. "What you doing out this early?"

"Not early, brother," the vendor replied, in a thick West Indian accent. "Dis late. I tried a new spot and sold more pretzels den ever. Hey, you want one? You look cold, mon. Here, it'll be on me. On de house."

The blonde waved inside the building to the burly black man standing near the elevator. He looked out and noticed his partner tearing into a big, soft, hot pretzel. Smiling, he waved to the third ground floor guard, and they both marched out the door. They stood in a circle, their breath smoking out. All accepted the peddler's gifts and celebrated his good fortune with him. They felt warm for a moment, and a bit friendlier. They grinned and waved as he headed up the block a few minutes later, the wheels of his cart squeaking rhythmically as he went.

\* \* \* \* \*

Across the street, Felicity watched the trio from the darkness of an opposing doorway. She was dressed in her work clothes, holding a pair of opera glasses. She smiled broadly when she saw the first man yawn. After all, if it worked on guard dogs it would work on these hastily hired extra security men. The first one was leaning against a wall. By now she knew Morgan was around the next corner, peeling off the facial hair, the slouch hat and the padded, ragged coat. And he would be putting on more appropriate footwear for the work ahead.

Guard number two crouched in the hallway as the drugged pretzel took full effect. The third man was trying to rouse his two partners. He had a little more body mass, which may have been slowing the effects, but his own groggy mind appeared to be just coming to the realization that something was amiss.

From her right, Felicity could see Morgan jogging in toward the target building, all black in his own "business suit". The only standing guard staggered back into the building. Three seconds later, Morgan followed. Five seconds after that, a black glove reached out the door and beckoned. She nodded, smiled, and sprinted across the street. Inside, she followed Morgan as he dragged the big man through the door into the fire stairs. She wished they could ride up but, unfortunately, elevators always have lights that announce an approaching car. Not the safest way to travel in a guarded building.

"I'm still not sure about your boots," she said as the stairwell door closed behind her. "They might make too much noise on the steps. I've got to get you a pair of these special crepe soled boots."

Morgan turned and closely examined the steel door they had just come through. "Don't sweat it, Red. These fire doors are almost completely soundproof. Now, quit stalling and let's get up there."

She smiled a challenge in response to Morgan's remark and launched herself forward. She moved beside him as they took forty-one flights of cement stairs in four quick jogging bursts. Every five minutes she reported elapsed time. During each of three rest stops, one minute each, the pair breathed deeply but did not speak. In the dimly lighted stairwell, seemingly infinite above and below, they simply watched each other. She checked his face for alertness and tension level, and she knew he was checking her as well, looking at looseness of muscle, depth of breathing, lightness of tread. They both searched for any hint of hesitation or loss of sureness. She wasn't disappointed, and his subtle nod said that he wasn't either.

On the forty-first floor they faced a door and a cinder block wall. Felicity briefly thought she had miscounted, until she remembered how often these old buildings had no thirteenth floor. While Morgan pressed his ear to the heavy steel door, she produced a small container of lubricant with which she doused the door hinges. She crouched at the door while Morgan, above her, pressed the door handle and held it down, barely cracking the door open.

Three long minutes of silence passed. She imagined Morgan's hand had to be starting to ache, locked around the handle, but he never made a sound. His closed eyes told her he was keeping his mind relaxed. Finally, the slow, easy tread of a bored hall guard approached.

As the footsteps moved past them, Morgan pressed forward and the door eased open without making a sound. His steely right arm snapped out, his gloved hand clamping over the patroller's mouth. His other iron hand locked around the guard's throat, dragging him into the stairwell with startling ease. Felicity pulled a hypodermic from a pocket on her belt, dropped the protective plastic sleeve and slid the needle into the man's forearm, through his shirt. He could only have caught a fleeting glimpse of her beautiful, smiling face as she pulled the needle out. He struggled pointlessly for a few seconds, but then his movements slowed and the light went out of his eyes.

While Morgan sat the guard in a corner of the stairway, Felicity stepped into the hall. Using a tiny jimmy and screwdriver, she removed the cover plate from the controls of Seagrave's exclusive elevator. Morgan was soon looking over her shoulder, but she knew her silent ritual held no meaning for him. Felicity was staring into the blackness of the hole in the wall, while she produced a tiny black box.

As they had rehearsed, Morgan shined a pencil torch's thin beam into the workspace, barely five by three inches. Three wires hung from the black box. With a penknife, Felicity loosened connections and peeled insulation in the control access. Using alligator clips, she attached the black box to three contact points. Once the contacts were solid she turned and smiled at Morgan. He pressed a gloved finger into the elevator call button.

Seconds later, steel doors wheezed open and Morgan and Felicity played "Alphonse and Gaston" four or five times before she finally entered the elevator first. They were still grinning about their "after you" routine a moment later as the doors whispered open again three stories higher. Morgan stepped out, turned right, and came face to face with a yuppie playing hall monitor.

Felicity hung back for a good view. This part she loved. The guard was about fifteen feet away. He had been scanning a folded newspaper as he walked, humming softly to himself. He dropped his newspaper, his right hand snapping jerkily for the weapon under the left arm of his tweed jacket. Morgan took three quick loping strides and had him by the wrist before his hand could clear the blazer. Morgan's right hand moved in a blur, stiffened fingers driving into his opponent's solar plexus. As the man doubled over, Morgan's elbow crashed down onto the base of his skull. Snatching the back of the blazer's collar, Morgan lowered him to the floor without a sound.

Felicity's movement's matched Morgan's efficiency. On her first visit to that building, she was on a fishing expedition, but this time she knew exactly which room she wanted to enter. Picking the lock on the target door took her exactly nine seconds. Once inside the now familiar conference room, she waved Morgan in behind her. He eased the door closed behind himself and stopped to listen for a moment. Apparently satisfied, he moved to the desk and turned on the lamp. Felicity nodded to him and stepped across the room. He called to her in a loud stage whisper.

"Red. Are you sure?"

"Of course I'm sure," she said, backtracking closer to him. "I've met him, remember? And I heard everything Aaron told us about him, didn't I? This is the kind of man who would strictly separate his family life from business. His ego and sense of self-control are obvious. On top of all that, he's the type who'll be wanting to keep his real treasures near at hand. He'd want to be playing with his toys."

Morgan nodded. "Still sounds like a wild guess to me."

"Morgan, I have to trust my guts," she said. "All my experience, all my instincts are telling me the brooch has got to be in his living area, I'm betting in his bedroom. And surely he'd have the hallway outside his apartment upstairs heavily guarded, so this is the way to go in."

"If it is the way in," Morgan said. "I'm still not sure that elevator you noticed last night when you stared Seagrave down goes to his apartment. What if it goes to the warehouse?"

"There's no reason on earth to have an elevator here, going there. Common sense and all my experience tells me it's Seagrave's back door. Trust me."

Morgan's face reflected his concern. "What if you meet a guard up there?"

"What, in his own apartment? In his home?" she asked. "Not a chance. Not if I understand the man at all." She slapped his shoulder playfully and headed for the other end of the room. As expected, she needed no special gadgets to open it. The silent movement of the doors, folding open to welcome her, was a pleasant surprise. She stepped inside and waved to Morgan as the doors closed.

Seconds later, gilt-edged doors slid back, and the elevator opened onto a cozy study filled with expensive electronic toys. It was what she expected to see based on her read of Seagrave, and she would bet most of the stereo and video equipment was never used. She stepped out of the elevator car, keeping to the edges of the room. Floors, she knew, usually creaked least at the edges.

The darkness was as thick and deep as the ankle covering, wine colored carpet she walked on, yet Felicity moved through it with ease, as a shadow at home among shadows. She brushed past the velvet sofa followed only by the sound of her own heartbeat.

At the master bedroom she listened in rapt attention to the slow, steady breathing of its two occupants. Satisfied that those in the room were both asleep, she peered inside. There lay Adrian Seagrave in yellow silk pajamas, beneath burgundy satin sheets, in a king size water bed. His wife lay face down, two feet away. One of them had kicked the covers down to their ankles.

Mrs. Seagrave wore an expensive nightgown, rucked up around her hips. She was taller than her husband, blond, and the kind of plump many shapely women become when they no longer have any reason to watch their figures. But Felicity was struck most by the contrast between the two sleeping faces. The woman's face was relaxed, untroubled. Few wrinkles showed. A slight smile rested on her lips. She slept the sleep of the innocent. Was this woman aware of her husband's brutal life of crime? Did she know he ordered people killed just to increase his profits?

Perhaps not. Maybe she thought he was just a typical American businessman.

Oh lord, thought Felicity. Perhaps this really is a typical American businessman.

She pulled a tiny nose clip and mouth filter from her belt. It held a four-inch cylinder of compressed air. She was certain it would be more than enough for her plans. The miniature aerosol can she sprayed into the room contained a mild sedative mist that would merely cause those in the bed to sleep more deeply. Next she plugged her familiar earplug into place and began scanning the room with her metal detector.

While she probed the room, her mind was probing the situation. Morgan had stated it quite simply. Their problems would not be ended unless Seagrave was, as he put it, "signed off." An interesting euphemism, that. After she had the brooch, she would ride the elevator back to the conference room. Morgan would ride upstairs in the little elevator and quietly slit the man's throat. Self-defense, and he started it, and all that. It all seemed pretty simple at the time, but she had not considered the wife. Besides, what gave them the right to calmly commit cold-blooded murder?

After all the trouble she had gone through, Felicity found the safe behind a cheap velvet painting of a matador. The moral situation continued to plague her as, moving automatic precision, she placed the stethoscope in position for opening the combination lock. Could she and Morgan pass the death sentence on this man? After all, he was not really evil, just greedy. If that became a capital offense, she would be next on the gallows herself. On the other hand, he had tried to kill her. Or, more accurately, to have her killed by others. And he was responsible for the death of some of Morgan's friends. But even if he did deserve to die, what about the woman, who would wake up beside a blood splattered corpse?

Her introspection was short circuited as she swung the steel door open. Feeling a wave of deja vu, Felicity reached into the cylindrical, felt lined hole and withdrew her diamond-studded prize. She stared into the heartless, flawless stone, silently scolding it. How much trouble you have caused, she thought. How much pain. And how many deaths have you caused since your ancient creation? How much blood have men spilled in pursuit of a green piece of stone carrying a chunk of polished carbon with little white marbles around it?

Felicity sighed and shook her head, honest enough to admit to herself that none of that really mattered to her. At last her quest was ended and the reward was indescribably sweet. It had been so easy in the end. With Morgan for backup, anything was within reach. Again she considered the idea of them continuing as a team in the future. She wasn't sure how that could work, but it certainly felt comfortable thinking it.

One small snag was nagging at the back of her mind. She pulled the solution from a squeeze pocket at the side of her black denims. She removed the safety sleeve from another thin hypodermic needle and very gently slid its tip into Marlene Seagrave's exposed hip. The mist she had previously sprayed merely deepened the sleep of those who inhaled it. This injection would knock the woman out. She would sleep through anything now, even a gunshot in the same room.

Not that she would need to. Morgan planned to do his work with a knife, up close and personal as he put it. The mental image still rattled her. She wished that Morgan had brought some sort of poison with him instead. That would finish Adrian Seagrave off more neatly. As it was, she figured she would at least convince Morgan to put the man's mortal remains elsewhere after the deed was done. No woman deserves to wake up beside a bloody corpse.

\* \* \* \* \*

Leaning back against the bar in the darkness, Morgan watched the small elevator for movement. He sipped some of Seagrave's Napoleon Brandy with a smile. When Felicity landed he would ride up and quietly push seven inches of steel into Adrian Seagrave's throat. For Crazy Mike. For Smitty. For Josh. In fact, one inch of blade for each of the men he lost when Seagrave ordered them abandoned in the jungle. It would not be fun, and he would relive it a few times in his sleep, but in his mind it was a matter of expedience. Then he and his new partner would be out of the building before anyone knew they had been there.

His new partner. He liked the sound of that. Maybe if he had a real partner he could finally settle somewhere, before his luck ran out. He did have that dream of going legit, setting up a personal protection business, providing a level of safety for executives who needed it against killers and terrorists. He was ready to become a defender instead of an attacker.

He swirled the brandy in its snifter, enjoying its sweet, biting aroma while he considered how smoothly he and Felicity worked together. They had known each other for only days, yet they breezed through this mission with hardly a word exchanged. Even when he did question her, her confidence convinced him that she had things under control.

He had never thought he could work with a woman. Of course, this situation was a bit different from anything he had ever considered because with this woman there could be no sex angle. He would never risk feeling both sides of love making again. So from that aspect, it was the same as working with a man. In all other ways, it was quite different. For example, he had never worked with a man who was such a talented creative thinker. While he worked in straight lines, she functioned well with no pattern whatever.

When the elevator door slid open, he marched over to Felicity, holding a glass out to her. She gratefully accepted it, taking a healthy pull. She bowed him toward the elevator but held his arm. Morgan turned toward her, and she pulled him toward her, craning her neck to whisper in his ear. Obviously she wanted to tell him something about the situation upstairs.

A piercing white light stabbed into their eyes. Morgan reflexes spun his head toward the door and sent his right hand flashing under his windbreaker. He froze as his eyes locked onto the newcomer through the blue dots dancing before them. Paul was just inside the door, his left hand on the light switch, his right hand halfway to the holster on his belt at his left side.

## -34-

Morgan eyes met Paul's, and both men froze. Then, to Felicity's surprise, both men slowly lowered their hands.

"I should have known it would be you," Morgan said.

"No one else thought anybody could get in here," Paul replied. "Me? I like to check everywhere."

Felicity did not really understand what was happening, but the moment felt too delicate to disturb without dire consequences. There was a long moment of silence. She was the only thing moving in the stillness. She stepped lightly toward the bar on Paul's right, feeling ignored. They were busted. Why wasn't this fellow sending up an alarm? And since he was being so quiet, why didn't Morgan shoot him or something?

"You can still walk away from this," Morgan said grimly. His mouth turned down at the futility of the situation.

"You know better than that," Paul said, his face equally stern. "I work for Seagrave. And I don't welch on a contract."

"You're good," Morgan said, pain showing on his face. "Very good. But you can't win."

"That may be, but I can't just let you..."

It happened with such unexpected quickness that Felicity had to replay the action in her mind to sort out what she had seen. Paul pronounced the word "let" with no emphasis, but as he said it his hand had snapped toward his holster. Morgan had dived left, landing hard on the conference table. His automatic appeared as if by sleight of hand in his right fist. The two gun blasts would have sounded simultaneous to a casual observer, but she could tell that Morgan fired earlier, by perhaps a tenth of a second. A bullet tinkled through the drape-covered window behind him. Paul's pistol dropped from nerveless fingers as he spun away to his left.

Before Paul even hit the carpeted floor, Morgan was moving toward him. Felicity bolted for the door. The caper was blown for good and all now. Those shots would surely bring curious guards, like sharks to a coral cut. She poked her head out the door, glancing quickly down the hall.

"Oh shite!" She grimaced as she saw a pistol round the hall corner, dragging a muscular man behind it.

Paul, clutching his left biceps, was staring up at Morgan. Bright red liquid seeped between his fingers.

"Thanks," Paul hissed through clenched teeth.

"For what?" Morgan asked, pulling a handkerchief from an inside jacket pocket.

Paul glanced at his arm. "It's not spurting out of my heart."

"My aim was off."

"Bullshit." Paul managed a pained smile.

"Move!" Felicity shouted, shoving Morgan's shoulder. "There's a bleeding army coming up the hall." With that, she took two long steps and dived gracefully into open air, arcing down behind the bar. On the floor, Felicity watched around the edge of the bar as Morgan scrambled to the back of the room. She heard the door slam open, and held her breath as two bullets scarred the conference table's maple top. She saw Morgan slam his body to the left and down into the elevator just before she ducked behind the bar.

The mass of gunfire made her cover her ears with her hands. Her head was ringing and somehow it made her mouth dry. Was this what it was like in combat, she wondered. It was all handgun fire but it was so dense that it sounded like machine guns to her. She was safe for the moment but she worried for Morgan, the intended target of all that shooting. That elevator looked uncomfortably small and soon the guards would work up the courage to move in for the kill.

One story above, Adrian Seagrave's eyes fluttered half open. The room felt like it was vibrating, as if some sort of construction was going on. He was having trouble waking up, but he had to investigate the noise.

Forcing himself to his feet, he staggered out of the bedroom and managed to reach his study. Yes, the noise was coming from below. His private elevator shaft was conducting it upward. It sounded like gunfire, but more than he had ever imagined. He leaned against the elevator casing, hesitating. He had to go downstairs and find out what was going on.

He reached toward the button, but hesitated and moved to lean both hands against the doors. He would rest for just a minute, and then summon his elevator car.

Felicity peeked over the edge of the bar, eyes bulging. She counted eleven men concentrating their gunfire on the elevator area. Revolver and automatic fire combined to create a deafening roar, reminding her of standing next to a waterfall. The air was thick with the stench of gunpowder smoke. She had heard gunpowder referred to as smokeless powder, but could hardly credit that name now. The acrid cloud was so dense she could taste it. The room literally shook with the blasts. The muzzle flashes reminded her of what Morgan had told her about the two hand grenades hanging on her belt.

She hefted one of the small black spheres. A "flash-bang" is what she remembered Morgan calling it. Some kind of stun grenade he said the British Special Air Service had first used to combat terrorists. They were designed to protect innocents in a hostage situation, and now this one might save Morgan.

Something, it looked to her like a bread tie, held the pin in. She twisted that off, pulled the pin out and flipped the spoon off. With her back to the bar and feet braced against the wall, she tossed the grenade backward, up and over the bar. Remembering what Morgan had told her about these devices, she clamped her hands over her ears and ducked her head.

\* \* \* \* \*

Crouching in a corner of the elevator, Morgan heard the clunk of pulleys engaging, and felt the elevator cables go taut. For less than a second he considered whether it would be safer to ride up or roll back out into the room. While looking toward the bar he spotted the small black sphere rising into the air, appearing to hang in space for a second at its apogee. He recognized it immediately and his face broke into a broad grin. "I love that girl," he whispered to himself as he covered his ears and buried his face in the elevator floor.

The small black ball arced over the crowd of shooters and dropped in front of them. It had fallen to waist height when the world seemed to explode. Almost no energy was expended in blast or heat. However, the star burst rivaled that of a thousand flashbulbs popping in concert, and even with his hands over his ears, Morgan could not be completely prepared for the concussive bang like a sonic boom that burst windows and shattered glasses on the bar.

Morgan felt the elevator lurch and rolled out of the little car as it started to rise. His ears were ringing but he was relatively unaffected, facing a room full of blinded and deafened gunmen. They were disoriented and frightened, with pounding heads and dazed wits. About half of them had dropped their guns in shock. He loved it.

With a running start, Morgan leaped into the midst of his dazzled attackers. The drop kick slapped two men to the floor. A quick spinning back kick, an edge of the hand slash to the neck and a jarring back fist put three more on the carpet. With his left, he thrust stiffened fingers into a guard's already aching eyes. He snapped a crisp jab into another's nose, putting him down for the count.

While all this was going on, Felicity slipped out from behind the bar. Morgan was purposely putting all of the attackers out of the fight without any further gunplay, and did not need any help, but he could see that she did not want to feel useless.

He saw Felicity seize a makeshift weapon from the bar, probably thinking she could bludgeon a few of the gunmen into submission. She stepped forward, hefting the bottle she and Morgan had been drinking from. He heard the dull thud behind him and turned to give her an encouraging smile. However, after her first swing he could see that the result startled her. As Morgan could have told her, the edge of a Napoleon Brandy bottle is a bit sturdier than the average professional strong-arm man's head. She must have expected her glass club to shatter, like they always do in the movies.

Morgan watched her dispatch the last four of Seagrave's hirelings with the same bottle, looking more confident with each swing. With the opposition neutralized, Morgan knelt beside Paul's unconscious body. He picked up the white handkerchief he had dropped beside Paul and tied it tightly around Paul's upper arm. Viscous red fluid was making his fingers slippery, but he did not care. In the past few days he had faced Central American soldiers, hired killers, bodyguards and ambushers. He was not about to let the only true professional he had encountered in the lot bleed to death.

While his fingers moved on their own, his mind was whirring like a high-speed computer, as he tried to calculate the time remaining for escape, Paul's survival odds, and what his next move should be. Backtracking to kill Seagrave might not leave them a sufficient getaway margin, but leaving him alive could turn out to be a fatal mistake.

All of that mental activity combined with an effort to monitor Paul's condition, track Felicity's position and observe the status of the dazed protectors to create a form of sensory overload. Together, it all made it impossible for Morgan to pay sufficient attention to his little inner voice. Too much was happening at once. Morgan's concentration was shaken by a single shouted word.

"You!"

Morgan looked up and to his right to see Adrian Seagrave, in yellow silk pajamas, looking aghast at the carnage in his main conference room. Time seemed to grind into slow motion.

Morgan glanced at Felicity, a flash of anger quickly fading as he remembered the pre-operational briefing she had given him. The sleep mist Felicity had sprayed upstairs was a mild sedative, but clearly not sufficient to block out the mass of gunfire that had flown through that room moments ago. Even if it had, the concussion grenade shook the entire building. But Seagrave must have rung for the elevator before that, which was why it began to rise while Morgan was in it. Now the man Morgan had gone there to kill staggered dazedly out of the elevator, looking like he had wandered into a nightmare.

Within the same second, Seagrave shouted his one word, Felicity gasped, and Morgan felt a massive hairy paw clamp onto his shoulder.

Monk, in a tee shirt and slacks, lifted Morgan into the air with one huge hand. The brute flipped Morgan casually, using no judo skill or leverage at all, and sent Morgan sailing across the room. He rolled with the fall as well as he could, but slammed hard into the wall. Through his haze, he could hear Seagrave shouting, "Kill him" again and again in a high, hysterical voice.

Blue spots bounced in front of Morgan's eyes as he grasped clumsily for his pistol. He managed to draw his weapon and get the safety off before Monk's grip on his wrist made his hand go numb, and the automatic dropped into the carpet. The other ape paw wrapped around Morgan's neck. He felt himself lifted from the floor, dangling as helplessly as a child.

If Monk had not managed a sneak attack, Morgan would have given himself pretty good odds against him. Now it looked as though this monster would literally tear him apart before he had a chance to fight back. Those arms were like twin oak beams. Morgan snap kicked into Monk's unprotected ribs with no apparent affect. Monk had a gut like granite.

Felicity moved in close and raised her brandy bottle like a baseball player waiting for a fastball to come across home plate. She smashed her bottle over Monk's head and this time it did shatter like the spun sugar bottles on a movie set. Monk shook his head, his hair spraying droplets of liquor, and turned toward her with a crooked grin. She looked around frantically, and the light of an idea came on in her eyes. She flashed a palm at Morgan, signaling him to hold on, and darted across the room.

Morgan wondered if she was looking for another weapon. He was not sure what Felicity had in mind, but he knew he had better coordinate his actions with hers. While she grabbed another bottle of brandy and ran to snatch something from the desk across the room, he dropped his free hand to his belt.

Monk was slowly pulling Morgan's head to one side, his right arm to the other, grinning like a child in anticipation of the cracking sound he loved. Morgan was strong and would resist to the last, but judging from Monk's face, that was a good thing, as if it would make the bone snap better when it came.

Felicity could see Seagrave at the other end of the room, behind Monk. His eyes showed white all around, his face alight with madness. She now realized how wrong she had been before. This was no simple ambitious businessman. This madman was truly evil.

Felicity jogged to the side, to get behind Monk. She jumped up and swung with all her strength. A full bottle of cognac shattered over Monk's head. The pungent odor bit into her nostrils and appeared to work like smelling salts on Morgan. The liquor ran like sweat into Monk's eyes. As if on cue, Morgan yanked off his belt buckle and plunged the three-inch double-edged push dagger into Monk's outstretched forearm. With a startled roar, the giant dropped Morgan to the floor but Morgan immediately sprang back up, smashing the first two knuckles of his right fist into Monk's throat, then slapping hard onto the giant's ears with both palms.

Monk rocked back with his mouth gaping, but he was not finished yet. He turned toward Felicity, his eyes reflecting the madness she'd seen on Seagrave's face. Monk, however, was clearly overcome by rage and in her mind was no longer human at all, but a crazed animal lurching toward her. That made her next action easier. She pushed her left hand forward, flipping the striker on the cigarette lighter she had swept up from the desk.

"Let's see how tough a bugger you are when we've turned you into an ape-man flambé," she said. Monk's brandy soaked tee shirt burst into a corona of flames that rushed up his back and swept around his head.

Still groggy, Morgan missed most of Felicity's comment, but his eyes were riveted to Monk's waving arms. Still dazed, Morgan crawled out of the way as Monk turned and staggered toward the only loud, continuous sound in the room, Seagrave's hysterical screams.

Adrian Seagrave was shouting for Monk to stop, but the maddened, blinded behemoth lumbered on. Seagrave backed away as far as he could. He hardly seemed to realize the he had run out of room. His feet continued to move, pressing him backward, crunching on the window glass shattered earlier by the concussion grenade. Frozen with terror, the businessman's fingers dug into the crushed velvet of the heavy drapes behind him. While Morgan and Felicity stared, Monk's huge frame wrapped itself like a flaming shroud around Seagrave's body.

\* \* \* \* \*

Morgan saw Felicity turn away, nausea showing on her face. The smell, he guessed. Human hair and flesh did burn with a distinctive stench. He also saw that a few of the building security guards had regained consciousness. Their eyes were locked on the scene in front of the window.

Morgan clenched his teeth, anticipating the end. Seagrave's pudgy hands poked out pathetically on either side of Monk's flaming frame as their combined mass tilted away. Wind whipped in through the already shattered window, fanning Monk's body into a giant pyre as it leaned outward. Morgan watched the two bodies, now fused together as one, pivot down and out of sight as if in slow motion, leaving a gaping hole where a wall-sized window had so recently been. A fierce flame lined that black hole, fanned by the suddenly noticeable breeze.

Morgan turned to see a small stampede headed toward the door, and it came as no surprise to him. The man who signed their paychecks was out the window. The group of hired guards, now all awake, could see the handwriting as well as the fire on the wall. Morgan was having similar thoughts. He scooped up his pistol on the run and moved to follow the pack out of the room. Felicity's hand on his arm stopped him.

"Wait," she said. "We can't go. Seagrave's wife is upstairs."

# -35-

Morgan stared past Felicity, who was backlit by a wall of flame. This was no time for conversation, but the strain on her face demanded a response.

"Red, you've got to be kidding. Seagrave didn't sleep through that firefight and neither could anyone else. She probably took a back way out of here long ago."

"I gave her a shot," Felicity whined. He had not heard her whine before. "She couldn't wake up."

"Fortunes of war, Red," he said grimly.

"No, damn it. I gave her a shot! If we leave her there, I will have murdered the girl."

Morgan stared into those pleading, deep green eyes, just for a moment. He did not debate further. He knew he would lose and time was depressingly short. He shook his head and ran back to the elevator.

The tiny elevator car was stifling, but the ride was short. The smell of smoke was already seeping into the luxury flat. He found the bedroom easily enough, and could see its only occupant was still sleeping, a deep drugged sleep thanks to Felicity. When he hefted Mrs. Seagrave's satin-draped form, his left shoulder screamed into his brain. He had all but forgotten the sprain. It hurt like a fishhook was jammed into the joint, but he did not drop his burden. With steely concentration he rolled the pain into a little ball and tucked it away in a corner of his mind, completely blocked off. Then he slowly returned to the elevator. The woman in his arms moaned as if in the throes of a nightmare. If she only knew, he thought.

At the bottom of the shaft, the elevator door slid open and the heat burst in. That end of the room was what firefighters would call fully involved in the blaze. Was this building too old to have a sprinkler system? Or did Seagrave pay someone off to get around fire safety code violations? Well, it hardly mattered now. Felicity stood by the open door, waving him on. The woman in his arms groggily mumbled, "What's going on?" He shifted her up onto his right shoulder and started across the floor in a crouch. The woman's perspiration dripped onto his back, blending with his own. He focused his attention on Felicity's face and the desperation he saw there.

Morgan had just stepped into the relative cool of the hallway when he heard a moan. It was not from Mrs. Seagrave. It was a deeper voice, and it came from behind him. Turning, his eyes were at first seared by the brightness of the flames. Heat washed over his face making it harder to breathe. Squinting, he sighted in on a figure on hands and knees, following a long shadow across the floor, but much too slowly.

Paul. Shit. Can't just leave him, Morgan thought.

Before he could put his thoughts into words, Felicity brushed past him. While he looked on, his mouth agape, she took the arm of the man who had kidnapped her and helped him regain his feet. After pulling Paul's left arm across her shoulders, Felicity shuffled toward the door. Morgan could see the pallor of blood loss and the extra creases of pain on Paul's face, but there was no time for additional first aid now.

"I can make it," Paul said in answer to Morgan's unvoiced question. He tried a smile of thanks.

Felicity passed Morgan in the hall and banged the call button. A long, tense minute passed before the private elevator door opened. The quartet hurried aboard for the short ride down three flights. When the doors opened again, the air was clearer, allowing everyone a deep breath.

"Okay, gang, let's go." With that, Morgan spun his load and headed down the hall. "Elevators are suicide in a burning building, I'm afraid. We had no choice before, since Seagrave had the stairs closed off from here up. But from here down we've got to take the safer choice." He pulled the steel door open and started downstairs.

"Wait!" Felicity shouted. "There's a wire. Six steps down." In the darkness Morgan managed to pick out the trip wire and carefully stepped over it. Felicity continued talking as they moved steadily down the stairs.

"It's an old habit," she said as they moved through the smoky gloom. "Whenever I go up stairs on a caper I leave a wire. If I have to exit quickly, anyone following me gets slowed down some."

Morgan's breathing got deeper after each flight of stairs, but the smoke also got thinner and the oven like warmth felt farther and farther away. He could feel Seagrave's wife beginning to fidget, fighting the drug still coursing through her veins. Paul, on the other hand, was less able to support himself, despite heroic effort. It was increasingly obvious that his weight was almost too much for Felicity to handle. Morgan wanted to help her, but he knew time was escaping them. He didn't know what businesses occupied most of the building, but Seagrave's business floors were warehouses filled with shipping materials, enough cardboard and paper to fuel a blast furnace. Beyond the stairwell he could hear the roar of the fire climbing down the building. If it ever got ahead of them, the stairwell itself could become a swirling blast furnace if any of the lower doors had been left open.

Morgan's thighs were burning as he proceeded downward, and his eyes burned with the sweat he didn't have time to wipe away. On the nineteenth floor landing Mrs. Seagrave's legs jerked in an awkward spasm. Thrown off balance, Morgan slumped against a wall. His eyes wandered up the stairs, focusing on the line of red spots Paul was leaving behind. Felicity's face was ashen and streaked with gray tracks left by her perspiration. Her hair hung in a clump, tangled under Paul's arm, and her eyes were vacant with concentration. Paul's face was ominously blank.

Morgan would not have left Paul behind, out of respect. He was still surprised that Felicity, unasked, had tried to rescue him. She had not dropped him yet, but it was obvious that she could not continue for long. He feared they would have to abandon someone, unless providence intervened.

"I think I can walk now." The woman's voice behind him took Morgan completely by surprise. Marlene Seagrave squirmed off his shoulder and smiled a woozy smile, trying to square her own proud shoulders and regain some dignity in her silk nightgown.

"Thank God," Felicity said, barely above a whisper. "This one's just passed out."

"Yeah, and I'm smelling more smoke," Morgan added.

"It is getting warm in here, isn't it?" Felicity said, nodding with her dramatic understatement. Morgan took three deep breaths and pulled off his light windbreaker, handing it to Marlene. "It is warm, but I thought you might want to cover up some."

Marlene nodded her thanks and accepted the jacket. Her reaction to his shoulder holster and knife was barely perceivable. Morgan noticed it, and he saw that Felicity did too. Marlene pulled the jacket on without comment. It hung past her hips and covered her hands completely.

Paul replaced Marlene in a fireman's carry across Morgan's shoulders, and the group continued descending the long vertical tunnel at a somewhat better pace. Morgan led, with Felicity close behind and Marlene Seagrave following. With each step, Marlene's mind seemed to become clearer. No one would mistake her for an athlete, but she was working hard to keep up, and to catch up in another sense.

"I have to ask you people something," she said in a breathless tremor. "I've been able to piece together a little of what's been happening here."

"I can imagine your confusion, eh..."

"Marlene," Mrs. Seagrave replied to Felicity's unvoiced query. "Thanks for verifying that we haven't met before. I don't recognize either of you. I know you don't work for my husband.

He makes sure they all know who I am. On the other hand, you hardly behave like police or emergency personnel or anything like that. So the most confusing thing to me I guess is why I'm here. I mean, my husband's staff all left me behind. Why didn't you?"

"That would take a bit of explaining," Felicity said, brushing some long red strands from her face. "It's a little complex."

"I think we have time," Marlene replied, out of breath but still able to manage a small smile.

"Well, alright then. You see, I was in your room earlier and I drugged you. If we left you there, in a fire like that, well, that'd be murder, wouldn't it?"

Marlene seemed to consider her words carefully, or maybe she was just having trouble catching her breath. "But you, well, this might seem a bit wrong to say under the circumstances, but you were there to hurt my husband, weren't you? "

Felicity rushed to say, "I was there to rob him."

Morgan appreciated Felicity's response. She must have liked Marlene Seagrave just for her straightforward attitude. She was trying not to hurt Marlene's feelings, but the woman persisted.

"I'm sure that's true," Marlene said, "but there are surely easier targets for a robbery. Why Adrian?"

Felicity kept pushing forward, not looking back at Marlene. "Sorry to tell you this, but he cheated me in a business deal. I wanted back what he took. We, eh, had a bit of a conflict with your security guards. Things got a little out of hand is all."

"The fire?"

"That was an accident," Felicity said with a raised index finger. After that remark, Morgan could not resist breaking into a grin. If he turned he imagined that he would see Felicity blushing.

Ten steps later, Marlene said, "I know the man your friend is carrying. He's one of my husband's business associates. A security specialist I think he said. He's probably one of the men you had your conflict with."

"So what?" Morgan asked over his shoulder. "Should we have left him to die?"

"Would he have saved you?" Marlene returned.

"Of course," Morgan said, but without much conviction. He wanted to end the conversation, because he found life easier when he did not examine his own reasons too closely. He got along just fine as long as he did what felt right at the time.

Morgan was moving forward on automatic pilot. Time lost meaning as he moved past identical flights of stairs. His back was screaming at him, but he shut it out. All his energy focused on simple tasks. Breathe. Step down. Maintain balance. Do you hear two sets of footsteps behind you? Good. Breathe. Step down. Maintain balance.

Walking in a daze Morgan felt his right foot thump to a halt inches before he expected it to, and he stumbled forward, nearly falling. With a shock, he realized there were no more steps to descend. They had reached the ground floor landing and he could hear sirens. No smoke wafted into the stairwell, but he would not expect any to pass under a fire door, even if noises did. Regaining his balance, he pressed his hand against the steel door. It was slightly warm. Morgan felt like a wrung out dishrag, despite the fact that his clothes were soaked through with his sweat, and the sweat of those he had carried. His lungs burned from dragging in all the air they could hold on his long overburdened descent. Fighting to keep his balance, he turned to face the girls and shifted Paul off his shoulder into his arms like a baby.

Marlene was breathing hard, wheezing like an old window-mounted air conditioner. Felicity held her arm to steady her. Felicity's eyes seemed a little out of focus, but her mouth was drawn into a hard line of determination he had only seen before on Rangers near the end of an all day road march. She was mad. Not mad at him or anybody in particular, but at the situation, and her anger was carrying her. His mind started playing an old Army cadence call.

*Had a dog, his name was Blue.*
*Blue wanted to be a Ranger too.*
*They made him march for 28 days.*
*Now old Blue's in a zombie haze*

He smiled. Felicity wanted to be a Ranger too. Morgan had been there and done that. When people got that tired they didn't think too well. His new partner was there now, and he had to fill in the thinking for her.

"Now listen," Morgan said. His words were clipped, his voice terse. "It's probably all smoke out there. You won't want your eyes open, but you've got to get out. If you get lost in the lobby, you're dead. Understand? The lobby door is about six paces to the right, then left about twenty. Got it?"

"Right six, left twenty," Felicity said in a robotic voice. "Right."

"When I push this door open, take a deep breath and crouch down as low as you can. Hold your breath, clamp your eyes shut and run. Hang on to Mrs. Seagrave and drag her if you have to. There's nothing in your way. When you hit the door to the outside, you'll know it. Ready? Go!"

Morgan slammed his back against the door's lever, swinging it open. Smoke curled in on him. The women slipped past, arms linked. He followed, hefting Paul in his arms. It was a long twenty seconds of darkness, following the sound of Marlene's feet on the marble floor. He was grateful that she was barefoot because despite her exhaustion, Felicity's boots were silent. Paul choked and gagged in his arms. Morgan's eyes smarted from the thick smoke, even with his lids clamped shut. Even his own saliva tasted of smoke while he held his breath.

Strong hands clamped onto his left leg, pulling him off balance. Someone must have gotten trapped in the lobby. It could be an innocent employee, or it might be one of the guards who ran from Seagrave's meeting room. Morgan didn't have the luxury of distinguishing. He managed to right himself on his left foot just long enough to manage a single stamp kick. It was enough to free him. He staggered forward, out of breath and out of time. He stumbled, almost dropping Paul. His shoulder hit something hard, but whatever it was, it moved.

The barrier slid aside and a blast of cool air froze the dampness on his face. Two sets of arms stopped him. He gulped fresh air and collapsed. He cracked his eyes open to see that a pair of firemen was helping him walk. Someone clamped an oxygen mask over Paul's face and lifted him away. The firemen holding

Morgan's arms lowered him to a seated position, leaning against the giant tire of a hook and ladder truck, and went back to work. His head hung between his legs, his eyes burning. Bull horns nearby blasted instructions to bystanders and emergency personnel.

Morgan's head spun, and the air tasted like water that had been in the refrigerator too long. It was all catching up to him now. His showdown with Paul. The shoot-out in the conference room, so much like a mad minute back in Vietnam. His brief, terrible battle with Monk. The fire. Forty-one flights of stairs, carrying a body all the way, racing against the blaze. And now, after all that, would come the moment of greatest danger.

There he sat, surrounded by police. His windbreaker was wrapped around Marlene Seagrave now, so there was no concealing the loaded gun he was carrying, not to mention three knives. Felicity was still laden with burglar tools and a live hand grenade. The building they just left was ablaze and two charred bodies were stretched out on the pavement around there somewhere. Any minute now, a nurse medical tech would be asking him how he was and what happened upstairs. He and Felicity were left with way too much to explain. What, he wondered, would they be charged with? Breaking and entering? Burglary? Arson? Murder? These days, maybe even terrorism. They were alone, with no witnesses and no defense.

Gathering his remaining strength, Morgan forced himself to his feet and trudged heavily over toward Felicity. She and Marlene Seagrave were talking to a police captain. Morgan had to step over hoses and avoid rushing fire fighters on the way. This scene of confusion, he realized, was all taking place inside a police barricade. Several trucks and emergency vehicles were parked too closely together in an overlapping pattern, like so many red and yellow pick-up sticks. What looked like an army of men was fighting what he could now see was a major fire. He looked around for Monk and Seagrave, but someone must have already cleared that mess away.

When he reached Felicity, he was surprised to find her looking solemn, but not worried or frightened. She raised a palm to

Morgan, cautioning him to stay silent. Marlene, still in her nightgown and Morgan's windbreaker, was speaking to a detective now. Morgan could barely hear her words over the fire fighters' clopping boots and shouted commands.

"That's right, Marlene Seagrave," she said, as a fireman wrapped a blanket around her shoulders. She was biting her lip and looking every bit the grieving widow. "My husband is, or was, Adrian Seagrave, the importer. We live, lived, in an apartment in this building. Our offices were here and he insisted on living where he worked."

"And these people?" the policeman asked.

"These people? Oh, they're in my husband's employ as, eh..."

"We're security personnel, sir," Felicity said, somehow looking helpful and supportive.

"Yes, that's right, security," Marlene said, nodding. "There were others, but they all ran off. This man and this woman risked their lives to save me and that other fellow, and I don't even know their names." She gulped back a very sincere and convincing sob. "I'll be happy to make a more extensive statement to you and the press after my new friends and I get a shower. Can I please go get some clothes on?"

As the police moved away, Felicity turned toward Morgan. Her confident expression melted like a wax mask. Exhaustion washed over her face and she fell into Morgan's arms. A man standing nearby turned from the police to point a camera at them. His automatic flash stabbed Morgan's eyes. Morgan twisted away, reflexively trying to avoid being identified.

"Who the hell are you?"

"Daily News," the man said, not even bothering to offer his name. Instead he pushed a pocket tape recorder toward their faces. "Fires happen every day. You guys are the story here. From what the other woman said, you two are real heroes."

## -36-

On a cool spring evening, a sleek black Corvette slid into a parking space in at an exclusive marina on the ocean side of Long Island. The passenger side door opened and a tall, powerfully built black man got out. He appeared vaguely uncomfortable in a navy blue suit and tie. His shoes were hand made Italian slip-ons. He walked around the car and opened the door for the driver, a slender, stately redhead. She was dressed simply in a jade silk gown that matched her eyes.

"That's her boat," Felicity said, pointing down a long pier.

"Boat?" Morgan snorted. "Red, when they get into the two hundred foot class, I don't think you call them boats. They become yachts. This old girl's two hundred eighteen feet from stem to stern."

"I just love that nautical talk," Felicity said. Arm in arm the couple walked slowly up a long gangplank. Its guide ropes were strung with small electric lights. As they got closer to the deck the subdued chatter of polite celebrants greeted them. The vessel ahead was jammed with smiling faces. Felicity scanned the tuxedo and gown crowd, but saw no familiar faces. As they were about to step aboard the vessel, their hostess appeared as if from nowhere.

"Thank God you came." Marlene beamed as she literally dragged them aboard. "My first party on my own and I'm a wreck. I would have died if you didn't show up."

Felicity took a good look at their hostess, as if for the first time. Marlene was somewhat older than Felicity, a little shorter and stockier. Still, she looked several years younger than the night they met. She had lost weight over the last two months. She may never be beauty pageant material again, but even in a tight fitting black evening gown, her figure was now nothing to be embarrassed about, and flattering highlights danced in her honey blonde hair.

"Well, did you enjoy your vacations?" Marlene asked as she hustled Morgan and Felicity into the center of the party. A buzz of polite, happy conversation enveloped them. A tray went by, and Marlene made sure they all collected drinks.

"You're certainly popular," Felicity said. "I have to apologize for Morgan. Tried to get him into a tux, I did, but he flat out refused."

Marlene turned to her, then paused, and the festive glow momentarily left her face. She forced the smile back into place and nodded toward Felicity's throat.

"I see you do wear it, at least." Felicity expected this moment. Marlene was looking into the antique brooch pinned at the top of her gown. It was the item that had driven the bizarre sequence of events that brought them together. And she saw that her friend was wearing a bittersweet smile.

"Wear it every chance I get," Felicity said. "Hope I didn't offend you by wearing it tonight. Guess I wanted you to know it wasn't just, I don't know. I didn't think of it bringing back bad memories."

Morgan leaned forward, interposing his body between the two women. "Why don't we go up top?"

Three minutes later they were standing alone on the upper deck at the stern of Marlene's motor cruiser. A warm wind whipped the women's hair and carried both the ocean's salty scent and the sounds of passing sea birds. Felicity's martini had started a glow in her stomach, matching the moon overhead. With her back to the shore, she was able to get lost in the endless black of the night sky.

Felicity stared into the faces of her two friends, and there was an undeclared moment of silence. They had not all been together since the excitement sixty days before. Two months had passed since that awful day of danger and the following day of police reports and news reporters. That had been a day of torture as well, a day of minute public scrutiny for three exhausted individuals who all had secrets to keep. Three, because the camera shy man known only as Paul had somehow slipped out of the hospital unobserved and disappeared, saving them the trouble of explaining a bullet wound.

"So?" Marlene said at last. "How did you enjoy your vacations?"

"Morgan just got back a couple of days ago." Felicity turned to watch the lights of an unknown nearby town. "He says he has a secret place he goes to after a bad time. An island he actually owns in the Pacific somewhere. Just a cabin he says. No electricity or plumbing or anything. Doesn't that sound romantic? Wouldn't take me, the git. Says no one else has ever been there. But he sure came back looking good."

"And yourself?"

"Oh, I had fun," Felicity answered. She chose not to mention exactly how she went off to relax as well. She spent three weeks at her Riviera place, wearing her newly acquired brooch at every opportunity. She gambled. She sailed. She took a lover. And she returned mentally and emotionally refreshed.

"Okay, what about the future?" Marlene asked. "When you left New York, you were talking about starting a business. Have the two of you discussed those plans further?"

"Extensively," Felicity said, her voice filled with energy and enthusiasm. "I've made contact with a number of security equipment manufacturers. And I've got to admit, the publicity after the fire helped a lot, especially when you publicly declared us your personal security advisors. I'll be marketing my services as a designer of security systems for businesses, museums, and the homes of the very wealthy. I'll be in the business of protecting the art and jewelry that I used to nick myself."

"And this will content you?" Marlene asked.

"Well, I suppose. And if one of my clients does take a loss, who better to recover what's been taken? That part sounds like fun. And with Morgan's help, I'll be able to provide security for major events too. He'll be training our security force, you see."

"Really?" Marlene turned to Morgan. "Do you have any experience in that sort of thing, or will you just fake it?"

"Actually, I've trained personal protectors and executive drivers in anti-terrorist tactics in the past," Morgan said. "I just haven't done it in the U.S. before. Overseas, a lot of that work is done my people with military experience. To tell you the truth, private companies do a lot of security work in other countries, often in conjunction with the U.S. military. Civilian paramilitary companies supplying contractors to Uncle Sam is a billion dollar business and I plan to take my share."

"Sorry, but you just don't strike me as the business type," Marlene said with a smile.

"Well, maybe I figure its time for me to settle down. A little." Morgan glanced at Felicity with a lopsided grin. "Besides, who says I won't be out there with my guys in Bosnia or Colombia or wherever?"

"I see," Marlene said, leaning back against the railing. "Well, I certainly wish you both success. I've learned a great deal about business in the past month, and I can tell you it's not easy."

"Well, don't get mad, but I did a bit of checking when I got back in the country," Felicity said. "It seems to me you've done all right by the Seagrave Corporation."

Marlene gave a short, sharp laugh. "I read a bunch of books on business. I was determined not to lose what I suddenly had. I've streamlined my husband's holdings and somehow managed to maintain control of it all. It's very exhilarating, really. I seem to have found some excellent managers. And, I find myself to be, after all the dust settled, quite wealthy. Oh, and my first official act as president of the company was to fire Stone." She paused, clearly steeling herself to launch into an unpleasant subject. Her voice lowered and lost much of its energy. "I've also learned a great deal about my husband's business dealings."

Felicity saw her partner looking more closely into Marlene's eyes. She could not, and ended up looking down at the deck.

"Yes, I know it all now," Marlene continued. "Or, at least, I think all. Anyway, I know how he cheated each of you. I know that he paid men to, um, to put you in danger. I guess I suspected for some time that he did this type of thing. But you've got to understand that to a twenty-six year old, over the hill beauty queen who hadn't done too well in school, who hadn't managed to get a modeling career going, who hated her parents, who was looking for a fast track to the upper class, well, Adrian Seagrave was a hard offer to refuse. And that was a lot of years ago. That's not by way of an excuse. It's just the way it was." Her lower lip was quivering, and she took a deep breath to regain control of herself. Felicity felt the chill that was shaking Marlene. She looked up, started to speak.

"Please don't say anything," Marlene continued. "I didn't ask you to come here to say that. Aside from just wanting to see you again, I really just wanted to thank you for saving my life now that I know all the reasons you had for not doing so. And to let you know there's no bad feelings here."

Morgan, leaning against the lifeboat, squirmed under her gaze but maintained eye contact.

"I know my husband's death was an accident. I blame you for nothing. And I wanted to help you get started in your future business. I wanted to give you this." Her voice sped up on the last sentence, and she rummaged in her purse, producing a small white envelope.

"And whatever might this be?" Felicity asked, without raising a hand to accept the offered envelope.

"It's a check," Marlene said. "Actually two, one for each of you. I feel I should pay you what my late husband owed you. You did work for him and you deserve to be compensated for it."

Morgan stared hard at Felicity. She eventually got the message that it was up to her to speak for both of them. After a deep breath, she accepted the gift from Marlene's hand. Standing beside her she turned into the breeze, her belly pressed against the railing. She watched the water eddying around the stern of the boat, looking solidly still, yet a part of the ever-moving sea.

"I think I can speak for the both of us," she finally said, tearing the envelope neatly in half. "You went way out of your way to help us from getting tangled up with the law that night, when we were total strangers." Felicity turned the envelope to rip it in quarters. "And that night, when you didn't know the whole story, you managed to get your own tale to fit in with ours so as to simplify the investigation." One more tear, and now the envelope and its contents were a stack of tiny paper squares. "I think we can consider all debts paid in full. We simply couldn't take the money, Marlene."

Felicity opened her hands, and a small stream of confetti danced on the night air before dropping to dot the sea with white spots. During the next few seconds of discomforting silence, Marlene seemed to weigh this new argument's validity.

"All right. Can I get you to contact my business manager, then?" Marlene asked. "He can make some introductions for you in business world, and with such a strong recommendation that I believe it'll guarantee you a good start in your new business. In fact, I insist on really being your first customer. I've got a small shipping line and a new banking concern and real estate holdings. You two have taught me in that my late husband didn't do a very good job with security. And when all is said and done, I have to say I appreciate the lesson."

Felicity's smile broke open, flashing her small, very white teeth. Marlene turned to her, and they fell into an embrace of genuine friendship. Morgan's deep baritone chuckling rumbled out across the water. Despite the hardships they had shared, or perhaps because of them, they were able to laugh together.

THE END

# Author's Bio

Austin S. Camacho is a public affairs specialist for the Department of Defense. America's military people overseas know him because for more than a decade his radio and television news reports were transmitted to them daily on the American Forces Network.

He was born in New York City but grew up in Saratoga Springs, New York. He majored in psychology at Union College in Schenectady, New York. Dwindling finances and escalating costs brought his college days to an end after three years. He enlisted in the Army as a weapons repairman but soon moved into a more appropriate field. The Army trained him to be a broadcast journalist. Disc jockey time alternated with news writing, video camera and editing work, public affairs assignments and news anchor duties.

During his years as a soldier, Austin lived in Missouri, California, Maryland, Georgia and Belgium. While enlisted he finished his Bachelor's Degree at night and started his Master's, and rose to the rank of Sergeant First Class. In his spare time, he began writing adventure and mystery novels set in some of the exotic places he'd visited.

After leaving the Army he continued to write military news for the Defense Department as a civilian. Today he handles media relations and writes articles for the DoD's Deployment Health Support Directorate. He has settled in northern Virginia with his wife Denise.

Austin is a voracious reader of just about any kind of nonfiction, plus mysteries, adventures and thrillers. When he isn't working or reading, he's writing.

Website: www.ascamacho.com
Email: ascamacho@hotmail.com

# ALSO BY AUSTIN S. CAMACHO

## *Blood and Bone*

An eighteen-year-old boy lies dying of leukemia. Kyle's only hope is a bone marrow transplant, but no one in his family can supply it. His last chance lies in finding his father, who disappeared before he was born. Kyle's family has nowhere to turn until they learn of a certain troubleshooter - that self-styled knight errant in dark glasses, Hannibal Jones. But his search for the missing man turns up much more: A woman who might be Kyle's illegitimate sister, the woman who could be her mother, and a man who may have killed Kyle's father. Hannibal follows a twisting path of deception, conspiracy and greed, from Washington to Mexico, but with each step the danger grows.

## *Collateral Damage*

Bea Collins came home from work to find that her boy friend Dean had disappeared. When she asked Hannibal Jones for help, Hannibal feared that his quarry had decided to run off with another woman after taking most of Bea's money. Little did he suspect that he would find Dean soon after he was accused of a bloody murder. Then he learned of previous killings linked to Dean's life - one of which took the lives of his father. It soon became clear that Hannibal would have to solve a series of murders in order to clear Dean's name.

## *The Troubleshooter*

A Washington attorney buys an apartment building in the heart of the city, but then he finds the building occupied by squatters: drug dealers, winos, and professional criminals intent on staying. Police are unable to empty the building for use by paying residents. No one seems willing or able to take on this challenge until the lawyer meets an intense young man named Hannibal Jones. He calls himself a troubleshooter, but he finds more trouble in Southeast Washington than he expected. The people holding crack pipes are backed up by people holding guns, and Hannibal soon finds himself up against a local crime boss and his powerful, mob connected father.